Domi lay writh...

The albino girl was hissing like a cat as the living stones ran across the flesh of her arm and up toward her shoulder, affixing themselves quicker than she could remove them. Domi snatched for another as it clambered toward her throat, wrenching it away with a tearing of her skin.

"Okay, Domi," Kane said calmly, "I'm right here."

Domi's scarlet eyes glared into his. "Kane, get them off me," she begged through gritted teeth.

His hands just a couple of inches away from her body, he stopped, staring nervously at the stones. Like a swarm of tiny-shelled insects, the hard backs of the stones had massed against Domi's arm, creating solid bands that wrapped around her like bangles.

He had had a similar stone embedded in him just a few months ago, and he could still recall the pain.

"Kane?" Domi squealed. "They're pushing into me. I can feel them!"

Other titles in this series:

James Axler
Outlanders®

GENESIS
SINISTER

A GOLD EAGLE BOOK FROM
W☉RLDWIDE®

TORONTO • NEW YORK • LONDON
AMSTERDAM • PARIS • SYDNEY • HAMBURG
STOCKHOLM • ATHENS • TOKYO • MILAN
MADRID • WARSAW • BUDAPEST • AUCKLAND

First edition November 2012

ISBN-13: 978-0-373-63876-5

GENESIS SINISTER

Copyright © 2012 by Worldwide Library

Special thanks to Rik Hoskin for his contribution to this work.

Printed in U.S.A.

"The clock strikes one that just struck two—Some schism in the sum—A Vagabond for Genesis Has wrecked the Pendulum."

—Emily Dickinson
1830–1886

The Road to Outlands—
From Secret Government Files to the Future

Almost two hundred years after the global holocaust, Kane, a former Magistrate of Cobaltville, often thought the world had been lucky to survive at all after a nuclear device detonated in the Russian embassy in Washington, D.C. The aftermath—forever known as skydark—reshaped continents and turned civilization into ashes.

Nearly depopulated, America became the Deathlands—poisoned by radiation, home to chaos and mutated life forms. Feudal rule reappeared in the form of baronies, while remote outposts clung to a brutish existence.

What eventually helped shape this wasteland were the redoubts, the secret preholocaust military installations with stores of weapons, and the home of gateways, the locational matter-transfer facilities. Some of the redoubts hid clues that had once fed wild theories of government cover-ups and alien visitations.

Rearmed from redoubt stockpiles, the barons consolidated their power and reclaimed technology for the villes. Their power, supported by some invisible authority, extended beyond their fortified walls to what was now called the Outlands. It was here that the rootstock of humanity survived, living with hellzones and chemical storms, hounded by Magistrates.

In the villes, rigid laws were enforced—to atone for the sins of the past and prepare the way for a better future. That was the barons' public credo and their right-to-rule.

Kane, along with friend and fellow Magistrate Grant, had upheld that claim until a fateful Outlands expedition. A displaced piece of technology…a question to a keeper of the archives…a vague clue about alien masters—and their world shifted radically. Suddenly, Brigid Baptiste, the archivist, faced summary execution, and Grant a quick termination. For Kane there was forgiveness if he pledged his unquestioning allegiance to Baron Cobalt and his unknown masters and abandoned his friends.

But that allegiance would make him support a mysterious and alien power and deny loyalty and friends. Then what else was there?

Kane had been brought up solely to serve the ville. Brigid's only link with her family was her mother's red-gold hair, green eyes and supple form. Grant's clues to his lineage were his ebony skin and powerful physique. But Domi, she of the white hair, was an Outlander pressed into sexual servitude in Cobaltville. She at least knew her roots and was a reminder to the exiles that the outcasts belonged in the human family.

Parents, friends, community—the very rootedness of humanity was denied. With no continuity, there was no forward momentum to the future. And that was the crux—when Kane began to wonder if there was a future.

For Kane, it wouldn't do. So the only way was out—way, way out.

After their escape, they found shelter at the forgotten Cerberus redoubt headed by Lakesh, a scientist, Cobaltville's head archivist, and secret opponent of the barons.

With their past turned into a lie, their future threatened, only one thing was left to give meaning to the outcasts. The hunger for freedom, the will to resist the hostile influences. And perhaps, by opposing, end them.

Chapter 1

Screams rolled across the waves.

On the deck of a fishing scow, a blond-haired woman was being dragged backward by her hair. She was shrieking and struggling as a pale-skinned man with tattoos down his exposed right arm yanked her across the decking against her will. A snatch of blond curls tore from her scalp as she tripped, and she slammed against the wooden deck with an agonized moan, tears streaming down her flushed face. Another man stepped before her as the one with the tattooed arm cursed. This one had dark eyes the color of midnight, a mop of black hair on his head and dark stubble along his jaw.

"Hold 'er down!" he snarled at his partner.

The man wore leather trousers and an open shirt, and where his chest was exposed the blonde woman could see dark chest hair tufting from his weather-tanned skin alongside a puckering of scars where he had been burned many years before. At his belt, the man had a holster in which he had jammed a long-barreled Colt revolver, its chrome finish marred from overpolishing. His name was "Black" John Jefferson and he was a pirate.

Fern Salt, his colleague with the tattooed arm,

obeyed with a nod, grasping the blonde by her wrists and slapping at her breasts to hold her down, stretching her taut as she tried to kick away. Salt pawed roughly at her left breast for a moment, laughing cruelly as he squeezed it. The woman was twenty-two, with apple-red cheeks and a belly already round with child. She screamed again, tears washing down her face.

All around them aboard the listing scow, the sounds of violence played out in a cacophonous symphony, gunshots and screams rolling over the waves. The sea was calm, and it seemed to urge the violence to hush with the sound of every softly lapping wave against the side of the boat.

One of the crew, a cousin to the blonde woman, scrambled across the deck to help her, alerted by her screams and followed by another of the pirates. Glancing over his shoulder, Black John snatched the Colt from its holster and squeezed the trigger, holding it upside down and blasting a single 9 mm bullet behind him. With the boom of discharge, the bullet cut into the sailor's right leg just below the knee, and he let loose a bloodcurdling scream as his leg exploded in a burst of blood and splintered bone. Another of Black John's crew, the man following the sailor across the deck, finished the job swiftly with a single bullet to the man's head.

Black John turned back to his task at hand. Unbuckling his belt and loosening his pants, he reached out for the screaming blonde. His fingernails had been painted as black as his nickname, and they glistened in the sunlight like the shells of insects.

"Quit shoutin', girl," he hissed, his eyes narrowed with fury. "Makes no diff'rence to me if you're alive or dead, just so long as you're still warm."

With that, Black John grasped the woman's skirts with one of his beautifully manicured hands, ripping away the bottom half of her dress to expose her crotch. Then, he got about his business as Fern Salt held her down with one tattooed arm. Salt's other arm was scrubbed clean and hairless, unnaturally pale where another tat had been removed. All around them, Black John's shipmates were rushing through the scow, sacking her and dispatching the last of her crew with cold professionalism as the ruined engine spit black smoke into the morning sky.

Beside the scow was a larger boat, and from a distance the pair seemed restful as they floated on the clear waters of the Bay of Campeche, far enough out from the coast that they couldn't be seen from the shore by the naked eye. The larger of the boats was a sleek sixty-foot cutter, its sides painted the same blue-green as the waves. The cutter was shaped like a dart in the water, flared at the aft with a long body that tapered to a brutal point like a stiletto blade at the front. The cutter's name was *La Discordia,* although papers filed in El Cuyo still had her listed by her original name, *La Vara de la Esperanza,* or *The Wand of Hope. La Discordia* loomed beside the smaller vessel like an older sibling, her dark shadow cast over the other's slanted deck.

La Segunda Montaña, the smaller vessel, was listing to one side where it had been wounded. The screams and shouts that had emanated from the scow as the crew of the larger vessel boarded her were dwindling now, the sounds as brief and sudden as bird calls, and, like those bird calls, they were ignored or unheard by anyone who might have intervened.

Aboard *La Segunda Montaña* all was pandemonium. Harpoons had been used to attach the two boats, trapping the smaller vessel as her captain tried to get out of the larger one's path. The scow had come all the way from the north, seeking freedom and a new life. Instead, one of those hooks had gone straight through the first mate's torso, gouging a hole through his chest even before the ships locked together. Now he was wedged upright, his body splayed against the safety rails that lined the scow's deck, screaming as the harpoon point held him in place, his ruined guts spilling down his legs.

Belowdecks, two pirates called Six and Xia were standing in the fishing scow's tiny hold. Xia held the sharp edge of his blade across a girl's throat while Six looked around the shabby little room. The girl had dark hair and pleading eyes, and Xia had already had his way with her.

"What is that?" Six asked, jabbing his outstretched finger at a box in the corner of the living quarters. The box had wooden sides and was open at the top, its lid propped against the wall. The box was half-full of stones, not one of which was more than an inch across; they looked like shale that had washed up on the beach.

The girl shook her head. "I don't know," she admitted, the glistening tears still drying on her pretty face. "It was here when we boarded. Belongs to the captain, I think."

"Belongs to us now, *hermanita,*" Xia growled, and he drew the blade closer to the girl's throat, six inches of knife glistening in the light cast by the round portholes. Xia was a large man, broad-shouldered and with a suggestion of Malaysian or Polynesian to his appearance, especially around the eyes and the golden tint of his skin. He wore an undershirt and cutoffs, and a long white scar ran almost the entire length of his left leg, from groin to well past the knee. He had gotten the scar in a knife fight on a plantation that had almost ended with the authorities hanging him. But only almost.

The girl struggled in his grip, trembling with fear.

"Floater this size don't need ballast," Six said as he nudged at the stones with the tip of his blaster. Six was broad-shouldered, too, with a gold hoop depending from his left earlobe. He wore his hair in a topknot on his otherwise shaved head, a gunslinger's mustache drooping down over his top lip. He licked the bristles absentmindedly as he spoke, eyes narrowing as he looked at the strange contents of the crate.

"Something in it, mebbe?" Xia suggested, gripping the girl tighter as she struggled. "You, keep fucking still."

Six rummaged through the stones with his free hand, turning them over as he plunged deeper into the crate. It was just a little deeper than a foot, and the broad-shouldered pirate reached down until he could distinctly feel the crate's bottom. "Nothing in there," he said. "Nothing but stones."

"Worth something, you think?" Xia asked.

As he spoke, the girl finally pulled herself free, wrenching out of his grip before Xia knew what was happening. Still pressed against her throat, Xia's blade cut through her flesh as she yanked herself away, and blood began to spurt as her carotid artery was compromised by its touch.

"Shit me, Xia," Six spit as the girl lumbered toward him, blood shooting from her nicked artery.

The blood seemed to blast out of her neck with the power of a jet, spraying the walls of the cabin and turning the lone porthole red in just three seconds as the girl screamed in agony.

Six leaped out of the way as the screaming girl barreled toward him, sidestepping as she fell toward the crate. The force of the rushing blood was lessening now, the furious jet turning into a steady stream of red that washed down the girl's tattered clothes. She slumped against the crate, blood flowing across its contents, and Six and Xia listened as her scream turned into a whimper and then to nothing.

"Damn, I liked her," Xia said. Then he shrugged as Six glared at him. "What? She got free," he added.

Six nodded. Then, after a moment's consideration, he reached down and pulled the girl off the crate by her long hair, tossing her to one side. She slumped against the wall of the hold, blood still running down her neck and turning her dress crimson.

Within the crate, the bloodied stones seemed to pulse and move where the blood seeped through them. Six watched for a moment before dismissing the thought as nothing more than an optical illusion. Then he grabbed the box and hefted it from the deck. "Shit like this gotta be worth something," he decided. "Only thing on this death trap that is."

Xia glanced at the dying girl before he followed Six up the little flight of wooden stairs and into the main cabin. She stared back, eyes wide with shock, the red pulse at her neck now turned to nothing more than a drizzle. In six minutes she would be dead from blood loss, and already her body was turning cold.

THE CAPTAIN OF *La Segunda Montaña* was a portly Latino called Alfredo. A man of indeterminate age with the leathery tanned skin and cropped hair that could place him anywhere from thirty-five to fifty-five, Alfredo struggled with the wheel as the boat listed farther to starboard. He was trying to bring the little scow back to true as his crew fended with their unwanted boarders. Alfredo had traveled a long way with his cargo; he still believed in a higher purpose.

He watched as one of the marauders leaped down from the cutter, brandishing a sword with a wickedly curved blade in one hand. The man had olive skin and brown dreadlocks that clattered with beads as he moved, and he smiled as he spotted the captain standing in his little box of a cabin, wrestling with the wheel.

"Please, *señor*," Alfredo called as the pirate approached him. "Don't hurt me. My ship, she will sink if I don't—"

The dreadlocked pirate drove the tip of his sword into Alfredo's chest, wrenching it down through his body from sternum to crotch as the man howled in agony. "What makes you think I'd give a shit about your boat?" he hissed, wrenching the blade free. The captain's guts came with the blade, spilling over the bloodied deck as he sank to his knees. And he screamed long and loud.

"For goodness' sake, shut him up!" Black John Jefferson commanded as he tightened his grip in the blonde woman's hair. "I can't concentrate on the task at hand with all that screaming."

The "task at hand," as Black John had described it, left the blonde sobbing, and the pirate cursed her even as he spilled his seed inside her. He pulled away from her and stood as his companion, Fern Salt of the tattooed sleeve, took his turn on the girl. All around them, mayhem reigned, and Black John smiled as he saw the bloody hell he had encouraged. The last of the ship's crew was being hoisted high in the air by four of Black John's crew as another used his bobbing form for target practice, shots clipping chunks from the helpless sailor's ear and cutting two of his fingers off his hand as they hit. Finally a bullet pierced the man's larynx as he screamed, and his scream turned to a gurgle as his ruined body was tossed overboard, the blood pouring down his flailing limbs.

Black John hurried over to the side of the ship as the man was thrown, wrenching his Colt Anaconda from its holster even as he ran. Steadying himself against the rail, Black John took aim at the bobbing figure before blasting a single bullet through the man's forehead, ripping his skull apart in an ugly red blotch. The sailor continued to bob in the ocean, eyes wide but their spark gone.

Black John turned back to his crew, eyeing them with his ferocious glare. "For goodness' sake, ex him when you're done," he berated. "No witnesses. Not ever. That's the code, lads."

Chastised, the pirate crew muttered their apologies as they checked the old scow's cabin for anything of value. Black John smiled grimly as he marched across the deck to where Fern Salt was having his way with the pregnant blonde. Gun still in hand, he shot the woman in the face, killing her instantly.

Delirious with passion, Fern Salt shook for a moment before realizing what had happened. "What did you do that for?" he shouted, his ardor disappearing like a snuffed flame. "I wasn't done pricking her, man!"

"No witnesses, Mr. Salt," Black John said in reply,

an ugly sneer marring his dark features. "No witnesses."

Still staring at the bloody body of the woman, Black
John aimed his pistol at her swollen belly and stroked
the trigger once more. Salt was splattered with blood,
and he growled as he turned and glared at Black John
as the sadistic pirate walked away, fury raging through
him. With a guttural shout, Fern Salt began to charge
across the sloping deck at his colleague.

Black John was a survivor who had relied on his
quick wits to keep him alive up to now. He heard Salt
charging at him and he stepped aside automatically,
his long coats swishing about him as he brought his
pistol around. Salt slammed into him still, knocking
Black John with his shoulder and shoving him a half-
dozen steps onward with a roar. Off balance, Black
John went down, tumbling to the deck with his first
mate atop him.

"What do you think you're doin', Mr. Salt?" Black
John bellowed.

Salt was too angry to respond. He scampered back,
reaching for the long-barreled Llama Comanche revolver he wore in an open shoulder rig. The Comanche
had a six-inch barrel and, at some point in its history,
someone had painted a naked, openmouthed woman
reclining along that length.

"You're a maniac," Salt snarled as he freed the Comanche from its holster.

Black John smiled as he brought his own pistol to
bear on the mutinous pirate. "Mr. Salt, surely you cannot be serious—"

Salt pulled the trigger, blasting a volley of .357 bullets into Black John's chest. Several missed, cutting
splinters from the deck in furious bursts of wood, but

three bullets hit, striking the captain with force enough to shake his whole body. Black John's pistol blasted, too, but he was a fraction of a second slower in getting that first shot in. His shots went wild, clipping Salt only once in the hard muscle of his upper left arm.

Salt bellowed in pain as the bullet winged him, jabbing with his Comanche and blasting another burst of fire at his captain. Black John lay writhing on the deck, blossoms of blood appearing on his clothes like opening poppies, a dark wound in each one's center.

"Bastard," Salt spit as his weapon finally clicked on Empty.

Standing there, his shoulders rising and falling as he breathed heavily, Salt became aware of his seven colleagues around him. They had boarded with him and Black John to take whatever cargo the ship might have.

"What happened, Fern?" Six asked, still hefting the crate of stones.

Salt became suddenly very aware that Six had a gun trained on him under the base of the box he held, a little snub-nosed thing, its finish the color of storm clouds.

"Cap'n's out of control," Salt muttered, shaking his head. "You seen it. You all seen it."

For a moment, Six and his companions stood in silence, each man poised with his own blaster. Then Six nodded and clicked the safety back on his pistol, the others following suit a moment later.

"Killed the girl an' the baby, just to make sure," Salt continued. "The unborn fucking baby. No witnesses, my eye, he just went kill crazy. It's sick, man."

Six took a step away, motioning for the others to follow with a tilt of his head. "Let's get back to *La Discordia* and get out of here. Time's ticking and the clock's never kind."

Xia looked Captain Black John Jefferson up and down for a moment, the man's blood pooling around him where he lay sprawled on the deck. "You want we should take him with us, Six?"

Six shook his head without looking back. "Screw him," he said. "Salt's right—he always was a sick bastard."

"Yeah," Xia agreed, plucking the Colt Anaconda from the dying man's grip. "An' he cheated at cards." With that, he blasted off a single shot into Black John's skull, finishing the job that Fern Salt had started.

Two minutes later, the graceful dartlike form of *La Discordia* was sailing away, cutting through the sea at some speed. Behind it, the little fishing vessel known as *La Segunda Montaña* lurched toward the water, its prow sinking beneath the waves. The pirate crew whooped as they departed the scene of the crime. They had gained only a few trinkets, a box of stones that had been washed in blood, but there had been women on the ship, and the men had been satisfied. Piracy was not always about goods; frequently it was simply an exercise in staving off boredom. The ability to live free, away from the baronies and their oppressive rules in the north, was something every crewman treasured.

Which was ironic, in that the passengers aboard *La Segunda Montaña* had also come in search of freedom. They were refugees, escaping a madness that seemed to engulf the northern territory of America. The villes had fallen but something had risen briefly in its place, a religion based on stone. Alfredo, the late captain of *La Segunda Montaña,* had lived the past few months of his life under the name of Alfredo Stone, in acknowledgment of his new faith. The people aboard his boat

had come south in search of freedom, trying to escape
the insanity that swept across the north after the fall
of the baronies, trying to find somewhere to live. Instead they had merely found somewhere new to die.

Chapter 2

Brigid Baptiste was sick of the questions. A member of the resistance group known as the Cerberus organization, Brigid had been deeply involved in a war between two would-be gods, Ullikummis and Enlil, who were in fact part of an ancient race of aliens called the Annunaki. With her Cerberus colleagues, Brigid had been battling the Annunaki for several years, striving to prevent their takeover of planet Earth and the absolute subjugation of the human spirit. But during the most recent skirmish with the insidious aliens, Brigid had been taken prisoner by Ullikummis, rogue upstart of the Annunaki. The stone god had turned her mind against her, brainwashed her into servitude. For a time she had taken the name of Brigid Haight and acted as Ullikummis's hand in darkness, helping to manipulate events so that Ullikummis could breathe new life into the reincarnated form of his mother and seize control of Earth and her peoples.

Gifted with an eidetic memory that granted her perfect recall, Brigid had used a mind trick to hide her own personality in a meditative trance, leaving her body to function solely as a shell controlled by the wicked purpose of Ullikummis. But she had become lost in the trance, and when her mind had finally been reawakened, Brigid found that her body had wrought terrible atrocities, killing innocents and betraying her closest friends.

The war itself was over. Less than a week earlier, Ullikummis had led his million-strong army in a final push on Enlil's stronghold on the banks of the Euphrates. Ultimately, the attack had failed, with enormous casualties on both sides. Cerberus had been in the thick of things, striving to the very limits of their abilities to halt the incredible God War that had erupted, twisting it from within. And for a while, almost to the very end of that final, cataclysmic battle, Brigid had stood with Ullikummis, opposed to the forces of man. She had a woman to thank for her final change of heart, a Cerberus fighter called Rosalia who had managed to break the meditative spell and free Brigid's mind from its hiding place beyond time.

Ever since then, Brigid had been plagued by questions. Her colleagues had been concerned for her, which was not only natural but touching—something so very human that it encompassed everything that the Cerberus organization represented. But Brigid didn't have any answers; she was still trying to put the pieces together herself. It was like waking from some horrible nightmare, only to be told that the nightmare had been real after all.

Now Brigid stood on the wide stone steps that led down to the River Ganges in India, the morning sun beating on her back. She was a tall and slender woman in her late twenties, with emerald eyes and flame-red hair that cascaded down her back in an elegant sweep of curls. Her skin was pale and she showed a wide expanse of forehead that suggested intelligence, along with full lips that suggested passion. In truth, Brigid could be defined by both of those aspects, and many more besides. She wore a white one-piece suit, the standard uniform of the Cerberus organization, and she had augmented this with a light jacket that was already making her feel too warm even before the sun had properly reached its full intensity.

Beside Brigid stood another woman dressed in similar clothes, enthusiastically gazing out at the rushing waters of the Ganges. This was Mariah Falk, a thin woman in her early forties, with short dark hair that showed flecks of white running through it. Though not conventionally pretty, Mariah had an engaging smile and a genial nature that put most people at ease. A geologist, Mariah had been with Cerberus a long time, ever since being awakened from a cryogenic suspension facility she had been placed in back in the twenty-first century. It had been her idea to travel to India, using the teleportation system that the Cerberus team relied on.

"Breathtaking, isn't it?" Mariah said, staring across the wide expanse of river where locals were washing clothes, hefting buckets of water for private use, and where the local holy men had come to wash the soles of their feet.

Brigid watched, too, as a clutch of children ran past them on the stone steps and leaped into the water, giggling as they splashed one another. All human life was here, she realized, going about its business, oblivious to the great war that had been fought just a few days before, a war that had been for their very souls.

The water itself was brown with silt where movements churned up the riverbed, and it had that smell to it, Brigid recognized, the smell of muddy puddles after a hard rainfall.

"Clem brought me here once," Mariah continued

enthusiastically. "He said that the Hindus believe the Ganges is the source of all life and that bathing in it will wash away a person's sins." She turned to Brigid then, smiling her bright, hopeful smile.

Brigid just stared, watching the water the way one might watch an insect bat against the outside of a windowpane, with distracted disinterest.

"Brigid, I don't know what happened to you," Mariah said gently, "but I like to think that Clem would have said to bring you here, if he'd still been alive."

Mariah had lost Clem Bryant in the God War, never having had the chance to tell him that she was in love with him.

Slowly Brigid dipped her head in the faintest of nods. "Clem was a good man," she said quietly.

"He was," Mariah agreed. "I really miss him. We all lost something in the war, Brigid. I lost…hope for a while."

Brigid looked at the geologist, saw the worry lines on her face and around her eyes. She looked older than Brigid remembered. The war had placed a strain on everyone.

"Do you want a dip?" Mariah asked, inclining her head encouragingly toward the river. "Wash away your sins, once-in-a-lifetime offer."

Brigid shook her head. "You go," she said. "I'll wait right here."

There, on the sandy stone steps that lined the riverbank, Mariah stripped off the white jumpsuit, revealing a modest swimsuit underneath. "Whether the river really does wash away people's sins or not, you can't keep blaming yourself for what happened," she told Brigid.

Brigid just looked at the rushing water, leaning

down until she was sitting on one of the wide steps, her legs stretched out before her.

Mariah didn't bother saying anything else. She had thought a trip to India might pull Brigid out of her blue funk. The Cerberus team was still engaged with the massive cleanup of their redoubt in the Bitterroot Mountains in Montana. The redoubt had been infiltrated and overwhelmed by Ullikummis and his army, but Brigid had seemed distant, emotionally disengaged, unable to be of any help. Yet the trip hadn't seemed to do anything for her mood. She remained withdrawn, as if in mourning.

Brigid watched as Mariah waded into the river, waters lapping at her ankles and then her knees, then higher until she was in it past her hips. The geologist crouched, letting the cool waters lap against her skin, smiling as it tickled.

It would take more than water to wash away her sins, Brigid knew. In her guise as Brigid Haight, she had been a part of the campaign to betray and cage humankind. To cleanse her of her sins would take a miracle, something with the power of a nuke. She watched in silence as Mariah ducked under the water, letting it run through her hair as all around her the locals continued going about their business seemingly without a care in the world. It was as if nothing had happened at all.

CERBERUS WAS A MESS. The familiar operations room that sat at the hub of the redoubt complex looked as if a bomb had hit it. No, not a bomb, Lakesh corrected himself—an avalanche.

Lakesh was in his mid-fifties, with dusky skin, clear blue eyes and an aquiline nose over his refined mouth.

His black hair was swept back in a tidy design, hints of gray showing at the temples. His full name was Mohandas Lakesh Singh and he had run the Cerberus operation since its inception. In fact, he had been at this redoubt, off and on, for the best part of 250 years, dating back to before the nuclear holocaust that had so dramatically changed the world at the end of the twentieth century. A physicist and cyberneticist of some renown in his day, Lakesh had worked on the original mat-trans system at this very redoubt. Cryogenic freezing and a program of organ replacement had kept Lakesh alive far longer than his natural years. In short, Lakesh had seen a lot in his life, and a lot of it had been in this very room in the heart of a mountain.

The room featured two aisles of computer desks, and one wall was dominated by a Mercator relief map showing Earth covered in lighted pathways that traced the routes available to the matter-transfer system at any given time. The mat-trans units were designed for military use back in the latter half of the twentieth century. The Cerberus mat-trans unit was located in its own chamber in the far corner of the room. Tinted brown armaglass walls encompassed its powerful machinery. With just the flick of a switch, the mat-trans could hurl a person across the quantum ether to a similar unit many miles away. Though primarily concentrated in mainland America, the mat-trans units stretched across all continents and even as far as the moon.

The operations room was staffed around the clock, with people checking the live feeds and liaising with field agents in their self-appointed role of protecting humankind. Right now, however, the room was mostly populated by a cleanup crew that was using a combination of ultrasonic generators and good old-fashioned brute force to remove the strange infestation that had threatened to consume the redoubt.

The Cerberus redoubt was initially a military facility located high in the Bitterroot Mountains in Montana, where it had remained largely forgotten or ignored in the two centuries since the nukecaust. In the years since that nuclear devastation, a strange mythology had grown up around the mountains, their dark, foreboding forests and seemingly bottomless ravines. The wilderness area surrounding the redoubt was virtually unpopulated. The nearest settlement was to be found in the flatlands some miles away, consisting of a small band of Indians, Sioux and Cheyenne, led by a shaman named Sky Dog.

Hidden away as it was, the redoubt had required few active measures to discourage visitors, so when it had been attacked by Ullikummis and his forces the personnel had been both surprised and dumbfounded. With a force of just fifty troops, Ullikummis had taken control of the redoubt, altering its interior dimensions and changing the very shape of the rooms themselves as he transformed it into a brutal Life Camp.

Ullikummis himself was the shamed scion of the Annunaki bloodline, and had been medically altered to look like a monster carved from stone. Among other genetic enhancements, Ullikummis exhibited a psionic control over rock, and had employed this to radically alter the whole of the redoubt, covering everything in a fresh skin of stone. Ullikummis had other powers, too, including his so-called obedience stones, semisentient shards of rock that could influence and control a person's thoughts. Ullikummis and his agents had secretly placed these obedience stones in several of the Cerberus personnel prior to the attack on the redoubt, and it had been these hidden allies within who had allowed the great stone Annunaki to take over the complex with such ease.

When the redoubt had come back under Cerberus's control, the personnel had begun the slow process of cleaning away the stone and replacing the damaged stock beneath. It had been four days now, and Lakesh wondered if he could see any progress at all. The ops room was still covered in a spiderweb of rock, thick stone fingers clawing across every surface and every wall, obliterating the old familiar sights he had been used to for so long.

Outside was little different. Just beyond the rollback door where the garish three-headed hellhound had been painted many years earlier, lending the Cerberus facility its name, thick posts of rock lined the plateau, barring the entryway to the redoubt for anything wider than a human. Even now, workers were chipping away at those pillars of stone, breaking them down into gravel and dust.

"I'm sorry it's such a mess in here," Lakesh said as he offered a seat to the beautiful woman who had come to speak with him. "You haven't caught us at our best."

Rosalia shrugged indifferently. "Don't worry," she said, "I'm not staying." Rosalia was long of limb with thick, dark hair that reached past her shoulders to halfway down her back. In her early twenties, Rosalia wore loose clothes, a pale skirt that brushed her ankles and a white cotton blouse that she had left half unbuttoned. Where her olive skin could be seen it was tanned a beautiful golden. Rosalia had first met one of the Cerberus field teams as an adversary, but she had joined their ranks during their campaign against Ullikummis and had proved her worth many times over.

"You've been a real asset to us, Rosalia," Lakesh told her. "Are you sure you wouldn't prefer to stay?"

Rosalia looked around the room, as if seeing it for the first time. "This? It's not my scene," she said. "You'll be fine without me."

And there it was, Lakesh thought. That remarkable arrogance that had typified Rosalia and her behavior within the Cerberus organization. The woman was competent—there was no question about it—but she was very aware of that fact. Whatever she had done, she made it clear that she had done it as a favor to Cerberus, not the other way around.

Kane, an incredibly gifted field agent and a lynchpin of the Cerberus team, had brought her on board. He had been trapped in the Life Camp at the time, and he had needed Rosalia's help to escape and thus free the other Cerberus captives. But he had seen something in her and had asked her to help them for the duration. With Ullikummis now destroyed, Rosalia felt that her time with Cerberus had reached its natural end.

"Where will you go?" Lakesh asked, raising his voice to be heard over the sounds of chiseling going on just behind his shoulder.

"Somewhere," Rosalia told him, as ever giving almost nothing away about herself.

"Cerberus owes you," Lakesh said, "and I would like to see us pay our debts. If there's anything I can do, or anything you need from the people of this facility, you need only ask."

Rosalia stifled a laugh. "The first time I met your people—" she began.

"The slate is clean," Lakesh cut in. "Whatever you did before you came here is forgotten. I promise."

Rosalia nodded with gratitude. "You know, there is

one thing," she said. "I was planning to go see some people I… Some acquaintances. They're down south. It's quite a journey or I would have gone there sooner. You have your tech, the interphaser and the mat-trans. Think you can maybe give me a little push in the right direction?"

A broad smile appeared on Lakesh's features. He was glad to be able to help the normally cagey young woman. "Where is it you need to go?" he asked.

"There's a town close to the border, Mexico," Rosalia said. "That side, not this."

Lakesh was already tapping at the computer terminal that dominated his desk. The screen still had tendrils of stone across it like a cracked windshield, but he could see enough to get what he needed. "Whereabouts, exactly?"

"The place has gone by many names," Rosalia said, "and it never once appeared on any map. I was told it was set up by a bandit who made himself its uncrowned king way back before the nukecaust. He meant it as a place where other outlaws could retreat and maybe retire. These days it's a place of tranquillity and learning, high in the mountains, away from the villes."

"Do you have coordinates?" Lakesh asked.

Rosalia nodded, tapping on the illuminated map on his computer screen. "Get me close enough, I'll hoof it from there."

"I'll have to track down the nearest entry point," Lakesh said, "which may take a while with the—"

"Everything?" Rosalia said brightly, gesturing around the ruined room.

Lakesh nodded. "Yes, with the 'everything' right

now. Leave it with me—you'll ship out before the day's over."

Rosalia nodded, pushing herself up from the swivel chair and making her way to the doors of the ops room. Rough stone ran along the edges of the doors, and they still wouldn't close properly. A worker called Farrell, with goatee beard and hoop earring, was using a hammer and chisel to slowly chip away the offending rock, piece by piece.

Looking up from his computer, Lakesh eyed Rosalia wonderingly. "What's there?" he asked, unable to contain himself.

"My old school," Rosalia said in response before leaving the room.

BLACK JOHN JEFFERSON drifted back to swirling consciousness, a burning pain urgent in his gut. His eyes flickered open, gazing straight up and into the glare of the sun overhead. He saw it but could not feel it; instead his skin felt cold.

All around he could hear the sounds of rushing water, as if someone had opened a plug and let the whole damn ocean in.

Beneath him the deck of the ship lurched, and Black John was sent sliding across it. He had to dig his heels in to stop himself going any farther. He felt as if he would be sick, and he tilted his aching head to one side, spitting out the warm mouthful of blood that threatened to fill it.

Suddenly the deck of *La Segunda Montaña* rocked violently to one side once again, and Black John struggled to pull himself up to a sitting position. The deck was wet beneath him, water mixing with his own blood and the blood of others as he tried to make sense of it. He stared at it, trying to remember what had happened, the blood swilling and churning in the clear water, eddying in little whirls of red.

He had shot him. That was what had happened, wasn't it? He had shot Fern Salt, turning on him after he had snuffed the straw-haired harlot before her screaming gave him any more of a headache. Hadn't worked. He had one hell of a headache now, so much so he reached up to his forehead with a curse. When he did so, he found the slick wound there, cried out in surprise and at the furious twinge of pain.

"Fuck!"

The boat lurched again, its prow disappearing beneath the waves once more, bobbing up for a moment before disappearing one final time. He was on a sinking ship, scuttled by his own men—shot and left for dead.

"Those mutinous bastards," he muttered, pulling himself up until he was standing, feeling queasy.

The wound in his skull was making him lightheaded, so much so he couldn't tell if it was the boat that was lurching or himself. Then another wave hit the sinking scow, and Black John stumbled as he tried to retain his balance.

The sound of rushing water was becoming more restrained, and Black John realized what that meant. The ship had all but sunk; there wasn't much left for the ocean to fill before she took her.

Beside him, a body floated past, a tanned man with a gaping wound across his belly, guts spewing forth like the writhing tentacles of an octopus.

"Better you than me," Black John muttered as the body floated away, even as the deck disappeared beneath his feet, covered by a carpet of ocean.

Beneath his feet, *La Segunda Montaña* finally sank from view, leaving Black John floating alongside six dead bodies on the ocean waves.

Black John was a pirate and sadist, but most of all he was a survivor. He would survive this. Somehow he would survive and bring bloody revenge on the crew that had betrayed him.

Chapter 3

The God War was over.

The mop-up, however—now, that would take a little longer.

Kane, Grant and Edwards stepped out of the rain and made their way past the open double doors of the old aircraft hangar and into the grumbling crowd that waited beyond. Within, close to forty or fifty people were waiting, the muttering sounds of their voices echoing from the high ceiling.

"Just like old times, isn't it?" Kane said under his breath as the three men entered the huge room.

Edwards nodded. "Yeah, it's a regular triple-P, all right."

"Triple-P" was slang for a Pedestrian Pit Patrol, a task all three men had had to perform in their past lives as Magistrates for ville authorities, lives all three had put behind them.

At some point in time, the building they entered had been used to store aircraft and automobiles, playthings of the very rich. That was before the nukecaust had changed the rules of the world, and civilization had been dealt such a blow that it had seemed for a while as if it might never recover. Even now, two hundred years later, these places still existed, abandoned and almost forgotten, relics of a bygone age just waiting to be put to use once more.

The ceiling dripped rainwater through gaping holes, and what glass remained in the windows was white with birds' droppings. Right now, even as the orderly crowd gathered, the sound of pigeons cooing trilled through the building, a sonic bed that was almost subliminal in its constancy.

Kane glanced up at the ceiling, watching for a moment as two pigeons took flight one after the other, a third joining them a moment later, weaving through the high girders that held the roof in place in a fluttering of gray feathers. The crowd ignored them.

In his early thirties, Kane was a tall man with a strong build that even his loose denim jacket could not disguise. With wide shoulders and rangy limbs, his physique resembled that of a wolf. He had the nature of a wolf, too, both a loner and pack leader depending on what the fates threw at him. His dark hair was cropped short and he was clean shaved for the first time in more than a month. As an ex-Magistrate, Kane was one of the enforcers of the now-fallen baronies that had dominated the former United States. He had been exiled from the barony of Cobaltville after stumbling upon a conspiracy that had threatened the very integrity of the system he was pledged to protect. Exiled along with his Magistrate partner Grant and archivist Brigid Baptiste, Kane had been recruited into the Cerberus operation in its infancy. Ever since, he had been battling against the Annunaki threat to Earth in all its myriad forms, and most recently he had taken down Ullikummis in a battle that raged not simply across Earth but through multiple planes of reality. Standing in a decrepit aircraft hangar amid a gaggle of other humans, Kane was glad to get back to something approaching normality once more.

The two men walking at Kane's side were similarly intimidating men. The first of these was Grant, Kane's longtime brother-in-arms whose relationship with Kane dated from way back to his days as a Cobaltville Magistrate. Tall and broad-shouldered, Grant was an imposing figure with ebony skin and not so much as an ounce of fat on his body. His hair was shaved close to his skull, and he had sported his trademark gunslinger's mustache. In his mid-thirties, Grant wore a long black duster made from Kevlar weave. The coat skimmed the tops of his boots, giving him a funereal look.

The other man was called Edwards, who was similarly well built. He had chosen to forgo a jacket, leaving his rippling arm muscles cinched beneath the tight sleeves of his dark cotton shirt. He was closer in age to Kane. Like Grant, his hair was shaved close to his skull, drawing attention to his bullet-bitten right ear. During the war with Ullikummis, Edwards had been duped into acting in the interests of the enemy through a hidden implant in his skull. That implant had been removed via ultrasonic surgery just four days earlier, but Edwards was in the field already—determined, as he put it, to make up for lost time. Kane and Grant kept an eye on him, neither of them sure that he could be fully trusted yet.

There was a fourth Cerberus agent in the room, an albino woman called Domi who had been tracking down information about this meeting for several days. She had patched through to Cerberus just a few hours before, confirming the time and location and giving the go-ahead for the others to move in.

The meeting itself was in the West Coast territory of the old United States of America, just forty miles

from the majestic settlement of Luikkerville. Built on
the ruins of Snakefishville, Luikkerville was a city
constructed from faith, its populace enthralled by the
preachings of Ullikummis and his followers. News of
Ullikummis's passing had done little to temper that
burgeoning faith in the region, and Domi was there to
ensure it remained at a manageable level. Where the
Annunaki were involved, that was often easier said
than done.

The crowd numbered close to fifty, and they came
from all walks of life, all ages and ethnicities. But
there was a definite atmosphere in the room. Kane
could sense an atmosphere of dissatisfaction and mis-
trust, the belief that some great betrayal had occurred.
Their god was dead.

Kane and his team continued moving through the
crowd, splitting up with assured casualness as they lost
themselves amid the ragtag congregation.

"…brother died," Kane heard one of the crowd complain as he walked past. "Disappeared in a warp and
never came back."

"Yeah," his companion agreed. "Same thing happened to my cousin. Ain't seen him since Sunday."

Kane moved on, gently pushing the occasional
crowd member aside as he found a good vantage point
to view the raised stage that dominated one end of
the room.

Elsewhere within the crowd, Grant and Edwards
made similar progress, making their way through the
throng without drawing attention to themselves. All
three men were trained Magistrates and they knew
how to work through a crowd, walking with that in-
herent authority and challenge to their step that made
others move aside.

A simple podium had been erected at one end of the hangar, just boards raised on piled blocks, and Kane, Grant and Edwards took their places as a woman stepped up onto it with the help of a man in a hooded robe. The robe was made of rough hessian material, and it featured a red shield insignia over the left breast. Kane winced as he recognized the design. Just a few years before, he and his colleagues had worn something similar in their roles as Magistrates; this new religion had appropriated much of the iconography of the dying villes in its manipulation of the populace. The woman looked to be in her late twenties, with mouse-brown hair to which she had added streaks of purple like an anarchic road map. She walked with a shuffle to her step, and Kane saw she carried a little extra weight around her middle beneath the loose, floaty dress she wore. The dress was white, and it billowed around her as it caught the drafts from the broken windows, clinging to her legs as she took each step.

To the side of the podium, two more of the robed Magistrate stand-ins waited, their hoods down revealing their emotionless expressions. They were watching the crowd warily.

The crowd came to a hush as the woman stood astride the podium, casting her eyes slowly over them, an appreciative smile forming on her lips. The woman raised her arms and, once the crowd was silent, she spoke.

"I was made a promise by Lord Ullikummis," she announced in a clear voice, "that stone would be the future. That stone would be *our* future."

A little rumble went through the crowd, and voices were raised in dissent.

"I heard it was over."

"Yeah, Lord Ullikummis abandoned us."

"He died."

The woman raised her hands for silence. "Please, people. Please."

Gradually, with a palpable sense of reluctance, the crowd quietened.

"Ullikummis is dead," the woman on the podium announced. "The rumors are true."

Someone in the crowd cried out, and others raised their voices in shock once again, taking a minute to finally quieten once more.

"Ullikummis ascended," the woman continued, "to watch over all of us, to better guarantee his utopia would come to pass. And he left us a gift."

The woman pulled at her waist then, and Kane saw that what she wore was not a dress after all but a skirt and top of the same shimmering material. She raised the top, lifting it up and over her belly until it cinched just below her breasts. Her pink belly was swollen, a little bump showing in line with her hips. At first, Kane had taken the bump for fat, but now he realized his mistake.

"He planted his seed in me before he ascended," the woman announced to the stunned crowd. "I am the Stone Widow, and Ullikummis's child grows within me. Our lord has departed, but his flesh shall live on."

Once again, the crowd began to talk, raising questions and surging forward to see and to touch the swollen belly of the pregnant woman who called herself the Stone Widow.

Careful not to draw attention to himself, Kane engaged the hidden receiver of his Commtact and subvocalized, "Edwards, what are you making of this?"

A moment later, Edwards responded, his voice crystal clear in Kane's head. "I need to be closer to be sure, Kane."

Commtacts were communications devices that were hidden beneath the skin of the Cerberus field personnel. Each subdermal device was a top-of-the-line communication unit whose designs had been discovered among the artifacts in Redoubt Yankee several years before by the Cerberus exiles. Commtacts featured sensor circuitry incorporating an analog-to-digital voice encoder that was subcutaneously embedded in a subject's mastoid bone. Once the pintels made contact, transmissions were funneled directly to the wearer's auditory canals through the skull casing, vibrating the ear canal to create sound. In theory, even if a user went completely deaf he or she would still be able to hear normally, in a fashion, courtesy of the Commtact device.

Kane bit back a curse as he saw Edwards's tall form pushing farther toward the very front of the crowd. The man's height made him conspicuous and, unlike himself and Grant, Edwards had never had much experience working in low-key ops like this one. Instead, he just barreled on, eyes on the prize.

"Cool off, Edwards," Kane subvocalized. "You're drawing too much attention."

"Well, shit, Kane," Edwards's voice came back. "Whatever's left inside me from that monster needs to get close to sense things. So, I'm getting close. You got a better idea, I'm all ears." As he spoke, Edwards peered across the heads of the crowd, fixing Kane with a challenging stare.

Kane looked away, his eyes automatically playing over the rest of the crowd. This wasn't right. This wasn't how it should play out. Edwards had been turned into a traitor against his will, and now that he was back on side he felt like he had something to prove. If they weren't careful, that desire to prove himself was going to land them all in very hot water.

MEANWHILE, CLOSE TO the rear wall of the hangar, the fourth agent of the Cerberus team had slipped past the celebrants and was making her way along the length of the room behind the stage. Domi was an albino with chalk-white skin and bone-white hair that was cut into a short, pixie-style bob. Barely five feet in height with eyes a fearsome red, Domi had the figure of a teenage girl, with tiny, bird-thin limbs and small, high breasts. Right now, she was wearing a simple, airy ensemble, a light dress that left much of her pale skin uncovered. Given her choice, Domi would prefer to wear less and perhaps nothing at all. A child of the Outlands, Domi found the feel of clothing on her skin restrictive.

She had been tracking this group for several days, and had already witnessed two of their "performances," for want of a better word. She balked at calling them sermons; there was nothing holy or reverent here that she could see. The group had come to recognize her, not in the least since her appearance was so distinctive, and she had told them her name was Mitra, a preferred alias she had used a few times while infiltrating similar pseudo religious groups. As "Mitra" she was trusted, a gentle-hearted innocent with a sickly parent who was looking for a new family in the form of this congregation. The story gave her enough credibility to pass herself off unnoticed as the false sermon continued.

While the crowd's attention was on the preaching Stone Widow, Domi ducked under the stage and peered at what lay beneath. The stage had been constructed of several sheets of wood, placed end to end and held aloft by piled cinder blocks at regular intervals. Visibility was poor underneath, but Domi could see that the area was being used for storage. She wanted to know what was being stored.

The woman speaker's coat was under there, neatly folded and placed by the open end of the stage. Other than that, the usual kind of things one would expect from travelers—several canteens filled with water along with some travel bags. Domi crouch-walked toward the bags—one of which was unbuckled at the top—and peered inside, spying a change of underwear along with some dried strips of cured meat in a separate bag with a clasp tie at its top. She sniffed the latter bag for a moment before moving on, head ducked beneath the stage. The height of the stage was about three feet, and Domi had to move slowly to find her way around.

Above her, the woman continued her proclamations about being the mother of the god's child, and the crowd oohed and aahed as prompted. Through the medium of the low stage, the voices sounded hollow and eerie, as if coming from a great length of tunnel.

Up ahead, Domi spotted a wooden box that had been pushed a little more than arm's length from the stage's edge and against the side wall, just enough to keep it safe. The box was about fourteen inches in height and roughly square.

Checking the edges of the stage for movement and confirming there was none, Domi made her way slowly toward the crate on silent tread.

UP AT THE FRONT OF THE crowd, the Stone Widow was continuing to explain her role in the New Order. Words like *messiah* were being bandied about, *child of god, saviour.* The audience was lapping it up. The sense of relief was palpable; these people craved something to believe in now that their god was gone.

"When this child is born," the woman continued, "he will be the first step in the evolution of our new world. A child born of god and woman. A force to lead us all."

Edwards had reached the front of the group now, and he stared at the woman, eyeing her belly. Edwards had been seeded with one of the semisentient stones that came from Ullikummis to fulfill his will. While most of the stone growth had now been removed from his skull, parts of it tenaciously remained—not enough to do any damage to Edwards, but enough that he could sense other obedience stones and their ilk. He sure as hell could detect something here, but it was dull, like a niggling itch.

"Well?" Kane asked over the Commtact. "Anything?"

"Definitely something here," Edwards replied. "Gonna have to pinpoint the source."

As he spoke, Edwards reached forward, hand outstretched, and slapped his palm against the speaker's ankle, the way others of the congregation had.

The woman was surprised by the hard grip, and she stopped midspeech to stare at the shaved-headed man who had grabbed her. "Let go, you're hurting," she said.

"Just wanted to touch the sainted lady," Edwards explained as the robed figures came hurrying toward him from the back of the podium.

"Get away from the glorious widow," one of the robed goons ordered.

The woman on stage kicked out and stepped back from Edwards, leaving him stumbling forward into the stage. The buzz in his head was there, but it was slight, and touching the so-called Stone Widow didn't seem to make any appreciable difference.

"I just wanted to," Edwards said, "to be close to the new life that's coming."

"So do I," another member of the crowd called. "Let me feel the new life."

"Let me be close," another shouted.

"And me!"

Suddenly, Kane and Grant found themselves being pushed forward in a human wave as the crowd surged to get closer to the Stone Widow, even as Edwards was shoved violently against the edge of the stage itself.

"Fuck, Edwards, what have you started?" Kane muttered into his Commtact link.

BENEATH THE STAGE, Domi's crimson eyes widened as the wooden box began to throb, its contents rattling within.

CONFUSED, BLACK JOHN Jefferson peered around him, trying to figure out where he was. He was surrounded by jungle, dense foliage thick with sap and the buzzing of insects like a wall of sound on the air. Tiny black flies swarmed about his wounds, feeding on his blood.

There was no real path to speak of, and Jefferson looked behind him, trying to recall if that was the direction he had come from. He had been on board the sinking fishing scow, had dipped under the waves when it had finally disappeared. The wound on his head had felt bastard hot where the sun struck it, but the salty water of the sea had made it sting even worse, doing nothing to cool either his skin or his temperament.

He had floated there awhile, the waves rolling about him, sending him on an undulating journey to wherever they chose. He remembered a beach, golden sand, a jungle running along its edge, palm trees and rubber plants. He had to have blacked out somewhere and had since been running on instinct.

He could recall nights like that when he'd been drunk, and his body had continued functioning anyway, whether his mind was really awake or not. Instinct could do that to a person—the deep-rooted instinct to survive.

Black John pushed the stem of a plant away as it tickled at his nose, shoving it aside with a groan of pain. His body ached and the wounds on his chest were still weeping, a clear pus coming from the broken skin where the bullets had struck, along with tiny slivers of congealing blood like red splinters. He'd kill them; that's what he'd do. Salt, Six, all of them. They should have followed his number-one creed—to leave no witnesses. Leaving him alive would be the last mistake those ungrateful sea dogs would make.

He battled on, fighting with the foliage, seeking something to vent his anger upon. Then, as he shoved the low branches of a towering palm out of the way, he saw the building. It sat there, nestled in the jungle's green embrace, as big as a cathedral. Constructed of stone the color of sand, the building had grand, sloping sides and a wide expanse of steps running up its center to a smaller structure that rested at its apex. The walls were notched with carvings, shadowed crevices in some script that the pirate couldn't recognize but assumed to be written words.

Black John eyed the building, estimating it to be more than three stories in height, but still shorter than the tallest of the palm trees surrounding it.

With nowhere left to turn, Black John trudged toward the structure, wondering if anyone was inside. He was in need of medical attention, he knew, and the blood-spot trail he left on the jungle floor informed him he likely didn't have that much time left. He reached down for the gun in his holster only to find it was gone. It didn't matter—whoever lived there would either help him or he'd execute them and then he'd help himself with whatever he could find. In the end, it was always that simple.

Chapter 4

Lakesh stared at the Mercator relief map that stretched across one wall of the operations room, narrowing his eyes to pick out the trails of lights that were currently dark. Like everything else in the ops room, the map had been covered by tendrils of stone during Ullikummis's violent assault on the redoubt. A tech on a stepladder was working at one side of the map, to the east, chipping away at the stone that had once overwhelmed it, removing its crust sliver by sliver. According to the map, there were plenty of pathways into the old states of Arizona, New Mexico and Texas, but there were no mat-trans-ready redoubts in the particular area that Rosalia had indicated. Lakesh shook his head with incredulity; it was almost as though military operations had been warned away from the region, deliberately kept at arm's length.

Swiveling his chair, Lakesh turned back to his computer, tapping at a key to reengage the darkened screen. While the Cerberus redoubt had been designed to manage the mat-trans system, it was not the only mode of transportation that Lakesh and his people had access to. The interphaser could also tap the quantum pathways and move people through space to specific locations.

While more amenable than the stationary mat-trans, the technology of the interphaser was limited by certain esoteric factors. The full gamut of those limitations had yet to be cataloged, but what was known was that the interphaser was reliant on an ancient web of powerful, hidden lines stretching across the globe and beyond. This network of geomantic energy followed old ley lines and supported a powerful technology so far beyond human comprehension as to appear magical. Though fixed, the interphaser's destination points often corresponded with the locations of temples, graveyards or similar sites of religious value. Clearly, ancient man had recognized the incredible power that was concentrated at such vortex points, which had been cataloged in the Parallax Points Program. These coordinates had been input into the interphaser.

Lakesh brought up a computer database of the known interphaser destinations; like most of the Cerberus endeavors, one of the IT experts had come up with a computer program that explored its properties.

Lakesh was still working at the problem when Brigid Baptiste and Mariah Falk returned, materializing in the mat-trans chamber like participants in a magic trick. Deep in his calculations, Lakesh had not heard the unit power up in the corner of the room, but when its door opened he looked up from his desk and watched Mariah and Brigid exit the chamber, returning home from their brief excursion to India. Mariah looked buoyant, smiling radiantly and—Lakesh fancied—walking with a skip in her step. A pace behind her, Brigid was solemn, her dour expression fixed. Lakesh had been Brigid's supervisor back when they had both been archivists in Cobaltville, and they had been colleagues—and friends—for a very long time. Right now, Lakesh was worried about her. What had happened with Ullikummis had put all of them through metaphorical hell, but Brigid had taken it worse than anyone, being turned so absolutely against her own will.

"Brigid, a word?" Lakesh called, raising his hand as the two women paced through the room.

Brigid turned to him, fixing Lakesh with dead eyes. "Yes?"

"I have spoken to Reba," Lakesh explained soberly once Mariah had left and Brigid had sat beside his desk. "She has agreed to speak with you about what you went through. She's been doing this with a number of our people. A lot of them are still quite understandably traumatized. We feel it might be of some help to you, as well. Do you understand?"

Reba DeFore was the facility's physician. Brigid had known her a long time, too.

"You mean a psych evaluation?" Brigid challenged.

Lakesh nodded. "You have been through a terrible ordeal," he said, "one we fear you are perhaps struggling to cope with. The sessions would be open-ended—and voluntary of course. I feel it would be for your own good."

Brigid glared at him, her brilliant emerald eyes piercing his. "No," she said.

Lakesh watched openmouthed as she rose to leave. Finally, he recovered his composure before she reached the doors. "Please, Brigid, there are so many questions that need to be addr—"

"No," she shrieked, turning on him. "I'm sick of questions. Sick, sick, sick. Do you hear me?"

Lakesh balked at the outburst, apologizing and defusing the situation by backtracking as quickly as he had suggested it. He watched as Brigid left the room, still mad.

Lakesh regretted that, but he was worried about her. They all were. He had known Brigid for a long time, and in all that time he had never known her like this. Her biolink transponder, the device that was injected into all Cerberus personnel so they could be monitored and tracked, had been shut off by Ullikummis, and without it she had been lost to them for almost two months. She had come back broken, no longer herself. And there didn't seem to be anything that Lakesh or anyone else could do about it.

BRIGID STORMED DOWN the main corridor that ran the length of the redoubt, the heels of her boots clumping against the hard stone floor. Wide enough to fit two ground vehicles side by side with ease, the corridor featured a high arched ceiling. It was always cold, like a cave at night, and always busy, running as it did the length of the redoubt mountain complex.

There was something about the feel of the corridor that was reassuring to Brigid right then, and she slowed her pace as she weaved over to the right-hand wall before pressing her hand against the rock. The wall was cold, the kind of cold that emanated just a little way beyond a thing's surface, that one could feel before touching. It felt real to her.

When Ullikummis had attacked her, overwhelmed her, destroyed her, Brigid had hidden her true mind away in a secret place that he couldn't reach. It was a higher plane of consciousness, accessible only via meditation. Its walls had been as white as lightning, and it had a sterile quality, with not so much as the hint of a breeze anywhere within it no matter how far she traveled.

Here, back in the redoubt with its rocky ceiling and

cold walls, Brigid couldn't help but notice the difference. It was real here. Everything was real. *Wasn't it?*

BLACK JOHN JEFFERSON had reached the top of the stone steps that ran up the outside of the building, and spatters of his blood now daubed each stair. It was a rectangular construction, the sloping sides reminiscent of a pyramid, although they failed to meet at the apex. Instead, there was a small covered area, fourteen feet by twelve, its flat stone roof marked with carvings. Black John examined those carvings for a moment, trying to make sense of them. The elements had not been kind to them, and much of the definition had worn away over time. Still, he saw geometric shapes and something that looked like a bird carved into the stone, but he didn't know what any of it meant.

Beneath the stone roof, there was another staircase, this one leading down into the building itself. The steps were dark and grimy, the detritus of dead leaves and dried insect shells lying amid swollen lines of moss.

Black John poked his head closer to the staircase and called out, "Hello? Anybody there?"

His own words echoed back to him after a moment, sounding hollow as they reverberated from the walls.

Jefferson clutched at his belly as another spark of searing pain ran through his guts where the bullets had struck, and when he brought his hand away it was slick with blood. The blood was thick, congealed with rough flecks in it from the edges of a forming scab.

Behind him, the jungle waited, bird caws and animal cries sounding distant and lonesome. Black John looked around him, searching the area. The tree cover was high, and the jungle was so overgrown that he could barely see ten feet beyond the edge of the stone

structure. It would not surprise him to learn that this
temple had stood here, unnoticed, for thousands of
years, utterly lost to the eyes of man.

Warily, the blood dripping from his stomach wound
with each step, Black John followed the stone steps
into the darkness of the forgotten temple.

STILL CONCERNED ABOUT Brigid's reaction, Lakesh threw
himself back into his work, unable to put the incident
out of his mind. The map of the Mexico border glowed
on the flickering computer screen, with several destination points highlighted that the interphaser would
be able to access. That posed a problem, too. While
Lakesh was willing to help Rosalia, the interphaser
would need to travel to the destination point, too, and
it was simply too valuable a unit for Lakesh to rely on
the feature that would return the device to the Cerberus
redoubt. Lakesh took a pen from his rock-scarred desk
and began to tap it against his teeth absently, wondering what his best course of action was. Brigid could
only be helped if she would let them. And Rosalia
needed to go home.

Lakesh was still pondering those problems when
Donald Bry came over to speak with him. With an
unruly mop of copper curls and an expression of permanent worry, Bry was second in command at the
Cerberus ops center, and was also Lakesh's closest
confidant. Many hours of experience had taught him
to pick up on the signs when Lakesh was worrying,
and seeing the man absentmindedly tapping at his teeth
with a pen was one sure giveaway.

"Something I can help you with, Lakesh?" he asked
cheerily.

Lakesh looked up from his calculations and smiled.

Bry had been overseeing much of the reconstruction work for the redoubt over the past four days, which meant that the two of them had spent little time in each other's company. "Donald, how are things progressing?"

"Slowly. Ever so slowly. But we're getting there."

Lakesh nodded. "I'll be glad when I can see my old map properly again."

"Ullikummis did a real number on this place," Bry said. "We've found things that look like carcasses up in the canteen area, round and as big as a dog but all withered up and dead now. The disturbing part is, they're made of rock."

"That sounds hideous," Lakesh said solemnly. "I fear what other surprises we might yet find."

Bry took a steadying breath, placing his hands on Lakesh's desk. "We made it back here, and that monster won't be coming again," he said. "We survived everything he did, and we'll make it through this, too. Whatever we find."

"I know," Lakesh agreed. "I'll just be glad when things are finally back to normal. I've spent too much of the past few months living out of a suitcase, not knowing what new horror the next day will bring."

"Life goes on," Bry conceded, as he glanced at Lakesh's screen. "But you look like you're puzzling over something there."

"Brigid," Lakesh said, ignoring the screen. "I fear that something has broken inside her, her spirit, if you will. What Ullikummis did took so much from her, and one can ill imagine what the effects of that are with her incredible memory. If she won't let us help her, I fear we could lose her forever.

"Am I an old fool to worry so, Donald?"

Bry chuckled. "If you are, then I am, too," he said. "Brigid's not herself…."

"She's more herself than she's been in months," Lakesh corrected. "That's the problem. She's grown—experience has shaped her. She almost bit my head off when I proposed she talk things over with Reba."

"Maybe therapy isn't the answer," Donald said after a moment's consideration. "One time when I was eight, my cat—Tiger—died. I really loved that cat, and my mom fussed and worried herself silly at what his passing would do to me. She asked if I would like a new cat, but I didn't want one. Eventually, she tried to get me to see a child psychiatrist."

"For a cat?" Lakesh asked.

"For a cat," Bry confirmed. "So, I saw her—a nice enough woman, though I'll be damned if I can recall her name after all these years. And we talked some, life and sorrow and all that. And it just made me realize that—you know, all I wanted was for people to stop asking me how I felt, to stop going on about it. I knew Tiger wasn't coming back, and it wasn't that I wanted a new cat. I just wanted to put that behind me and do new stuff."

"What happened?" Lakesh asked.

"Eventually the therapy sessions stopped," Bry said. "I probably only went for about four weeks, but that's a long time when you're eight. I think the shrink gave up when all I would talk about was some movie that I'd seen a trailer for. I can't remember what the movie was now, either. Go figure."

Lakesh laughed. "It was always something when you were a child, wasn't it?"

Bry nodded. "You've tried to help, Lakesh, but maybe Brigid can just figure this out in her own way.

No matter how much people care, probably all the questions aren't helping her right now. Nor is being here, with reminders of what Ullikummis did to us there to see on every surface."

"Perhaps not," Lakesh said, his eyes flicking back to the image on his computer terminal.

Bry watched as a smile crept across Lakesh's face. "I know that look," he said. "What is it?"

"You may have provided the solution to two problems," Lakesh said. "Rosalia requires the interphaser to travel to her next destination, but I am reluctant to leave it with her. However, if I were to send Brigid along for the trip, she could retrieve the interphaser and take a little time away from everything that's happening here."

Bry smiled. "Happy to help. Shall we say 'eureka'?" he asked.

"Oh, why not?" Lakesh laughed, and the two men punched their fists in the air.

"Eureka!"

Chapter 5

Those old stones were a-rattling.

In the darkened area beneath the stage in the old aircraft hangar, Domi pulled her hand back from the box. Her eyes widened as a sound came from it like the clip-clopping of hoofbeats. But already she was too late. A rush of stones came with her, racing over her hand and up her arm like insects, moving under their own power.

"No!" Domi cried out, scampering backward with her eyes fixed on the dark shapes running up her flesh. Before her, the box continued to tremble just slightly, as though it had been knocked, its contents rattling like cooking kernels of popcorn.

ON THE STAGE ABOVE, the Stone Widow was speaking of salvation. "The future will need strength," she proclaimed.

From his position in the jostling crowd, Kane watched as one of the three robed figures who were acting as the woman's assistants brought a wooden box over to her from its place at the edge of the stage. The box was roughly one foot square, and though Kane couldn't know it, it was an identical match to the one that Domi had just discovered beneath the raised stage.

"You all shall be that strength," the woman on stage continued joyously.

The crowd cheered in agreement, pushing ever closer to the orator. On stage, the robed man nudged the lid of the box aside, opening it so that the Stone Widow could reach within. From where he stood, Kane could not see what was in the box but he could tell it was heavy.

JUST FEET BELOW, Domi gasped as the strange stones ran across her skin. She brushed at them as their dark shapes moved along her right arm, watching in horror as they clung to her hand, ringing her wrist with a caking of stones. She grunted as she tried once again to pluck them from her flesh.

Several of the stones were sinking into the flesh of her right arm where they had first touched her, digging in with their sharp edges, forming the beginnings of a shell across Domi's skin. And all Domi could do was grit her teeth against the pain.

CLOSE TO THE FRONT of the stage, Edwards felt the pull of the box as the Stone Widow reached within. It seemed to be tugging at his mind, magnet to magnet.

"We are all grieving," the woman on stage proclaimed. "Ullikummis ascended, and we are left to grieve the passing. But the future is right here, within me. Within us all."

With the crowd transfixed, the Stone Widow plucked a handful of stones from the box, each one no bigger than her thumb joint. Kane balked as he realized that they were shards of Ullikummis. He searched the crowd for Edwards, saw the man reach a hand to his forehead and wince as if in pain.

The Stone Widow held her arm outstretched and, before Kane could do anything, opened her hand, palm down, above Edwards's head. A single stone—just a pebble really—dropped from her hand, falling onto Edwards's shoulders and the back of his neck. Edwards fell back, sweeping at the stone and brushing it away over the heads of the crowd. Beside him, another crowd member was receiving one of the living stones, arms outstretched to accept this precious gift from a god. But as the Stone Widow handed over the stone, there came a crash from below the stage and she turned.

One of the robed security men turned also, his brow furrowed beneath his hood. "What the heck—?"

Then there came more bumping from the underside of the stage as Domi bashed her head against it in her haste to get out, the living stones pouring across her skin, all the way up her right arm.

In front of the stage, Edwards shook his head to clear it of the buzzing before searching the crowd to locate his colleagues. "Kane—? Grant—?"

From his right, Kane came hurtling forward, swept along by the surging crowd eager to accept the eerie, living gifts. "Edwards, what's happ—?"

He stopped, spying the commotion at the far end of the stage where Domi had come barreling out from her hiding place. She had chosen to wear a light summery dress that left her chalk arms bare, and Kane could see immediately the dark spots rising along the right arm, rolling up it in some weird perversion of raindrops. Two of the robed acolytes were moving toward her, each of them reaching inside his billowing robes and pulling something free. Kane already knew that each of those figures would be packing heat.

"Domi, look out," Kane called, placing his left hand on Edwards's shoulder and using it to propel himself over the crowd and onto the stage. With his other hand,

Kane gestured forward, and the specific flinch movement of his wrist tendons activated the hidden holster he wore under his right sleeve, powering a weapon into his hand. The Sin Eater was a compact handblaster, roughly fourteen inches in length but able to fold in on itself for storage in the hidden sleeve holster. Once the official sidearm of the Magistrate Division, the Sin Eater fired 9 mm rounds. The trigger had no guard, as the necessity had never been foreseen for any kind of safety features. The absolute nature of that means of potential execution reflected the high regard with which Magistrates like Kane were viewed in the villes; their judgment could never be wrong. Thus, if the user's index finger was crooked at the time the weapon reached his hand, the pistol would begin firing automatically. Though no longer a Magistrate, Kane had retained his weapon from his days in service at Cobaltville, and he felt most comfortable with the weapon in hand.

Ahead of Kane, the two robed figures had brought what appeared to be slingshots into their hands, just simple coils of leather. Despite their primitive appearance, the slingshots could launch rock missiles at speeds that rivaled a bullet from a gun. These were the default weapon of the troops for Ullikummis, and Kane had been on the receiving end of their lethal projectiles on more than one occasion in the past three months.

"Kane, they've got stones," Edwards warned, recovering from his momentary loss of concentration.

"I see them," Kane muttered under his breath.

In unison, the two hooded forms spun the slingshots in their hands, gathering speed in a fraction of a second before unleashing the first of their stone ammunition. No larger than a knuckle each, two stones fired from the whirling slingshots like bullets, cutting through the air toward Domi's writhing form. At the same instant, Kane drew a bead on the hooded figure to the left and stroked the trigger of his Sin Eater, sending a single 9 mm bullet into the back of the man's leg. The man went down in a flutter of robes, crying out in pain as his leg gave way in a burst of blood.

Concentrating on protecting Domi, Kane was dimly aware that chaos was erupting in the main room behind him, the crowd startled by the gunshots in the enclosed space. But there was not time to worry about that now—Grant and Edwards could take care of it.

Kane charged across the stage as the figure to his left fell, bringing the Sin Eater around to take out the second. The figure in the robe surprised Kane with the swiftness of his response, spinning and bringing his arm up, batting away the muzzle of the Sin Eater even before Kane could pull the trigger a second time.

"Put the sling down," Kane demanded as he was knocked two paces to his left by the savage blow.

In response, the hooded figure simply smiled, reloading his simple but effective weapon in a blur of movement.

Down on the floor behind the stage, Domi was writhing in pain as two dozen stones rushed over her body, rolling like snail shells and leaving bloody welts in their wake. A complete line of the tiny stones had encircled her arm just below the elbow, forming a second skin there. "H-hurts," Domi hissed as she tried to pull one of the shell-like rocks from her limb. It pulled away with an audible popping sound, releasing her flesh with a spit of blood. Around it, the other stones shimmered and throbbed, shuffling to take its place.

Among the crowd, Grant and Edwards were calling for everyone to calm down.

"Just a little mix-up," Grant said, forcing that old Magistrate authority into his tone. "Everyone keep calm and no one's going to get hurt."

"Screw you!" yelled a man from just behind him, and Grant automatically ducked as his peripheral vision caught something being thrown at his head.

The powerfully built ex-Mag turned then, commanding his own Sin Eater into his hand from its hidden wrist holster. "We're busting this scam open, people," he shouted, targeting the man who had thrown his shoe. "You need to calm the hell down—right now."

Grant swept the blaster over the crowd at head level, warning them back as he backed toward the stage. Edwards was beside him, a smaller-caliber pistol now in his hands from its hiding place at the small of his back. As the two of them reached the stage, the Stone Widow and her remaining acolyte leaped over them, launching into the crowd and hurrying for the doors.

Dammit, Grant thought. Why was it that wherever he went with Kane he always ended up in situations like this? It was Kane, he was a magnet for trouble.

"Edwards, grab the box," Grant commanded as he chased after the woman.

Edwards charged after the retreating robed figure who was hefting the box of stones, shoving members of the crowd aside in his urgency to reach the man. Sensing the danger, the figure turned, his face a patchwork of wrinkled lines and puckered skin.

"You're one of us," the robed man hissed as he saw Edwards barrel toward him.

"Used to be," Edwards spit, pistol-whipping the man behind his ear.

The robed figure lurched forward, dropping the box at the strike, and its contents spilled across the room.

"Everyone back," Edwards ordered, skipping away from the strewed rocks. "Get back!"

Behind him, the crowd raised their voices in confusion.

AT THE REAR OF THE STAGE, Kane ducked as a volley of stones hurtled toward him from the shooter. As the rocks zipped over his head, Kane powered himself forward, charging at the man.

As he saw Kane charge toward him, the robed figure said one ominous sentence that Kane had heard time and time and again in the past few months: "I am stone."

Kane plowed into the man, knocking both of them back and off the stage. Although only a small drop, the robed man slammed against the floor with a loud crack of bone. Kane landed on top of him, and he brought the clenched fist of his left hand down in a swift, sharp jab. The punch struck the man full in the face, and Kane watched with satisfaction as his eyes flickered and he fell unconscious.

"No, you ain't," Kane muttered as he pulled himself off the fallen figure, moving to help Domi.

Back on the stage, the robed man's colleague was just recovering from the gunshot. An expert marksman, Kane had targeted him perfectly, clipping the top of his leg and hobbling him just long enough that he could not reload his sling.

Kane scurried across the stage to where Domi lay writhing on the floor. The albino woman was rolling back and forth, hissing like a cat as the living stones ran across the flesh of her arm and up toward her shoulder, affixing themselves quicker than she could remove them. Domi snatched for another as it clambered toward her throat, wrenching it away with a tear of her skin.

"Okay, Domi," Kane said calmly, "I'm right here."

Domi's scarlet eyes glared into his. "Kane, get them off me," she begged through gritted teeth.

Commanding his blaster back into its hidden holster, Kane kneeled next to Domi and reached for the shifting stones. Hands just a couple of inches away from her body, he stopped himself, staring nervously at the semi-living things. Like a swarm of tiny-shelled insects, the hard backs of the stones had massed against Domi's arm, creating solid bands there that wrapped over her skin like bangles.

"Kane?" Domi squealed. "They're pushing into me. I can feel them."

Kane had had a similar stone embedded in him just a few months earlier, and he could still recall the pain it had caused. Like leeches, Kane knew that the insidious things needed to be wrenched from the body before they gained any greater hold.

"Okay," Kane said, "let me work."

ON THE STAGE BEHIND KANE, the robed figure was pushing himself up, careful not to put pressure on his wounded leg. As soon as he was standing, the slingshot began to revolve again in his hand, cutting through the air with an audible whoosh as he targeted the man who had shot him.

Still standing over the spilled stones like a barricade, Edwards saw the hooded figure rise, saw the slingshot picking up speed in his grip. Edwards assessed the situation in an instant and concluded that taking a potshot at the man was too dangerous in this crowd. So he ran, knocking aside several of the congregation as he rushed for the stage and leaped. Before the robed man could launch the stone projectile, Edwards threw himself at him.

"No way, buddy," Edwards growled as he slammed full force into Kane's would-be attacker. "Fight's over for you."

The hooded man dropped to the stage with a crash under the weight of Edwards's attack, crying in agony as his wounded leg was wrenched painfully to the side.

Edwards turned to the crowd that was warily approaching the spilled stones he had been guarding. "Nobody touch anything," he warned, "for your own safety."

The Stone Widow weaved through the crowd, hurrying toward the main exit of the hangar with the last of the robed guards stumbling after her, recovering from Edwards's attack. "What happened?" she asked. "The stones…"

"We'll come back for them," the robed man said. "Let's just get out of here."

They both looked up as Grant stepped from the shadows to block the door. "You ain't going nowhere," he warned.

Beside the Stone Widow, the robed figure turned on Grant, throwing a handful of stones in the ex-Magistrate's face. Grant lifted his arm to protect himself, batting the stones aside as they slapped uselessly against the Kevlar of his coat sleeve.

Before the robed figure could follow through, Grant had his Sin Eater pressed against the man's forehead, whip fast. "You try that again, you'll be doing it without a head on those shoulders," Grant warned ominously.

Seeing the futility of arguing, the robed man slowly raised his hands in surrender.

OVER THE NEXT FIFTEEN minutes, Kane used a knife to pluck the stones from Domi's arm while she lay there, biting her lip. "Evil things," she hissed, and Kane was inclined to agree.

Removed, the stones moved only for a few moments before lying still on the floor. It seemed that contact with flesh triggered them, and separated from the warmth of Domi's body they ceased functioning, returning to their dormant state.

Once he was done, Kane produced a little medical kit from a pouch in his belt. The kit included several antiseptic wipes, and he used these to clean the grazed sections of Domi's arm where the stones had tried to bond.

"Does this mean Ullikummis isn't dead?" Domi asked.

"He's dead, all right," Kane assured her as he wiped at one of the grazes. "Saw it with my own eyes. Just a few last bits of his crap to clean up."

Domi watched the unmoving stones for a few seconds. "They tried to—" she began and Kane nodded.

"I know."

While Kane nursed Domi's wounds, Edwards guided the confused congregation to the doors, assuring them they had been duped and that this was just another old-time scam, the kind of thing their grandfathers were either pulling or falling for in the Deathlands.

"Go home and find a better life for yourselves,"

Edwards told them. "'Cause you won't find it here in a bunch of empty promises."

Whether the congregation took his warning to heart, no one could say, but the sight of a man with a bullet-bitten ear brandishing a blaster and ordering them from the hangar was enough to dissuade them from asking too many questions. Once they had left, Edwards carefully retrieved the spilled contents of the other box of stones, piling them together with his booted feet, careful not to let them touch his skin. They seemed dormant now, dead things, but he had felt them call to him earlier, deep in his skull where Ullikummis had touched him.

While his companions were clearing up the mess, Grant brought the Stone Widow to the rear of the stage along with one of her robed assistants. The other sec men had been disarmed by Edwards, and both were still unconscious. Edwards proceeded to tie them up with strips of their own robes while Grant interrogated the two who remained awake.

"Where did these stones come from?" Grant asked, fixing the Stone Widow and her guardian with a no-nonsense stare.

"What's it to you?" the robed figure challenged.

Beneath his hood, he looked tired and drawn, a man of twenty-five with the skin of a man of sixty or seventy. It was as if something was eating him up from inside. Grant had seen this before when he was a Magistrate, drug users hopped up on jolt or some other stimulant, burning through their own bodies in just a few years. In the case of the robed man, Grant suspected he knew what it was. His robe indicated that he had been one of Ullikummis's elite guards, the people whom Cerberus had dubbed "firewalkers." Each firewalker had a sentient stone embedded within his or her skull that could simulate the physical properties of Ullikummis, turning flesh to stone during bouts of incredible concentration. The stones had been linked to Ullikummis himself, and with him destroyed they were withering and dying, eating away at their hosts like parasites.

"Come here," Grant said, grabbing the man by the scruff of the neck and marching him over to a window of the hangar.

Edwards remained with the Stone Widow, sitting on the edge of the stage and holding his blaster ready in case she tried anything. She looked defeated, biting her lip in futility.

"See this?" Grant said, shoving the robed man face-first toward the window. "Your face, you see that?"

The man looked at his reflection in the glass. "What of it, man?" he replied contemptuously.

"You've got a stone inside you, right?" Grant said. "Just like the ones that attacked the white girl over there."

"Mitra?" the man said. "She shouldn't have been—"

"Never mind what she should and shouldn't have been doing," Grant cut in. "How old are you?"

"What? Twenty-three. What's it matter to you?"

"You're even younger than I'd guessed," Grant said sorrowfully. "Take another look at your face."

The twenty-three-year-old man looked at his reflection in the dropping-spattered glass of the window.

"You're looking old," Grant told him. "No escaping it."

The robed man look irritated, but he seemed unsure of where to direct his anger. "Is there a point to all this?"

"You have a stone inside you," Grant told him. "Just like the ones that tried to attach themselves to Mitra there. They've burned out, my friend. They're past their due date. Whatever that stone used to do for you, now all it does is eat you up. You need to get it removed. Your god is gone and he ain't coming back."

"You have no idea of the power—" the man began.

"Yes, I do," Grant said solemnly. "Try it. Go ahead, tap the stone field and show me what you can do."

The man glared at him, suspecting a trick. Grant encouraged him with an incline of his head. "Go on."

Standing there by the wall, the man clenched his fists and spoke three words: "I am stone."

Grant drew back his fist and, without warning, smacked the man in the jaw. The man was knocked back by the force of that blow, staggering backward until, three steps later, he slammed against the wall behind him.

"Stone, huh?" Grant taunted.

The robed man wiped at his chin, swiping blood away from a loosened tooth. "What…?" he asked, confused. "You… What happened?"

"Stones don't work anymore," Grant told him. "Trust my people, and we'll get it out of you and anyone else that needs it. Leave them in there, and they'll burn through your body in next to no time. That's your choice. Are we clear?"

The man nodded, still rubbing at his sore jaw. "So what do you want me to do?"

Grant pointed at the second box of stones that Kane had now carefully retrieved from under the stage per Domi's instruction. He had sealed the box to ensure nothing could touch his skin.

"The stones," Grant said. "I want to know where they came from."

The man looked at Grant with resignation, a shining droplet of blood budding at his split lip. "Okay, man, I'll tell you what I know. But you said you'd help me, right?"

"That's what we're here for," Grant assured him.

Chapter 6

The graveyard was silent, its stone slabs overgrown, the ancient gravestones broken and ruined. A mausoleum stood in the center of the small plot, its faux-Roman columns subsumed by creepers, their leaves as red as sunset. Overhead, the sun itself was still bright as afternoon prophesized evening, a place marker burning whitely in the blue sky. For a moment, the leaves of the creepers bent in a breeze that could not be felt, and the chipped and broken gravestones seemed to shake and bulge in their spots. Then a burst of light appeared from nowhere, all the colors of the spectrum swirling in its impossible depths.

Brigid and Rosalia materialized in that lotus-blossom swirl of color as the twin cones of light shimmered. The beautiful light burst cut more than a dozen feet into the sky and, impossibly, the same distance down into the earth, creating an hourglass shape in the once-still graveyard. This was an optical illusion generated by the opening of a window through the cosmos, and it had been created by the ignition of the interphaser.

The interphaser was a simple metal unit, one foot tall and the same on each side of its square base. Its sides reached up to form a pyramid shape, and the light burst seemed to emanate from somewhere within it before disappearing a moment later with the speed of a popped balloon.

"Nice place," Rosalia observed as she lifted her foot from the tangled vines that crisscrossed the ground. "Cerberus would feel right at home, huh?"

Working the controls of the interphaser, Brigid looked up to see what Rosalia was indicating. It was a statue of a dog on a stone plinth. The dog was a pointer, sitting obediently, its head cocked as if waiting for instruction. Vines had grown over the plinth and wrapped most of the hound's body.

Brigid looked around as she packed the interphaser in its carrying case, seeing similar statues of dogs and cats poised amid the thick undergrowth. A pet cemetery, then.

"Do you know where we are?" Brigid asked her dark-haired companion.

Rosalia was pacing around the little graveyard, peering over its low walls. "I think so," she said. "House over that way, I've seen it from the road a few times."

Brigid looked where Rosalia indicated, spotted the house between the trees. It was a big mansion-type place, and the pet cemetery lay on its grounds. Presumably its one-time owners had thought a lot of their animals, Brigid guessed.

Standing, Brigid made her way across the overgrown graveyard and joined Rosalia at the gates. The gates themselves were missing, probably stolen and melted down sometime after the place had been abandoned. The nukecaust had dramatically culled Earth's population at the start of the twenty-first century. A lot of things had been taken and applied to new uses by the struggling survivors.

"How far away are we," Brigid asked, "from this village of yours?"

Rosalia smiled enigmatically. "Not far."

With that, Rosalia stepped over the single fallen gatepost and tromped off toward the house. Back in the graveyard, Brigid watched for a moment, wondering about the logic of what she was doing. Kane trusted this woman, despite their previous run-ins, she knew that much, and his word had always carried weight for Brigid. She and Kane were *anam-charas,* soul friends linked throughout eternity, bonded at some spiritual level to always find and watch over each other. As such, their relationship ran to a far deeper level of trust than most people would ever know.

And what about their *anam-chara* bond, anyway? It wasn't as if Kane was the center of Brigid's world; they weren't lovers in any traditional sense, even though they felt love for each other. Ullikummis had forced them apart, turning Brigid into something she could barely recognize. While under Ullikummis's influence, Brigid had actually shot Kane, blasting him in the chest. With her photographic memory, she could replay that moment over and over if she chose to, and it haunted her every time she looked at Kane. Their *anam-chara* bond had meant so much, yet now she wondered if she could even bear to be near him after what she had done. Of course, Kane had said nothing of the incident, had only joked nonchalantly, making light of the whole wretched escapade. But it festered in Brigid's mind, lurking in the shadows like a sinister face from a child's nightmare.

To Brigid, it felt as if they were losing the *anam-chara* bond that had held them together for so long. No matter how much she wanted to reach out, something stopped her, emotionally stunting her.

"Are you coming, Red?" Rosalia called from across

the mansion's abandoned grounds, intruding on Brigid's melancholy.

Brigid nodded firmly before tromping from the cemetery and trudging across the long grass, the carrying case holding the interphaser swinging at her side. Maybe Lakesh had been right. Maybe she needed to get away.

THEY TREKKED FOR TWENTY minutes, the evening sun warm against Brigid's back even through the weave of the shadow suit she wore. The shadow suit acted as an independent, temperature-controlled environment for its wearer, but Brigid chose to ignore that, preferring instead to feel everything that the real world had to throw at her. She had been away from that for too long.

Rosalia set a fast pace, keeping to a comfortable jog as she led the way out of the overgrown grounds of the dilapidated mansion and onto the dusty road beyond. Rosalia kept herself in the prime of physical fitness, and Brigid noted how little the exertion seemed to affect her.

There was a paved road a little way beyond the forgotten mansion, and carts and scratch-built automobiles rolled down the street now and then, passing the two women as they made their way to their destination. Beside the road it was mostly open ground, sandy red earth giving the whole area a blushlike tint. Now and then the two travelers would pass a shack that had been constructed at the side of the road, and Brigid might spot a woman there by the porch, sitting down to darn the holes in a pair of man's socks or leaning over to water the potted plants proudly arrayed by the front door.

"Who lives here?" Brigid asked as they passed one of the shacks.

Rosalia looked around her. "People. Just people. Why, what did you expect? *Caballeros* and *banditos,* swashbuckling their way down the streets?"

Brigid shook her head. "It's just you forget sometimes what the world really is, all the people who make up its diversity and color."

Marching onward down the road, Rosalia turned back and smiled. "I thought you never forgot anything," she teased.

"I don't know," Brigid mused. "The world we inhabit—Cerberus—it's all so frenetic. I guess I do forget sometimes that a normal world is out here."

"Life's not just memory, is it?" Rosalia observed. "It's for living."

Together, the two women continued along the road until Rosalia found the junction she had been searching for. The road itself continued on, but a rough dirt track had begun to run parallel to it at about fifteen feet away, rutted wheel marks crisscrossing between the two.

"Come on," Rosalia instructed, stepping off the paved road.

Brigid followed, joining her companion on the other track.

Before long, the track veered away from the paved road once more, following a gentle incline that ultimately led into the mountains.

They walked for another quarter hour, following the path through the foothills and around the mountains themselves.

"Do you know where we're going?" Brigid asked once, gazing around the desolate, uninhabited path.

Rosalia simply turned to her and smiled, offering nothing more than the incline of her head.

Eventually the narrow path dropped again, and Brigid saw buildings waiting in the distance, hidden within the recess of the valleys. The buildings were white-painted stucco, no doubt to reflect the sun's heat during the daytime, now turned pink by its setting glare. Most of the buildings were just one-story, sprawling structures that accommodated perhaps five or more rooms, but there were a few two-story buildings, one with a high steeple dominating its western side. A few people could be seen milling between the buildings, and the occasional sound of voices and laughter came from below.

"Does this place have a name?" Brigid asked as she trekked with Rosalia along the pathway.

"Not anymore," Rosalia told her with a shrug.

Brigid knew better than to probe her reticent companion too deeply, and together she and Rosalia marched past a sprawling graveyard that sat about a mile from the town itself. The graves were indicated by simple gravestones, each one marked not by a name but merely a number. Some of them looked more than a hundred years old, and not a single one had flowers.

All around, fields of crops were waiting to be harvested, a herd of cows and a sheep flock grazing in other fields patterned with long grass. It didn't take much imagination to realize that this hidden community could feed itself. Brigid guessed it had perhaps sprung from some old survivalist troop dating back to the nukecaust that had reshaped the world.

"Do you come from around here?" Brigid asked as they walked toward the town's outskirts.

"No," Rosalia said. "I was schooled here. In the nunnery, over there."

Brigid looked, saw the little chapel with its bell tower. It was just two stories high and built of stucco like the rest of the town, and it was probably the largest single building here.

The sun setting to their left, the two women walked past the simple stone marker that indicated the town limits, with Rosalia leading the way toward the nunnery. "You'll like it here," she promised. "It's quiet."

Brigid thanked her. She had agreed to come here when Lakesh had proposed it because it meant relief from the incessant questions from her colleagues. Rosalia was different. She didn't ask questions; she just seemed to listen and to observe. Before they had left Cerberus, she had assured Brigid that she would take her to a place of tranquillity and meditation. It sounded preferable to therapy from Reba DeFore and, away from Cerberus and still carrying the interphaser, Brigid knew she could just run and keep running if she chose to, until she finally disappeared.

They walked through the open gates to the nunnery, an arch that was high enough to accommodate a horse and cart, and stepped into the courtyard within. Whatever Brigid had expected, she was left dumbfounded by what she saw. Women, all of them young and many of them still just girls, were involved in various forms of combat, throwing one another on straw mats, engaged in swordplay, shooting arrows at targets and working nunchakus in a furious display of fighting prowess.

"What kind of place is this?" Brigid said, taking everything in.

"I told you already," Rosalia explained. "It's a school."

How long had it been? Black John Jefferson's eye-sight was dimming as he trudged heavily along the stone corridor. The walls to either side of him sloped subtly inward, narrowing the tunnel at its roof, four-teen feet above his dipped head. The walls themselves were solid, and the whole tunnel echoed with each heavy footstep.

"Where is this place?" Black John muttered, his words echoing.

He had climbed down the stone steps, slowly and heavily, his blood spilling onto each one as he passed. In his weak and wounded state, the stairs seemed to go on for a long time, and the light from the sky above had narrowed to just a single foot-wide shaft by the time he found the bottom stair.

Down there, Black John had trudged on, step by la-borious step, following the only path he could see in the dim light from the stairs. There should be sconces here, or some other way to light the area, he felt sure, but he could find none. His head was reeling too much to care.

It took twenty minutes to walk the corridor, each footstep like running a marathon now, blood filling his blouse and streaming down his legs. His wounds just wouldn't scab over anymore; they had been pulled about too much.

Ahead of him a doorway led into an open room. He stopped on its threshold and leaned heavily against the wall, his breath coming in ragged, wheezing gasps that echoed through the underground maze. In the dark-ness, he could only see hints of the room beyond. It was wide, roughly circular, and it seemed to take up the whole expanse of the building. Furthermore, there didn't seem to be any furniture in the room, only a broad floor covered in dust.

Well, he had come this far, hadn't he?

Black John removed his hand from the wall, and when he did so a bloody handprint remained there, clinging to the stone like some awful, red arachnid. He walked into the room, bent almost double, the pain in his ruined guts like a burning blade.

Maybe there is treasure in here, he thought. He was delirious now from the loss of blood, and he had all but forgotten what had brought him here in the first place, forgotten that he was dying.

Three paces were all he could manage. Three paces, and then the vicious pirate keeled to the floor, the clatter of his fall echoing through the stone temple.

As he lay there, dying and burning for revenge, his blood leaked onto the stone floor, filling the intricate pattern that had been carved there ten thousand years before. The carvings formed one huge symbol, and the symbol represented just a single word:

Engage.

Chapter 7

"There were five boxes in all," the Stone Widow's assistant explained as Grant loomed over him in the interrogation room. "Everyone split up once Ullikummis disappeared, and the stones were divvied up between the acolytes."

"Where did the other boxes go?" Grant asked. He had been talking with this man for more than three hours now, and he was starting to form a picture of what had happened after the God War. Cerberus had been on the run from Ullikummis's people for so long that they hadn't had time to stop and examine his legacy. From what the man, whose name was Daniel, told him, it seemed that Ullikummis had to an extent been a force for good, bringing people together. Despite the advances brought by the Program of Unification, the world was still recovering from the greatest tragedy in human history—the nukecaust that had recast the world as a radioactive deathland. Under Ullikummis's influence, new communities had begun to form, and new territories had taken shape.

In the company of the Stone Widow, Daniel had traveled from the East Coast all the way across to the West. He had met friends all over—and by friends, Grant knew he meant people faithful to the dead stone god—and had seen grand construction projects like bridge building and river damming taking shape as the outlanders finally worked together. "They're still pockets right now," Daniel had said, "but it will grow."

Now, as they sat together in the interrogation room in the basement of the Cerberus redoubt, Grant jotted notes in a small notebook, occasionally consulting a map and asking Daniel to mark up areas of interest. Daniel had agreed to all of this once Grant had brought home what the stone was doing to him, but there was a catch—Grant had promised that his people here would remove the parasitic stone, but no one was really sure that such a thing could be done.

Unlike the rock lining inside Edwards's skull and the other obedience stones that they had managed to excise, the stones in the firewalkers were seeded very deep, and they tapped into the nervous system at a symbiotic level. A pragmatist, Grant had kept this information from Daniel, certain that the end justified the means and knowing his people would try. Grant's team had brought the others back, too, the Stone Widow and her men, and those three were in a holding cell while Lakesh and his team decided what to do with them next.

"I don't remember what happened to the other boxes," Daniel said, tugging nervously at his sleeve. "They could be anywhere by now."

"These things are alive," Grant reminded him, "and they're dangerous. You see what it's doing to you, burning you up from the inside like so much human fuel. A whole crate of these things could kill a ville—women, children, everyone. You don't want that on your conscience."

Daniel shook his head infinitesimally. "What are you people, anyway? Why do you care?"

"We care because it's the right thing to do," Grant told him.

"And who are you?"

"We're the people who care, that's all you need to know."

With that, Grant got back to his questioning.

ON THE OTHER SIDE of the one-way glass that over-looked the interrogation room, Kane and Edwards were watching the whole exchange in a darkened ob-servation booth.

"Oh, Grant's good," Kane said cheerily. "Answer the guy with Zen logic. I like it."

As he spoke, the door opened and Lakesh stepped in to join the two ex-Magistrates listening to Daniel's interrogation. "How are things going here?" he asked.

"Slow but sure," Kane said.

"And we're out of snacks," Edwards added, pluck-ing the last cookie from the plate resting on the shelf that lined the one-way mirror.

"How's Domi?" Kane asked as Lakesh peered through the window at Grant and the rapidly aging acolyte.

"Reba proposes to keep her in the infirmary for a few hours," Lakesh said, not turning away from the view window, "just to make sure there are no long-term ill effects from her bout with the stones, but in essence I am told she is fine. Thank you, Kane, for moving so swiftly to help her."

"You're very welcome," Kane said. "She's a fighter. She would have done the same for me if our positions had been reversed."

"THINK BACK," GRANT URGED. "Where did the stones come from? Originally."

Daniel leaned heavily forward against the single desk of the well-lit interrogation room, trying to recall the details Grant was probing for.

"We were on pilgrimage to Bensalem," Daniel began, "out on the East Coast, when we heard the news of Lord Ullikummis's passing. Hit us all really hard, you know? We had passage on a ferry at the time, me, Mel and the others. Rickety old boat, hit the waves with all the dynamism of a brick."

"Then what happened?" Grant prompted.

"The message came through the same way the call had, in our minds. We were at Bensalem by then."

"Little island off the coast here," Grant clarified, indicating it on the map. "Go on."

"Mel said she didn't want Ullikummis to be dead," Daniel recalled. "None of us did. It was like losing your own life. And so we did the pilgrimage anyway, landed at the island and looked at the thing he had built there."

Grant didn't know all the details, but he understood that the island fortress of Bensalem had been raised from the ocean bed by Ullikummis just a few months before.

"We found the buds there, the stones," Daniel said. "The ferryman had some old crates on his boat, so we divvied them up. Mel took one and it settled into her skin, which proved they still worked. You see—they still worked then."

"He hadn't been dead long," Grant surmised.

"Then we left, went our separate ways," Daniel told him. "Mel and me stuck together. She felt the stone growing inside her like a seed."

"The Stone Widow," Grant muttered, shaking his head. Was there no end to the idiocy these people would bring upon themselves? "What happened to the ferryman?" he asked.

"I don't know," Daniel admitted after a moment's consideration. "Said something about heading back home."

"And where would that be?"

"You're kidding me, right?" Daniel asked. "I spoke to the guy for maybe two minutes. I don't remember if he even told me."

"It's okay. What was his name?" Grant said patiently.

Daniel thought. "Al. Alfred," he said. "Alfred Stone." Of course. Every convert to the faith of Ullikummis changed his surname to Stone. It would be like searching for a needle in a haystack to locate the man by name alone.

"Anything else you remember?" Grant asked. "The name of the boat?"

"Now you're asking," Daniel said. "It was a foreign name, I had to ask what it meant. *Second Mountain,* that was it."

"Second Mountain," Grant repeated, writing the words on his pad. "But you translated it. What did it say originally? What language was it in?"

"Seg—? Oh, I don't know, man," Daniel whined. "Look, can I get a drink or something? I thought you were going to help me."

"I am helping you," Grant said with no room for apology. "Now, answer the question. After that, I'll get you your drink. Heck, I'll get you a banquet if you want me to."

Daniel nodded, pushing a weary hand against his old-too-soon features. "He looked tanned," he said, "like a Latino. Black hair. South American, I guess. That's all I can remember."

"Latino," Grant repeated. Then he scooted his chair back and stood. "Thanks, Daniel. You stay here a little longer and someone will bring that drink for you. Hang in there, man—it'll all be fine."

With that, Grant exited the interrogation chamber, locking the room behind him.

"'*La Segunda Montaña*,'" Donald Bry read from the computer display less than an hour later. "Owner, one Alfredo Rodriguez, born in Papantla, Mexico, married, wife's name's Juanita. Migrated north in search of work four years ago. Fisherman by trade.

"The boat itself is a fishing scow with a long history. Alfredo isn't the first owner. He purchased it at a registered sale in Tuxpan."

"Where is that?" Kane asked, leaning closer over Bry in the Cerberus ops center. Grant stood at his side, blowing on a cup of green tea to cool it.

"It's a port located very close to Mexico City," Bry explained. "Papantla's just a little way to the south, part of what used to be called Veracruz."

"Used to be?" Grant repeated doubtfully.

Bry shrugged. "Map's been cut and recut a few times since then," he said. "I'm going on what data we have."

Kane stared at Bry's computer screen for a moment, scanning the information there. "Well, it's something to go on." He had been a Magistrate for a long time before joining the Cerberus operation. He knew any lead was valuable, however slim it might seem.

"We struck lucky with the boat connection," Bry agreed. "People move from place to place without anyone taking much notice, but boats have to be registered. Mexico's a relatively narrow strip of land surrounded by water. The port authorities there are pretty diligent with their record keeping, took about two seconds to tap into it once we nailed the country."

Grant took a sip from his tea before he spoke. "I guess we'll head to this Tuxpan place and see what we can find. Any evidence of the stones being used is going to be hard to hide."

Supervising the work on the ancient Mercator relief map across the wall behind them, Lakesh had been listening to the whole exchange. He nodded as Grant spoke, making his way across the understaffed operations room. "Brigid has just traveled to an area close to the Mexican border with Rosalia," he said, and Kane raised an eyebrow with interest. "Perhaps you could arrange to meet up when you're all done."

"Yeah," Kane said with noticeable resignation. "Sounds like a plan."

Then, the two ex-Mags left the room to prepare themselves for a return to the field the next day, passing beneath the ongoing repairs on the huge map.

Kane hurried out and into the main artery of the mountain redoubt, and Grant found he had to trot along just to keep up.

"Everything okay?" Grant asked.

"Sure, it's fine," Kane said.

"With you and Brigid, I mean," Grant pushed.

"What?" Kane asked, keeping up his fast pace as he walked down the tunnel-like corridor.

"Didn't seem all right in there, Kane," Grant said.

Kane ignored him, not even bothering to respond as he continued his fast pace along the corridor.

"Maybe you can fool the others, but I know you,"

Grant said, matching Kane step for step. "What's happening, man? Let me in."

"You've seen Baptiste," Kane muttered bitterly. "You know how she is right now. The whole Ullikummis thing really messed with her."

"You speak to her?" Grant asked.

Kane nodded. "Yeah, we spoke. She told me she didn't want to remember any of it. Baptiste, the memory freak, didn't want to remember any of it."

Together, the two men passed through a side door and entered a stairwell. Once tiled, the steps had been marred by rocky growths like the rest of the redoubt, leaving them rough and uneven. Their boots clattered against the steps as they ascended, making their way toward their private quarters to clean up and get a night's rest before shipping out again at dawn.

As they reached the turn where the staircase became wider, Kane stopped, looking at his partner for the first time. "You know what?" he said. "Maybe she's right. Maybe we should all just forget about it."

Grant shook his head. "Uh-uh, we're still mopping this up," he reminded Kane. "We're about to zip across to Mexico to try to locate a missing batch of parasitic stones that we think budded from Ullikummis's body. This shit's going to be with us a long while yet."

"If it is, then Baptiste won't be," Kane said. There was a note of chilling certainty in his voice that Grant had rarely heard before. "We lost her once, Grant. If it happens again it'll be because I pushed her."

"*You* pushed her?" Grant repeated, emphasizing his confusion.

"We," Kane corrected. "All of us."

Grant looked at Kane, trying to read his face. He had known the man such a long time, and yet Kane could still surprise him. Kane met Grant's questioning gaze with his own, steely gray-blue eyes fixing with his. Grant saw the anger there and the bitterness.

"You think you're responsible, don't you?" he said.

"I should have killed Ullikummis when I had the chance," Kane explained. "That way none of this would have happened."

"When?" Grant challenged. "When did you have that opportunity?"

"You remember when we went deep-sea diving to the Ontic Library?" Kane said. "We found Ullikummis there in some kind of coma, plugged into the living datastream of the library itself."

"I remember," Grant said. "You wanted to kill him, and Baptiste stopped you. I was there, too."

"I should have tried harder," Kane said.

"That library contained the raw data for the structure of the universe," Grant said. "It was a living thing. Brigid said that killing Ullikummis while he was wired into it ran the major risk of sending a quake through reality itself. She was the only person who could hold it together long enough to make him disengage and leave the place alone. The stakes were higher than just shooting or not shooting someone. Much higher."

Kane stared at Grant, taking a deep breath before he spoke. "We saved reality but at the ultimate expense of losing Baptiste to that monster."

"You can't possibly know that," Grant said. "Way too many ifs to factor in."

"We're here and she's not," Kane said, "and even when she is here, she's not. That's the factors, all of them."

"No, it's not," Grant corrected his younger partner gently. "We've all been run ragged by this, but we need to keep our heads, Kane. Now more than ever."

"I just thought…" Kane began, and stopped himself. "I just thought that when I finally did kill Ullikummis that that was it, that it was finally over."

Grant stood there, watching his friend, wondering what he could possibly say. Finally, Kane spoke for him.

"Screw it," Kane said. "Let's go kick some Mexican stone ass."

Grant laughed. "Yeah," he agreed.

The rest would have to figure itself out with time.

SOME FOURTEEN HUNDRED miles to the south, the subject of Kane and Grant's conversation was just making her way into the courtyard that lay in the middle of the nunnery, following Rosalia's lead. All around them, girls and young women were continuing with their exercises, judo chops and wrestling holds being demonstrated and mimicked beneath the red-gold rays of the sun. An arched terrace ran along the outside of the courtyard, providing shade or shelter as the elements demanded, and Rosalia walked beneath it, encouraging Brigid to join her.

"Have to be careful here," Rosalia said. "Don't want to get hit by a throwing knife gone astray."

Brigid nodded, watching the courtyard for a moment as a girl no older than twelve—rake thin with gangly limbs and long dark hair tied back from her head—leaped high into the air from a standing start. In the air, the girl whipped her leg around to kick a dangling punch bag with a resounding thump while a half-dozen girls watched. The girl landed with swan-like grace, shuddering just slightly as she regained her footing on the ground, and her audience clapped politely while the nun overseeing them nodded once. "Well done, Catherine," the nun said, "but be careful with the landing. You stumbled."

As the two women made their way around the courtyard, Rosalia was greeted by several nuns in full habit, taking a moment from their instruction of the girls to welcome her home.

"Well, well, if it isn't little Rosalia," one said, smiling broadly. She was teaching a class on archery, and she held up her hand to the four girls she taught, instructing them to cease. "Let's look at you, young lady," she said, hurrying over.

Rosalia smiled demurely, brushing loose strands of hair from her face self-consciously. "Sister Michelle, you look well."

The nun smiled, creases appearing around her eyes and mouth. "I look old." She laughed. "You, however— well, you look more beautiful than ever. Does Mother Superior know you're here?"

"It's a surprise," Rosalia said. "And I brought a friend."

Brigid stepped forward, holding her hand out to shake Sister Michelle's. "Pleased to meet you, Sister. I'm Brigid."

As the nun welcomed her and asked about her stay, Brigid noticed the girls behind her, the four that she had been training in the art of archery. Each girl was waiting patiently, standing erect and watching the conversation without any show of emotion. At nine years old they had already been taught to observe, Brigid realized, just like Rosalia.

"Now, then, Rosalia," Sister Michelle said, "I have been trying to instill in my girls here the necessity to practice. Might I call upon you to show them why that is so important?"

Rosalia smiled self-consciously, walking across to the staging area before the targets. Sister Michelle handed her her own bow, the only one that was adult-size, and Rosalia hefted it for a moment, feeling its weight. Then, plucking an arrow from the contents of a high-sided bucket on the ground, Rosalia raised the bow to shoulder height and loaded the weapon.

Without any sign of strain, Rosalia drew back the string and launched the arrow, firing it into the black bull's-eye of the central target.

"Straight and true," she said, handing the bow back to Sister Michelle.

Beside the nun, the girls began muttering excitedly, impressed by the show of marksmanship.

"Notice how swiftly she was ready, girls," Sister Michelle told the class, continuing with her lesson.

"You do that a lot?" Brigid asked Rosalia as they made their way through the northernmost set of doors and into the building.

"I graduated top of my class," Rosalia told her. "Come on. We'll find you a room."

Brigid followed. She still wasn't sure that she would be staying, but her meeting with the nun had reassured her of one thing—these people wouldn't bother her, and they wouldn't inquire about her well-being unless she asked them to.

Chapter 8

At the Cerberus redoubt, two guards stood at the doors to her medical rooms while Cerberus physician Reba DeFore checked over the woman who had called herself the Stone Widow. DeFore was a buxom woman with long ash-blond hair that she had knotted into an elaborate French twist to keep it out of her face. Like other people in the ex-military facility, Reba wore a white jumpsuit. The Stone Widow had dressed in a medical gown, and Reba was careful as she gave the pregnant woman a physical. The other Cerberus personnel, such as Kane and Grant, might have considered the woman an enemy prisoner, but DeFore thought of her only as a patient who had potentially been exposed to a highly dangerous substance.

"Why don't you tell me a bit about yourself," DeFore said encouragingly as she held her fingers to the woman's wrist and counted her pulse.

"There's nothing to tell," the woman replied truculently.

"Everyone has something to tell," DeFore said gently. "I've been a physician long enough to recognize that. Why don't you start with your name? I assume you weren't born 'Miss Stone Widow.'"

Her patient laughed at that. "No, I guess not," she said. "It's Mel. Melanie. My parents named me after some vegetarian granny I never had a chance to meet."

"And where was that? Your parents, I mean—where did you grow up?"

"Beausoleil," Melanie said wistfully.

DeFore knew of it well. Beausoleil was one of nine villes that had dominated the United States during the twenty-third century. Beausoleil had been secretly overseen by one of the Annunaki, the would-be goddess called Lilitu. The ville was located in the area once known as Tennessee, though it had suffered a devastating air attack during one of the frequent spats between the feuding Annunaki more than a year earlier that had left it little more than rubble.

"Were you there when it got hit?" DeFore asked, satisfied that the woman's pulse was normal.

"Yeah." Melanie nodded. "I was…working in a tavern when the first bombs hit. The Tosspot Tumor, someone's idea of a joke though it never seemed very funny to me—just kind of childish. Things had been normal for as long as I could remember but this one morning there was, I don't know, an atmosphere, like there was static electricity in the air. I don't even remember if there was a noise. All I recall now was that there was this massive burst of light and then the windows blew in." She reached down, hiking up the hem of her gown a little more to show the top of her leg. There was a long scar there, an eight-inch white line running across her otherwise tanned skin. "I got hit by flying glass, but I was one of the lucky ones."

"Luck has a lot of different ways it manifests," Reba agreed as she slipped a short black sleeve over the woman's arm to check her blood pressure. As she worked the pump, her patient continued her story.

"Big pane of glass went into Vi, my boss, cut right through him. And as I lay there, listening to the explosions rattling overhead, I saw something come scuttling across the bits of broken glass that had been shitted all over the floor," Melanie said. "You know what it was? A roach. My boss was dead, but the roaches had survived."

And so had you, DeFore thought, but she didn't say anything. The woman's blood pressure was a little low, but that wasn't unusual for someone heavy with child. She made a note of it and continued her examination, letting the woman speak.

"I guess it was pretty much then that I made up my mind," Melanie explained. "I couldn't stay in that shithole any longer. I didn't mind the men, y'know, they just did what they had to do. But the bugs and all that, that's what I couldn't stand. Well, it weren't like the place was still standing after that bomb struck it.

"So I upped and left, and when I walked out, bleeding right down my leg, I saw these silver things in the sky," Melanie continued, "like big saucers, with snakes coming out of them."

"So you ran?" Reba asked.

Melanie laughed. "Damn right I ran. Straight to the gates, into the Outlands, didn't even bother to look back."

"So what brought you to Ullikummis?" DeFore asked, shining the light of her otoscope down the woman's right ear.

"I'd grown up in the ville," Mel replied. "Okay, not the best part, what with being down there in the Pits, but still. But the Outlands, that was a whole 'nother world. People are different, nasty sometimes. It wasn't a good place for a sixteen-year-old kid to be running around alone."

"You're…seventeen?" DeFore asked, unable to hide the surprise from her voice.

"Eighteen," Mel corrected, "just turned a few weeks back."

"You look…" DeFore stopped herself. "You look good for it." She had been about to say "older." Melanie, the Stone Widow, looked closer to twenty-seven or twenty-eight, her skin lined. As the woman continued to speak, DeFore ran a comb through Melanie's hair, checking for mites. That was always a risk with outlanders.

"So I heard about this promise," Mel continued, "all about the future. And I figured, I want me some of that. I want to be a part of this glorious future. They said there was a stone angel at its center, one who had been sent down from heaven to enlighten the world. Like Promen…Proman…Pro—"

"Prometheus?" DeFore suggested, parting the woman's hair gently.

"That's it," Mel agreed. "And we wanted to see him, me and Danny and some others. Did the pilgrimage, went out to his island, y'know?"

Though she was listening, DeFore's brow had creased in vexation. "Has your hair always been this thin?" she asked. She was running the comb through the woman's scalp, and as she parted the hair a wide area of baldness—in itself unusual in a woman—showed between dyed strands.

"Whussat?" Mel answered. "I don't know. I mean, I dye it sometimes and I guess that makes it brittle."

"Yes," the medic agreed. But she could tell straight away that this wasn't damage from dyeing. This was aging. The woman may be eighteen years old, but her body was anywhere between twenty-five and seventy-five. Finishing her checks, DeFore walked across the room and pulled a seat up to join Melanie, coming close so she could look her in the eye.

"Tell me about the stones," she prompted thoughtfully, patting the woman's hand gently to encourage her.

Mel nodded. "So we made it to the island, but Ullikummis weren't there," she said. "He'd died was what we heard. There were people on the boat who had the stones already, and they said they felt it. I wish I could have.

"We found this stash of stones, and I placed one against my skin just like I'd seen, here." Melanie tapped at her left wrist. "It felt weird, a bit like when a dog has finished licking you and you feel the spit dry. This stone thing went into me, hid itself there. It was weird, but kind of…enlivening. I felt really alive. To be at one with God in that instant."

"Is it still inside you?" DeFore asked.

"Yeah."

"Do you know it's killing you?" Reba asked gently. "From the inside. These things were linked to Ullikummis, but when he died they became autonomous. There's no purpose to them without Ullikummis, so they simply consume the things they touch. My colleagues believe this will kill you if we don't remove it soon."

The Stone Widow looked horrified. "No way. You can't…"

"How old was Danny when you met him?" Reba asked.

"What? I don't know. Twenty-three. No—twenty-two," the woman said, confused. "We did this thing for his birthday down on the beach where I stripped—"

"Never mind that," Reba interrupted. "You understand that Danny is getting older, much older. He's aging far more rapidly than is normal. You must have noticed that. Melanie?"

Slowly, reluctantly, the woman nodded. "It's the stone?"

DeFore nodded, placing her hand once more over that of her young patient. "We will get the stones out," she said. "It's the only course left, if you want to live. If you want your baby to live."

"I wanted to be closer to God," Melanie whispered, and Reba saw tears run from her eyes.

"I know," DeFore reassured her. "I know."

Chapter 9

La Discordia crept into the port like an ink stain on the ocean, drifting silently toward the docks before weighing anchor. There she waited, poised just beyond the mouth of the docks themselves, her crew making its way to shore via a tiny flotilla of just two rowboats led by Mr. Six. He stood in the lead rowboat and breathed in the salty air of the ocean with a mixture of familiarity and contempt.

"I can taste the sea, boys," he complained in a loud voice. "Must need more rum, and damn soon."

His colleagues on the small boat laughed as they rowed toward the dock, cheering Six on as he took a swig from the bottle he had brought along with him.

A moment later, Six's boat butted against the wooden docks like a restless goat, followed closely by its twin containing his shipmates. El Cana was a small port on the eastern coast of Mexico that strictly speaking didn't really exist. Its name was a joke, because El Cana—the cops—never much bothered with the scooped bay. As long as the bar owners and brothel managers paid their taxes or their bribes, no one in authority was much bothered about what went on here. Truth be known, the authorities would even come visit when their wives were out of town and their mistresses were angry with them.

The docks were quiet, a few children bustling about

in the dwindling sunlight, rolling marbles or stones across the stained wooden planks of the pier.

Six clambered from the rowboat and up the ladder to the pier, followed by Fern Salt and another crewman called Tuska. Tuska was a mahogany-skinned brute of a man, with a gap-toothed smile and a sequence of thick gold rings running like a strip across all four fingers of his right hand, four more running up the outside of his right ear. A good man to have on side, Tuska had both the temperament and the conversational skills of a thunderstorm.

As they passed the children, Six reached into his pocket and tossed them a rounded pebble, one of the mysterious stash they had found on the little fishing boat. He had been examining them all day, trying to figure out their purpose. They were stones, yes, and yet they seemed to have a presence in the galley of his ship where he'd looked them over, a presence as if alive. He had pocketed a handful before leaving *La Discordia,* wondering if perhaps someone at the bar there might be able to shed any light on what they were. He had a whole box load if they proved to be valuable, and if they were *really* valuable then he'd find these kids again and convince them to hand the stone back. As it was, making friends never hurt, especially thieving little whore brats like these whose loyalty could be bought for next to nothing.

Fern Salt followed Six, stepping over the kids' game with a growl, a grim sneer on his scarred face. All that Salt could think of was that pretty blonde on the scow, and how Black John had ruined his little not-so-private party with her. "Fuck Black John, let the sea have him," Salt muttered under his breath as he helped Six to Sal's Bar, close to the wooden pier.

"Y'still thinking of him," Six said, laughing, "when you should be thinking of all the fillies we'll make happy before the night is out."

As he spoke, the two men, accompanied by their crewmates, walked through the open door of Sal's. Fractured music oozed through the air from an old recording, spluttering along as it tried to find space amid the smoke fug that clouded the low roof.

The barroom was small and cramped, with a low ceiling and numerous private booths and nooks littered around its irregular angles. Sal himself stood behind the bar, his permanent five-o'clock shadow as reliable as his terrible taste in music. Beside him, Sal's daughter, seventeen years old and wearing a white dress that doubtless fitted better before she hit puberty, was pulling glasses of beer from the pumps that lined the bar top.

As ever, the bar was crowded and sweaty, peopled by men who had spent too many hours at sea and no longer knew when to stop drinking.

While Xia and Six found a table—which involved Xia gently shoving a dozing drunk aside—Salt made a beeline for the bar with Tuska accompanying. Their other shipmate, a man called Drake, had remained with the boats outside—it takes a born thief to truly know never to leave anything sellable unattended.

Salt staggered against the bar and eyed Sal's daughter. "Beer and gin and rum," he said. "Gimme it all."

The dark-haired young woman eyed him through thick lashes. Her name was Duendecito and she was no stranger to men. She could tell straight away what the pirate was thinking.

"A flagon of beer?" she asked. "Two maybe?"

"Make it three," Salt slurred. "No, four. Yeah, four."

Behind them, a fight had broken out between two men who had been playing cards, the old bottle caps they used as betting chips flying across the room as they came to blows. Tuska watched them and laughed before turning back to Sal at the bar.

"See you finally got some entertainment in this shit-hole, eh?" he said mockingly.

"Yeah, yeah, yeah." Sal hurried out from behind the bar brandishing his shotgun. He drew a bead on the two men as they traded punches, uncocking the safety. "All right, *cucarachas*," he warned them, "take it outside my bar or you won't take anything out."

After a moment, the two men ceased fighting and held their hands up in apology and defeat, brushing themselves down.

Standing at the bar, Tuska and Salt took their drinks and made their way over to their table. "Keep 'em coming, Legs," Salt instructed the woman at the bar. "As much as you've got."

At his table, Six had laid out the five remaining stones he carried and was studying one under the side light with a jeweler's eyepiece, turning it this way and that to see if he could find any clue as to its purpose.

Watching him, Xia grinned. "Shitty haul, right?"

Six laughed, flicking the stone back onto the table. "You can't fight shitty haul."

THE WOMAN WHO RAN the nunnery was called Ungela, and she met Rosalia with a long hug. Ungela was at least fifty, with hair the color of wire wool tucked beneath her blue cowl. She was dressed in the blue-and-white robes of a mother superior, and she had a slight limp that caused her to shuffle when she hurried across her office to meet Rosalia, the wide smile defining her face.

"You look so, so well," Ungela said in Spanish, and Brigid thought she could see tears glistening in the older woman's eyes.

Sparsely decorated, the office featured chestnut walls and a small desk with a well-worn blotter covering its surface. There was a picture on the wall showing the Crucifixion in stark black and white. Behind the desk, a large window looked out into the courtyard. The window had been propped open to encourage a cooling breeze, and the continuing sounds of combat could be heard as Ungela invited the two visitors to sit.

"This is my friend Brigid," Rosalia explained as they took their seats.

Mother Superior nodded, a smile creasing the lines across her face. "Brigid? An old Irish name, isn't it?" she said in accented English.

Brigid nodded. "Sadly, I'm only from as far afield as Cobaltville."

Ungela thought for a moment before she responded. "Just over the border, then," she said. "Almost a local girl. And what brings you here? Forgive me, but you strike me as a little old for our program of learning."

Brigid smiled obligingly. "No, I just…" She trailed off. Why exactly was she here?

"Brigid is a part of a team called Cerberus." Rosalia picked up the conversation, speaking in Spanish. Her words were automatically translated by Brigid's hidden Commtact. "I've been working with them over the past few months. They operate as investigators. Brigid became…a little lost. She came with me to seek guidance."

The mother superior raised her eyebrows. "Guidance?" she asked in English. "Is that it?"

Brigid wasn't entirely sure. "To be honest, I've not been myself for a while," she said, cagily referring to her brainwashing at the hands of Ullikummis. "I feel...adrift."

Ungela nodded. "You've forgotten who you are," she said, "and you want to find that person once more." She spoke English with an accent, emphasizing the wrong syllables and thus making it sound more lyrical than Brigid was used to. The effect was strangely soothing.

"It's only natural," Ungela continued. "But that person may not exist anymore, Brigid. We grow as people and, even if we don't like the way we grow, that growth is as intractable as the growing limbs of a tree. The tree grows with the sun, reaching for it. Merely willing its limbs to reach for something else does not change the nature of the tree."

"But people are not trees," Brigid said. "They can change."

"Can they?" the mother superior asked gently. "In my experience, we have as much past as we choose to have, but we remain shaped by its tides. I am a teacher, and this convent is a place of learning. We take children—girls—at a young age and we shape them into women, making them independent and capable in both thought and in action. When they leave here, they do so with the tools to remain themselves no matter what challenges they may face. Where they go from there, only they will know. The tree is planted, the stem becomes a trunk and the trunk grows branches. But it can only ever grow forward, never back."

Brigid nodded.

"You will find yourself in time," Ungela assured

her, "whoever you turn out to be. In the meantime, you may stay here for as long as you wish. We don't have much out here. Our food is simple but fresh, and our beds are old but hardy. But we do have time in abundance.

"However, you will forgive my lack of hospitality if I ask Rosalia to show you around. My sciatica is playing its games again today. I'm not good for much but hobbling."

"Thank you," Brigid said, bowing her head slightly.

"Dinner is in a little under an hour," Ungela added with a kindly smile. "You are very welcome to join us. You will hear the bell, and Rosalia will show you where to go. You remember, sweet Rose?"

Rosalia nodded. "Of course."

In Spanish, Ungela added, "Take room seven. Dear Tia had to leave on urgent business, so it's free and can sleep the both of you."

"Do you expect her back?" Rosalia asked.

Mother Superior Ungela nodded. "I hope so."

With that, the two younger women left the mother superior's office, and Rosalia led the way upstairs to the sleeping quarters.

AFTER THEY HAD SET their meager belongings in the room they would share, which included Brigid placing the encased interphaser in a lockable wardrobe, Brigid and Rosalia made their way to the dining hall. The complex was large, and it had the spaciousness of old architecture, all high ceilings and intricate nooks, a pleasing decorative flair to the design. They passed several classrooms, their doors propped open to keep the air flowing through the warm, old building. Brigid saw well-stocked bookshelves running across the back walls of both classrooms, and the children themselves appeared obedient and worked in silence.

The dining hall was a large room with a wooden floor and tall windows along both sides. The floor had been beautifully polished and reflected the red sun as it sank behind the mountains to the west. Brigid made a quick count of the long tables, estimating that the room could accommodate seventy people at one sitting. Just now it was empty, only a few of the nuns bustling about preparing food and placing jugs of water at the center of each table. A large round clock dominated the wall above the serving area, its hands making their unhurried way toward seven o'clock.

Rosalia led the way to a table to one side of the room and sat. It was close to the rear of the room, looking out over the courtyard. Brigid glanced out the window, but the girls had finished their training for the day. Only Sister Michelle remained, packing away the archery equipment with the aid of one of her young students. The girl was slim with dark hair, her limbs long and angular, elbows and knees jutting awkwardly as she moved.

"I brought a boy in here once," Rosalia said, interrupting Brigid's thoughts. "Snuck him in wearing my spare robe."

Brigid looked at her and snorted. "Really?"

"He was a farmer's son, worked in the fields to the south." Rosalia shrugged. "I was twelve—there were hormones."

Brigid laughed. "Did you get caught?"

Rosalia nodded, running her tongue across her top teeth. "Oh, yes. Mother superior was Nicole in those days, not Ungela. She made me repent the ways of the flesh over and over until I promised never to do it again. This at the same time they were teaching us to dance, to use our bodies to attract men's eyes. I couldn't make the two things work together in my mind. It was only later I realized what it was about. Power."

"And did you dance?" Brigid asked. "For him? The farmer's son?"

"Yes," Rosalia said. "He couldn't take his eyes off me."

"I'll bet."

From somewhere above them, the bell chimed seven and other people—pupils and teachers—came striding into the dining hall, lining up at the counter, where each took a tray and waited to be served. Rosalia encouraged Brigid to stand, and together the two women joined the line.

MOONLIGHT LIT THE BAY at El Cana, a white sliver like a winking eye hanging steady in the ink-black sky. A girl was running across the sand there, her white dress billowing about her, laughing as her bare feet sank into the wet sand. It was Duendecito, the barman's daughter. Behind her, Fern Salt ran with his head down, his breath chugging like an old gas heater.

"Come on, big man," Duendecito trilled. "Catch me if you can."

Salt growled something unintelligible as he ran, picking up the pace as he chased the young woman across the beach.

BACK AT SAL'S BAR, Sal kept one eye on the restroom. "Where is Duendecito?" he asked himself, shaking his head as he turned the stir fry.

He hadn't noticed when she had left, but she had

been gone too long, he realized. She was a good girl, had her mother's eyes and the same fire in her belly that he had had in his youth; he recognized it even twenty years later. Sal looked up, scanning the room one last time. The cardplayers were playing their game and, over in the corner, domino players were working their slabs for money, too. The bar itself had quietened a bit. One of the boats had to have left dock, taking her crew with her. But there was no Duendecito.

Sal walked across the wooden floor to the restroom door. He tapped against it once—"Hello?"—before pushing it open and peering inside. A couple was in there, a whore servicing one of the sailors. Sal knew she was a local girl.

"You seen Duendecito?" Sal asked.

The woman looked up and gave Sal a slow blink—No.

At their table, Six and his crew were busy downing shots as if it was a race. As Tuska slammed his glass on the table, he noticed Sal pacing anxiously about the bar.

"Six," Tuska growled, gesturing to the barman.

Six followed his nod. "Yeah, I see him," he said. "Where's Salt?"

"Went chasing Sal's little girl, I think," Xia said.

"Shit," Six spit, shaking his head.

"She was up for it," Tuska elaborated.

"Yeah, but even so—shit," Six said, shaking his head. Black John would have kept Salt in line. *He* should have, in John's absence. "Let's go find them."

Three chairs scraped across the wooden floorboards as the pirates rose and made their way out the door.

OUTSIDE, ON THE SLIVER of beach that crouched against the water, Duendecito was still laughing as Fern Salt reached out for her with one of his well-muscled arms. His tanned fingers snagged in her long hair and he pulled, yanking the girl back even as she giggled and ran, his tattooed sleeve rippling.

The pull was harder than she was expecting, and Duendecito shrieked as she stumbled and fell. "My hair," she said, still half laughing, her limbs splayed on the sodden sand.

Salt loomed over her, a sneer crossing his lips before wiping his mouth on the back of his hand. "Game's over now, little pixie," he intoned.

Duendecito was still laughing when Salt mounted her, cinching her white skirt aside and bracing her legs apart with more force than he needed. This close he smelled of drink, sweat and festering rage.

The girl stopped laughing as he tore at her middle, pawing at her insides with sweaty fingers. Duendecito gasped.

"Y-you're hurting…" she pleaded.

But Salt didn't care. He had wanted that blonde on the boat so badly, spent the whole day feeling like his pants would burst with the pressure, his seed burning inside him. He thrust into Duendecito, and as she screamed, she saw the metal of a blade appear in the drunken pirate's hand, glistening in the single shaft of moonlight.

Duendecito shrieked once again, and Salt shoved his hand in her mouth, trying to silence her. She bit down on it, sharp teeth clamping into the ball of his thumb until he pulled it away with a curse.

Angered, Salt brought the blade closer to the girl's face, nicking her across her left cheek, where tears were already washing, unbidden.

"Shut up," the brutal pirate commanded, but Duendecito was too deeply into her trauma to hear. She kept shrieking and gasping, and the hell if that didn't just turn Salt on even more. He reached into the pocket of his britches, pulling something free. It was a stone, a little bigger than his thumb knuckle; he had picked it up from the table once Six had finished examining it along with another, palming them to ensure he got his cut of the spoils, whatever they were worth. It was a seasoned thief's move, the urge to take whatever wasn't covered or nailed down. Six had already had too many drinks to notice or to care.

Salt brought his tattooed hand up to the pretty girl's mouth once more, the stone clasped between thumb and forefinger.

"This'll quiet you," he gritted, holding her mouth open with one hand.

"D-d-don't," Duendecito begged, her plea more urgent than ever.

But Salt ignored her, shoving the stone into her open mouth where it rolled down her tongue and snagged against her throat. She lay there, choking as the stone bit against her windpipe, her body writhing, trying to cough it free.

But Salt didn't care. He drilled his shaft into her, not bothered that she no longer wanted him, nor caring if perhaps she never really had, if it had all been attention seeking. The writhing only made it better, her pelvis bumping against his as he pounded against her in that ancient rhythm.

It took less than a minute, just a few forceful thrusts and then it was done, Salt's seed spilling inside the girl. She had stopped moving by then, the obstruction in her throat halting her breathing, leaving her wheezing faintly as she clawed to life. Tears streamed down her face, washing into the damp sand as the sea rolled up to meet their bodies. There was blood between her legs; Salt had forced her, and she had bled with him still inside her.

Salt kissed her once, licking his tongue down the side of her face before pulling himself up to a standing position, where he adjusted his pants and buckled his belt. Duendecito lay there, a bloody pool forming between her legs, its thick lines lengthening like red tendrils as the sea came to greet them.

"Mr. Salt, what the hell did you do?" Six shouted from off to the pirate's left.

Salt looked up and saw Six, Xia and Tuska standing on the pier behind him, twenty feet away. He was drunk, and he felt that strange moment of giddiness as something familiar but entirely unexpected roared up against his consciousness.

"Salt?" Six demanded. As Salt watched, Six trotted along the pier to where it was a little closer to the sand, then jumped down, landing with little grace on the moist sand before storming over to meet him. "Salt? I asked you a question."

Trotting along behind Six, Xia smirked. "Think it's pretty obvious what he did," the broad-shouldered pirate said.

Tuska laughed at the comment until Six held up his hand in angry warning.

"All right, all right," Six said, looking all around, eyeing the tatty buildings along the shore. It was empty out here—for now. "I see what you did. She still alive? She better be still alive, Salt, because Sal is going to be hell enough mad as it is. We're friends here, we don't rock the boat. What the shits were you thinking?"

Salt stared at Six with a glazed expression. It was as if he couldn't quite make sense of the man's words.

Six clapped Salt over the shoulder and walked him away from the scene. "Shit, you're drunk," he spit. "Shit. We need to get you out of here. Come on."

With the help of his colleagues, Six hustled Salt to the pier and from there back to the rowboats that Drake was supposed to be guarding. Hunkered down in one of the boats, Drake had fallen asleep, the glowing stub of a cigarette filed between his twitching fingers like a cat's eye in the darkness.

Back on the beach, Duendecito's slender form undulated as the sea slapped against it, foam fingers reaching out for her, rearing back.

And the blood ran into the sea. And the violence continued to spread like a rash.

Chapter 10

In the dining hall of the nunnery, the meal had long since finished. Brigid and Rosalia remained sitting at their table as some of the students cleared away their plates. They were honored guests, a graduate and her friend, and they were treated with reverence. Several of the younger girls spoke about Rosalia within ear-shot, discussing wild escapades she was rumored to have undertaken

"I heard she fought dinosaurs on a forgotten island," one said.

"I heard she danced for a pharaoh," another said, as if to top her friend's story.

Rosalia smiled, stifling a laugh.

"They think a lot of you here," Brigid said quietly as the girls were ushered away by Sister Annette.

"Mother Superior always told us that we would be welcomed back anytime," Rosalia said, speaking the words in a bored manner like a mantra.

Brigid smiled. "What is it that they teach you here?"

"To be women, of course."

"No," Brigid said, "there's more to it than that. These girls are disciplined. I can tell that just by being in their presence for a few hours. They are warriors, like samurai."

Over by the serving area, a wide expanse of floor space had been cleared, and two girls stood to provide entertainment for those who wished to remain. One played a wooden recorder while the other accompanied her on a violin, working her bow across its strings in a mournful sonata. Both girls played acceptably, though there was no soul to their playing yet. It was simply an exercise in reading music and repeating its notes. Brigid guessed that neither girl was older than twelve, and she hoped they would improve in time. Some of the other students and nuns remained to listen to the recital, while others departed to their rooms.

"Do you play an instrument?" Rosalia asked.

Brigid thought for a moment. "I can," she said, "but I've never taken the trouble to learn."

"But you can…?" Rosalia queried.

"My memory," Brigid explained. "If I watch closely, I'll memorize the movements, and I could repeat them if I put my mind to it. I don't know that it would sound good, though."

"Brigid, why are you here?" Rosalia asked, the non-sequitur surprising Brigid with its directness.

"I needed time away from Cerberus," Brigid said. "They kept following me with their questions, and I don't have answers that I care to share. Reba and Lakesh and…"

"Kane?" Rosalia prompted as the redhead fell silent.

"They're all driving me mad," Brigid said with a heavy sigh. "I'm not proud of what happened before, with Ullikummis. I don't want to keep dwelling on it."

"I didn't ask you to," Rosalia pointed out. "You complain about people worrying about you, and yet you run away so that they'll worry some more."

"I don't…" Brigid began.

"What is wrong with you?" Rosalia asked. "You have people who care about you, who genuinely care.

People who look out for you and worry about you, and that's something that's rarer than you realize. And you come here, you run away."

"If you don't want me here—" Brigid began.

"I didn't say that," Rosalia interrupted. "You run away from here, and then where do you go? What? You going to keep running until you find somewhere where no one gives two shits about you, and you think then you'll be happy? Is that it?"

At one end of the room, the two musicians brought their first movement to an end, pausing for a moment before they launched into the second. Brigid watched them, a strange kind of fury welling within her.

"I don't mean to run away," Brigid said firmly, staring into Rosalia's dark eyes, the challenge clear.

"And yet it's exactly what you are doing," Rosalia told her. "In my experience, you shouldn't run away unless you have somewhere to go."

HAVING WASHED, KANE was alone in his room in the Cerberus redoubt. It had been a long day. The operations team had been tracking Domi through the past three nights and had finally received word from her a little after dawn. Kane and his squad had been ready to go, suiting up and prepping their weapons before launching into the quantum ether via the mat-trans where they could rendezvous with Domi and the Stone Widow out on the West Coast. He had been keyed up for upward of forty-eight hours, and the sense of relief when they had finally moved into action against the Stone Widow and her acolytes was palpable. Remaining at that level of preparedness for so long weighed heavily on a man, even those of such discipline and training and Kane and his ex-Magistrate partners.

Now Kane lay atop his bed, shoes off, running through the mission briefing for the following day. He and Grant would head out to Tuxpan, first thing. Kane had excused Edwards from this mission; he didn't know how long they would be in Mexico, and Edwards was still suffering from the head trauma he had suffered at the hands of Ullikummis. The man was trying his best to contribute positively to the Cerberus operation, but his health was still borderline and he was prone to nagging headaches. A quick-strike op like the one outside Luikkerville was fine, but the more open-ended remit of their mission to Mexico ruled him out on health grounds. Over the past few weeks, Kane had suffered some health issues of his own, thankfully past now but briefly pulling him out of active duty. He understood where Edwards was coming from on this; the need to be back in the field was an urge that drove all Magistrates.

But by the same token, Kane was quietly pleased that Edwards would be benched this time out. Kane and Grant had shared a lot of adventures together, and it did them good to work together once more, just the two of them. Of course, it should be three. For years now, their Cerberus field team had been made up of three people—Kane to judge the risks, Grant to provide the muscle and Brigid Baptiste to supply the brains. Without her, their efficient little group was compromised, Kane knew. It was more than just losing a friend; Brigid provided a crucial balance for their field team, something that had been sorely lacking these past few months in her absence.

Without meaning to, Kane's thoughts drifted back to the last time he and Grant had been called in to help Domi, back while Brigid was working as an agent for

Ullikummis. They had finally met up in a cave beneath the earth outside Luikkerville, where a woman calling herself Maria Halloween had snagged Brigid out of the quantum stream in an audacious plot to drain the soul energy that entwined her with Kane via their *anamchara* bond. Halloween had been defeated, but the battle had left Kane exhausted as Brigid approached him.

"Baptiste," he had gasped, "I can't believe you're here. I thought I'd lost you forev—"

The sentence had died in his throat as he saw Brigid unholster the TP-9 semiautomatic pistol that she wore at her hip, even as the hybrid child called Quavell watched from behind her.

Kane had thought she was delirious, confused. She had been plucked out of the quantum ether, drawn here against her will and held in stasis as Halloween tried to drain her life. He didn't know about the mental reprogramming she had been subjected to by Ullikummis. Not then, anyway. He tried to calm her, speaking softly, gently.

"Baptiste," he had said, "it's me. It's Kane. Everything's okay now. It's okay. The good guys won."

In reply, Brigid had raised the blaster and pulled the trigger, unleashing a stream of 9 mm bullets into Kane's chest. Worse, though, Kane had seen her eyes narrow just a fraction of a second before she pulled the trigger, seen that moment of recognition before she tried to kill him. His shadow suit had saved him, its armored weave dulling the impact of the bullets even as he was forced back by their barrage. Kane had crashed into a pool that dominated the cave, his chest crying out in agony as the bullets drilled against him until, finally, Brigid's weapon had clicked on Empty. And then she spoke, words so callous they chilled his heart.

"Didn't you get the memo, Kane?" she whispered. "All the heroes are dead."

Moments later, the woman he had known as Brigid Baptiste had disappeared, leaving Kane for dead.

He had survived, of course. But now, as he lay on his bed, gazing into the nothingness above him, Kane replayed those moments again in his mind. Brigid had tried to kill him. And the strangest part was, even though she was back, it was she and not he who was having trouble trusting her.

Kane sighed.

There was so much still to fix.

OUT LOUD, HER LIFE SOUNDED like a madman relating a dream.

"I spent three years in hell," Brigid began. She was in the room that the mother superior had assigned to her and Rosalia, sitting on the wide windowsill that overlooked the courtyard. The courtyard was dark now with the moon sliver barely touching it. Rosalia sat on the bed, listening and occasionally nodding, saying little.

"About a year ago," Brigid said, "we went on a mission to old Russia, me, Kane and Grant. There was an ancient military base there, hidden under the ground but blocked up hundreds of years ago to prevent anyone from discovering the experiment being performed inside.

"The Soviets had a secret project called Chernobog, and it had produced a weapon called the Death Cry. It was designed by the Soviet regime to combat the threat of interstellar aliens—extraterrestrials, you understand? The old socialists had been insular and protective, but they were pretty much on the money with this. They had this Death Cry up and running by 1928, almost twenty years before the Roswell visitation."

Rosalia looked at Brigid with bemusement.

"The incident in Roswell is seen by experts as a touchmark for alien encounter," Brigid clarified. "It occurred in the middle of the twentieth century, and informs a lot of what we consider modern alien experience.

"So anyway, the Soviets had designed this incredible weapon, but they had run into an unexpected problem—where to store it. Keep in mind that this thing was designed in a climate of paranoia. They were genuinely afraid that aliens might come and suck out their brains. There was, according to the Cheka agency that oversaw the project, nowhere on Earth that one could hide the Death Cry without it being found by a potential alien invader. Even the best hiding place would be revealed under torture, and the Cheka were acknowledged masters of torture, so they knew what they were talking about.

"So the scientists behind Project Chernobog struck upon an idea, one so outlandish that it might actually deflect an alien interrogation. They looked at meditation, that oh-so-human ability to still one's mind and search deep within oneself. They found a frequency that could be shared, a realm of higher human consciousness that could be experienced mutually, allowing for construction and providing the perfect place to hide their weapon. They called it Krylograd after the scientist who made the discovery.

"Even if an alien were to read the mind of a person involved in the project, the Soviets reasoned, the alien would have no means to infiltrate a plane set within higher human consciousness. To do so would be like, I don't know, trying to enter the dreams of a cat.

"Of course, to get a whole munitions factory up and running on this mental plane involved a lot of personnel, and the scientists needed to find a way to ensure everyone was tuned to the same meditative wavelength. They did this by creating a mandala, a pictorial meditation tool that the personnel memorized. Once they did so, they could make the leap to the Astral Factory within shared human consciousness where they would work on the weapon.

"However," Brigid continued, "there was a problem. Just like dreaming, the factory workers' sense of time went haywire once they accessed the factory. Something about delving into the human mind throws one's ability to perceive time accurately, and people went there never to return, their bodies decaying in the abandoned redoubt, their project pretty much forgotten. That was until Cerberus came along.

"We found the mandala and I used it to access this other dimension."

"You used it?" Rosalia repeated, incredulous. "Are you some kind of yoga guru, Brigid?"

Brigid shook her head. "I have an eidetic memory, which means I can perfectly visualize everything I've ever seen. Sometimes people call it a photographic memory. The mandala worked by memory—once memorized it would stimulate the brain to this higher level of human consciousness. It probably took the soldiers and scientists of Project Chernobog six months to get it right, maybe longer. It took me just a few hours."

Rosalia nodded in acceptance. "So, you accessed Krylograd and then what?"

"The Death Cry proved to be a bust," Brigid said

dismissively. "It worked, but it sustained damage when we tried to launch it, and ultimately the whole thing was taken out of our hands.

"But the people there, living in this vast complex—bigger than you can comprehend, like one of those villes you dream about that just go on forever—they had lost all perspective. They thought they'd been there for a few months, not three hundred years. The place, the experience, it had changed their minds. They couldn't comprehend that so much time had passed since they had last spoken to their Soviet masters. These were mental constructs, self-projections—they didn't age. So they just carried on tinkering with this incredible weapon, waiting for the day they'd be called upon to use it. A day that never came and, after the nukecaust, never would. I was there for only a few hours, and I could already feel myself losing my sense of time to that astral world. It was frightening."

"I'll bet," Rosalia agreed.

"When I got out, it was fine," Brigid said, "but I'd seen the mandala. And once seen, I couldn't unsee it. It was there in my mind, waiting to be recalled.

"Two months ago, Ullikummis attacked Cerberus, plunging the whole redoubt into chaos."

"I know," Rosalia said. "I was there." She had been on the wrong side then, struggling for self-preservation, but now Brigid understood why.

"He took me away," Brigid said. "Did you know that? He took me away and he… *Tortured* is too strong a word. He made me think differently, brainwashed me, changed me so that I could see things in the way of the Annunaki, the alien. It was like—did you ever see that picture of a vase that's also two faces staring at each other?"

Rosalia nodded.

"It was like that," Brigid said. "Suddenly I could see both things, entirely contradictory and yet existing in unison. I knew he was trying to reprogram me, to rebuild my mind, and I tried to resist. But there came this moment where I realized I would lose. He was too strong, Ullikummis was too strong. I was losing my mind, being reshaped into something dark, something he required to execute his plan. And it struck me that I had to hide or I'd die—my mind would become his forever. So I remembered the mandala, pictured it in my mind. There had been a trick to it before—gold on blue, green and red. A pattern. I remembered that, and I sent my mind—my *real* mind—to Krylograd once more, to hide while Ullikummis shaped what was left into his automaton. He renamed her, called her…" Brigid stopped, her mouth suddenly dry.

"Haight," Rosalia finished for her. "It's okay, Brigid—I'm not going to judge you."

"You should," Brigid said. "I did terrible things, my body became his weapon, his hand in darkness. As first priest of the New Order I killed people, burned down their houses with their screaming bodies locked inside. I ordered people to be executed—children. And with my face, I hurt my friend Balam and his child, abused the trust we had built, using my face to infiltrate his once-safe world. And I shot Kane.

"I saw it all, while I hid in Krylograd, well away from the Astral Factory and its people. A part of me was always aware of what my body was doing, as if seen at the edge of my peripheral vision, and yet I couldn't engage with it. I couldn't get back. Brigid Haight existed for just seven weeks, and yet to me it was years, trapped on that astral plane, watching every sick and twisted thing she did in my name, time stretched beyond all reason.

"Ullikummis had blocked me out of my own mind, not perhaps deliberately, but the way he had retooled my thoughts—my brain rejected my mind like a patient rejecting a donor's heart. I just could not get back."

"You did it eventually," Rosalia said.

Brigid nodded solemnly, gazing out the window and into the lonely courtyard below. Rosalia had been there when she had finally recovered her own will, the Baptiste part of her overwhelming and replacing the spiteful persona of Haight. It had taken a Herculean effort of will coupled with the use of a nutrient bath designed to rebuild Annunaki from their genetic template. She had almost died.

"I want things to be right," Brigid said, "but I keep seeing all the wrong, over and over."

"Dismiss it," Rosalia said. "It's the past. Your friends have forgiven you."

Brigid turned back, facing Rosalia once more, and her expression chilled the dark-haired mercenary. "I have seen so many things," she said. "I went to a place under the sea where the rules of physics are written, tapped my brain into the storehouse of reality itself. When Ullikummis turned my mind, he made me see multidimensionally. The Annunaki are not like us. Their lives are immense, their perceptions different. In opening my mind to that way of thinking, he let me see things I couldn't process, couldn't cope with. I hid because they would—unknowingly—give me away to the Annunaki, those things I saw.

"I told you about the vase with two faces. I see both. Two existences that could not fit together and yet still do. It's like a sickness, a sickness of vision, of comprehension. And I know that I need to forget it now, or I'll be mad. Perhaps I already am."

"No," Rosalia assured her. "Don't say that."

"Shadow flowers make up our bodies," Brigid said, "and there are fingers that paw at the petals, trying to reach our hearts, to reach into our lives."

"You need to let this go, Brigid," Rosalia said. "You're torturing yourself, going over and over it like this."

Brigid turned on her, hot tears streaming down her face. "I have an eidetic memory," she shouted, "and all I want to do is forget."

"I know," Rosalia said. "I have seen terrible things, done terrible things, too. The nuns here taught me to be strong. They taught me how to disengage. They'll show you if you let them."

"Why?"

"Survival," Rosalia said. "That's always the answer to every question. We're built to survive, we humans. You protecting your mind in Krylograd only proves that."

"I hid," Brigid said contemptuously.

"No," Rosalia told her gently. "You survived. Remember it like that, and you'll find you can live with it."

Brigid looked at Rosalia, and her eyes glazed over until she was looking through her. "The faces and the vase," she said quietly. "I need to unsee the faces."

Rosalia checked the chron by the bed. It was almost 4:00 a.m. "You should get some sleep," she told Brigid.

"I'm afraid to close my eyes sometimes," Brigid admitted, "in case I wake up as someone else again."

Rosalia looked at the woman with the flame-red hair, saw the fear in her red-rimmed eyes. "I'll be here," she said. "I was there last time when you came back. I'll be here again."

Brigid nodded wearily. "Thank you," she said quietly.

Chapter 11

After she spoke to Rosalia, Brigid's racing thoughts recalled what had happened in the cavernlike prison on the artificial island of Bensalem. Ullikummis had infiltrated her mind somehow, his thoughts becoming hers, his godlike will overwhelming her merely human one, as it surely had to.

"Each step forward changes the next one you must take," Ullikummis told her. "Upelluri taught me that."

Brigid felt his presence in her mind then. He had spent so long with her, concentrated his energies on her for so long, determined to change her way of thinking. And she saw it, an inkblot across her mind, her old thoughts becoming smaller, irrelevant to her. No, that could not happen. Ullikummis had changed her through the softest of coercion, made her see things that weren't there, that did not exist as anything more than...

She looked up, past Ullikummis to the shining things that waited at the edge of the cave where he held her, things that did not exist as anything more than reflections on the surface of the mirror, Brigid realized.

It had occurred to Brigid then that she could not possibly hope to halt this thing's progress in her mind, could not possibly hope to survive intact as it overwhelmed her. She could do nothing but embrace the mental might of Ullikummis, scion of the Annunaki, and in so doing become one with them, commune with their very way of thinking. And in doing that, she threatened to lose Brigid Baptiste forever.

There had been a trick to it before, Brigid recalled. Gold on blue, green and red. The weaving threads of destiny.

"My father required a weapon," Ullikummis said, "a physical expression of his hatred."

The words seemed to echo in Brigid's mind as she remembered the multicolored threads. She was losing the continuity of memory, fragmenting into something less than she had been before.

"I was that weapon," Ullikummis continued. "I was the hatred that my father unleashed upon his enemies."

Brigid concentrated, remembering the colors and the pattern they created. She could see it now, in the mind's eye of her prodigious memory. It had been woven into a carpet the first time she saw it, hidden in an underground bunker in the part of the old Soviet Union that had once been known as Georgia. The pattern had the cerulean-blue color of the sky as its base, a foundation on which all the others were sewn. Each intricate line had been woven there in golden rings, green highlights, red lines.

"And now I need a weapon of hatred, too," Ullikummis was saying. But his voice was so distant now, she could feel herself withdrawing with each word as time itself seemed, if not to stand still, then at least to slow. "A weapon so devious, so powerful, that it can shape the future."

Brigid concentrated on the colors, the familiar pattern that the threads wove, even as her surface brain sank into the mental embrace of the great god Ullikummis, knowing it could no longer fight him. In that

moment she was gone, concentrating not on his rumbling words, but on the mandala that was patterned in
her mind, perfectly remembered, a tool for astonishing mental concentration.

The mandala threw her out of her body just as it
had almost a year before. Her thoughts—her mind—
had broken free of her physicality and was set adrift,
cast into the astral plane. Tibetan monks had devel-
oped this trick of concentrating on and memorizing the
complex lines of a single image, a mandala designed
to bring them spiritual enlightenment. When she had
explained it to Kane and Grant, she had compared the
mandala to a tuning fork that resonated with God; if
users could re-create its entirety in memory then they,
too, would tune in with God and achieve enlightenment or spiritual wholeness.

But the technique had been turned into a weapon by
a Russian scientist called Krylova, who had employed
it to tap a hidden mental space that could be shared and
used to construct increasingly elaborate machines. The
mental space had been dubbed Krylograd after its dis-
coverer, and the Soviet military of 1928 had set about
using it to build the formidable Death Cry weapon,
which they intended to turn on potential alien invaders.

Brigid stood on the brink as she had once before,
seeing the shimmering pattern of the mandala rip-
ple like liquid, overwhelming her vision. It appeared
poised tauntingly close, as if she could reach out
and touch it. Somewhere in the distance, the gravel-
churning rumble of Ullikummis droned on, driving another nail into her empty brain, taking absolute control
of her body, unaware that her psyche—her self—had
departed the vessel. Her body was left as if in coma,
the mind floating free like steam from a kettle.

Brigid reached forward, pressing her hand to that liquid wall of the mandala pattern, pushing her hand through it as she had once before. Her body—or, more accurately, her *perceived* body—felt afire with the budding of her chakras, the miniature suns that drove the body and the mind, the points that formed the *soul eternal*.

Brigid felt taller now, so vast that she felt as though she could straddle Earth and touch the stars. Her physical limitations had been exceeded; this was her astral self now, and for all her vaunted memory, it felt as if she were doing it again for the first time. Within her, the seven chakras were blossoming like flowers, each one opening like a glowing star of furious intensity, each change bringing a new and different experience of the self in its wake.

Brigid Baptiste stared at the mandala just feet ahead, seeing its impossible depths, circle on square, over and over, each depth opening into further depth, an ouroboros of detail.

If her body—her real body—wanted her back, it never said. Instead, it trusted her to find her own path in the astral world, assured of the umbilical that would always link them, certain she could never become entirely lost.

With a decisive push, Brigid reached for the mandala and stepped through.

The transition was like stepping into a waterfall, the sudden rush of energy crashing down and streaming the body with its sheer power.

Beyond the mandala lay the lightning world, just as she had left it. When she had been here before, she had located the Astral Factory, met with the Soviet scientists who still worked there, laboring under the misapprehension that they had been there but a few months. One, a doctor called Djugashvili, had befriended her. He was a good man whose prodigious intellect and lust for security had been wasted on a weapon that no one would ever dare to fire, a weapon that had ultimately been forgotten.

Djugashvili had died, a victim of the same brutal regime that had exiled him to work at the Astral Factory in the first place. But with his death, perhaps, the factory had altered, its complement of staff finally becoming aware of the awful, unconscionable trick that had been played on their wasted lives. They had been exiled to a place without time, and they had lived their lives, on and on, following the same routines as their bodies died and their project was forgotten.

When Brigid had told Lakesh, out on the stony plateau that sat beyond the Cerberus redoubt's rollback doors, he had suggested that perhaps now those same people would live anew, carving new lives and a new society in the astral plane. Brigid had dismissed his suggestion as fancy. There were ten soldiers here and a handful of lab technicians; everyone else had been killed over time.

And that was another thing—even though she had hidden her mind from Ullikummis, Krylograd wasn't safe. If she was "killed" here—an all-too-credible supposition with the trigger-happy Soviet soldiers running around—her astral form would fizzle and die, becoming nothing more than a memory with all the validity of a Rorschach ink stain.

Thus, if she was to stay here, she would need to do so well away from the Astral Factory and its warmongering agenda. Which meant that, even here, she would have to hide.

Before her, a wide-walled, impossibly high corridor stretched off into the distance, its walls the color of lightning, no further illumination needed. If she followed it, Brigid knew, she would find herself at a fork, and from there she could explore the rest of the vast plane of reality known as Krylograd. Therein lay her best chance at survival.

Brigid looked behind her, reminding herself of the way she had come. A convex bud seemed to rest against the lightning-white dead end, its curve shimmering as if not quite real. It was the gateway to the real world, but it was a one-way valve, allowing her through but barring her return. To go back, to return to her physical body, would take concentration, the same incredible meditation that she had employed to reach here.

Shell-shocked by the interrogation, yet still determined, Brigid began to stride down the corridor away from its cul-de-sac terminus. Ten feet across, the corridor had an auditory quality to it like no other. There were echoes, but they seemed dull, her footsteps sounding like the distant dripping of a water tank. The walls were smooth and unchanging, that fierce illumination like staring into the heart of a light bulb. It took—subjectively—hours, and with the singularity of design, Brigid could not see where the corridor ended until she was almost upon it. There, just as she remembered, the corridor broke into a T, one branch going left, one going right. She gazed back, her eyes searching the way she had just come. The convex bubble remained on the far wall, just out of reach, as if perhaps a dozen feet away. She had been walking for hours to get away from it, and yet it was still only there, just behind her, no more distant than her shadow on a summer wall.

This place, the mental plane designated Krylograd, did not follow the rules of normal perception. Space here was different, and Brigid knew that her time sense could no longer be trusted. That two-hour walk down the lightning corridor might have been a day in real time, or a week, or just a second.

A part of her mind flickered with images, perceiving the real world as if through the distant lens of a reversed telescope. She stood beside the monster Ullikummis on an expanse of rocks, gazing out to sea as the sun set. She spoke with him, but her voice seemed different there, drained of its emotion, its warmth. She was his plaything now, his puppet, his hand in darkness. She acknowledged that in her dead tone, christening herself anew:

"Brigid Haight."

Brigid Baptiste shut her mind to this, concentrating on the white-walled corridor, its high ceilings and dazzling floor. Last time she had been here she had turned right and found the Russians where they worked at their death machine. This time she turned left, skulking down the corridor, glancing warily over her shoulder with every fifth step.

Eventually, Brigid found a place where she could hide and be safe. It was a room, once again colored like lightning, its ceiling impossibly high. The walls were smooth, with a curve to them that one only knew in molded plastics in the real world. It contained a boxy lump that dominated the floor, also glowing with the white radiance, and large enough to hide a small automobile inside. Its walls were solid, and there was no door, no way in. Brigid hid behind it, trying to remember what had happened to bring her here, the deadly assault that Ullikummis had launched on her home.

How long she remained there, she could not say. There was no need to eat in Krylograd; it was a meditative state and its people needed no sustenance. Outside, her body would feed as it always had, or wither and die if she let it. She had left just a sliver of her mind to keep the physical body working, but that sliver had been enough for Ullikummis to retool and shape to his will.

How long she remained there, she could not say. Did one hundred days in hell feel different from one day? Did a thousand feel different from a hundred? Besides, who could judge?

All she knew was that she was here and she was safe, and all the things that occurred outside, in the physical world, happened to that other Brigid, one whose soul had been corrupted, painted the darkest black of midnight. But the whole time, as her sense of time receded, she saw the things she did as that other her, the beast of Haight who rampaged across the globe, burning with the fires that ran through Ullikummis's veins.

To see everything, to know every misdeed, but to do nothing would have driven a lesser person mad. And even now, Brigid still could not look back on that time without regret. She had shot Kane, and that was not the worst thing she had done as Brigid Haight. Haight had done the dark deeds, but it was Baptiste who knew where the bodies lay, where the charred corpses sagged in the ruins of their burned-out houses. It was Brigid

Baptiste who had to live with the memory, the terrible things she had done, the terrible thing she had been.

Brigid Baptiste, the woman with the flawless memory, wanted only to forget.

Chapter 12

Twin Mantas streaked through the predawn air, rocketing away from the hidden Cerberus redoubt. Kane and Grant sat in the respective pilot seats of each vessel, their heads immersed in the bronze-colored tactical helmets that covered their skulls and masked their features entirely.

The Mantas had the shape and general configuration of seagoing Manta rays, flattened wedges with graceful wings curving out from their bodies, and an elongated hump in the center of the craft providing the only evidence of a cockpit. They were alien in design, transatmospheric and subspace vehicles that had been acquired by the Cerberus team for long-range missions, after being discovered by Kane and Grant during one of their exploratory missions, after being left discarded on Earth for several millennia.

The adaptable vehicles were mostly used for long-range and atmospheric work, but they could also be employed for stealth operations where a lot of rapid movement could be foreseen, as with the case in the mission to Tuxpan. Each Manta had a wingspan of twenty yards, and a body length of only fifteen feet. The beauty of their design was breathtaking, an effortless combination of every principle of aerodynamics wrapped up in their gleaming burnt-gold finish. The entire surface of each craft was decorated with curious geometric designs: elaborate cuneiform markings, swirling glyphs and cup-and-spiral symbols.

"Skies clear and looking good," Kane reported over the Commtact.

From the Cerberus ops room, Donald Bry's voice responded, speaking as if inside Kane's head. "Safe journey, Kane, my friend. Keep us apprised of any developments once you reach the border."

"Will do," Kane said, signing off.

Overnight, Bry and the team had amassed a little more information about *La Segunda Montaña,* including a photograph and full description of her appearance, incorporating the boat's dimensions. The photograph showed a green lick of paint along the bottom half of the hull with a white flash running through it. The paint looked old and peeling. The boat had made her way down the East Coast from close to the Bay of Fundy, making several stops along the way. She had picked up passengers at one of those stops, in the disputed territory of Beausoleil, after which her progress had been lost. The assumption that she was headed home was reasonable enough, although it was impossible to extrapolate a definite picture from the available data. There was no record of her docking; she had disappeared.

As soon as Kane shut down that communication, Grant's voice came over the Commtact in place of Bry's. "So how long do we have in the sky? Two hours, did we say?"

"Ninety minutes," Kane said as the identical craft blasted over Hyndman Peak. "Might as well sit back and enjoy the view. May be the last chance we get to relax."

"I hear ya," Grant agreed.

The two men had traveled alone this time. With Domi still recovering from her ordeal outside Luikkerville, and Edwards suffering on-again, off-again migraines from the junk still in his head, the two warriors had preferred to travel alone. This was a stealth mission; any loose cannon needed to be excised before they took off. Edwards had complained, of course, but he was in such rotten shape even he wasn't up to arguing the issue much when it came right down to it.

Thus, Kane and Grant rocketed across the air to the Mexico border way down south, the sun rising to their left.

TUXPAN SMELLED OF FOOD. The ville was more built-up than Kane had expected, a swathe of low-storied buildings crammed one on top of the other as they backed away from the harbor. The harbor itself was surprisingly well kept, the docks modern and well organized, a marvel of concrete and steel.

Kane and Grant had left their Mantas in a free yard at the southernmost point of the docks, bringing them into a landing on the tarmac there where they sat incongruous among the local vehicles. The locals stared at the sleek, bronze aircraft in amazement, and several commented to their pilots in their own language, which the Cerberus men's Commtacts automatically translated. Kane approached a man who waited in a sentry box by a set of iron gates, shuffling a few credits in his hand so that the coins clinked together, while Grant dogged his heels. The man in the sentry box was in his forties, with thick black hair that was beginning to turn white at the temples. He wore a smart uniform with a peaked cap, and Kane pegged him right away for whatever passed for a Magistrate to the locals, a private sec man maybe.

"Hey, have a word?" Kane called.

Stepping out from his sentry box, the local Mag could hardly take his eyes off the beautiful Mantas as the morning sun was brilliantly reflected from their metal skins. "What can I do for you, *señor?*"

"My friend and I are here on a little business," Kane explained, slipping easily into the mannerisms of conversing Magistrates.

The local nodded. "Flying some pretty heavy-duty stuff there," he observed.

"Sure are," Kane agreed. "Wondered if you'd be able to keep an eye on it, nothing special, just check in now and then to make sure no one tries stripping them down while we're gone." Kane shook the credits in his hand again. "Might be a little in it for you, if that's going to be a concern." With the stones somewhere nearby, Kane didn't have time to wait around, so putting the bribe out there right up front seemed prudent.

The local Mag offered an ingratiating smile. "I'm sure we can come to some arrangement, *señor.* What kind of duration did you have in mind?"

"We're not sure," Kane admitted. "You know where the harbormaster is?"

The sec man pointed up the street. "Way up there," he said, and he gave Kane directions. "I'm only on until twelve, *señor.* Anything after that would be classed as overtime."

Kane reached for the man's hand to shake it. "Well, if that becomes necessary, you let me or my partner here know, okay?"

As the two men shook hands, Kane passed him the credits, palming them with ease. It was a small amount, to be sure, but should be enough to keep the man on side for a few hours at least.

The local Mag smiled. "You smell that?" he said. "Radiation leak maybe, probably nothing but I should look into it. Safety, you understand. I'd better cordon off this area until I have it under control." He went back to his sentry post and drew out a chain, which could be strung across the entry to the parking zone. As he went about setting it up, he looked at Kane. "Radiation can be tricky. You have any idea how long it might take, *señor*?"

Kane shrugged. "Radiation's tricky," he agreed. "Use your own judgment."

With that, Kane walked past the cordoned-off area with Grant matching his step. People in the immediate vicinity backed away from the cordoned-off area as the guard closed the gates. Grant looked at Kane and smiled. "Slickly done."

Kane raised his hand to his face, brushing his finger to his nose in an old code that the two friends shared. "Let's hope so," he said. The gesture was known as the one-percent salute, a wry reminder that no matter how certain things seemed, something could always appear that altered the odds.

Grant laughed. Old habits died hard.

THE TWO EX-MAGS MADE their way through the harbor. Even that early in the morning, the docks were bustling with people, as vessels were tied up and unloaded as they drew into port. Tuxpan was a busy place these days, serving much of the east coast of Mexico. While the place was bustling, there didn't seem to be much in the way of innovation. Unloading was still being done by hand, old vessels clunking into the port.

Kane had dressed in a battered denim jacket while Grant wore his long duster with the Kevlar plating. Though big men, neither particularly stood out in this haunt of dockers and seamen, working men who used their brute strength to get things done. Like most docks, the streets were a haphazard warren, piers jutting out with unsecured planks bridging them to give passersby a route while the contents of the boats were unpacked.

As they walked, Kane and Grant kept an eye out for *La Segunda Montaña,* the fishing vessel that they were here to find. There were large boats and small, many of them rust buckets that no longer looked seaworthy. There were several fishing boats that matched the description of a twenty-five-foot scow, but on reading their names none proved to be the vessel they were looking for. Unless the boat had been renamed and repainted, the Cerberus team hadn't seen it.

Positioned toward the center of complex of piers and a little way back, exactly as the sec man had indicated, sat a two-story building that housed the harbormaster. Kane and Grant made their way to the entrance, a door propped open by a brick to let the air flow through.

Inside, a battered transistor radio spit a tinny rendition of what sounded like an old folk tune, though it struggled to be heard over the whir of the air con.

A tanned, bespectacled woman with gray streaks in her dark hair sat behind a counter. She looked up and smiled, greeting Kane in Spanish.

"We're trying to find a boat," Kane explained. "A fishing scow called *La Segunda Montaña*, should have docked here sometime yesterday."

The woman assessed Kane for a moment, her eyes flicking to Grant, who stood like a solemn gargoyle by the office door. "You come far?" the woman asked, reaching for a loose-leaf folder that was propped at one end of her desk.

"A little way," Kane said vaguely. A place like this was used to foreign visitors. It was no surprise that the woman thought nothing of two strangers appearing looking for information.

The woman frowned as she ran her finger down the column of handwritten names, and, after a moment, she looked up at Kane with an apologetic smile. "Sorry, no *Segunda Montaña* here, *señor*."

Kane leaned over the counter, scanning the facing page of the folder for a moment. "Is there any chance it would have been missed? Or registered under another name?"

"Not that I can think of," the receptionist admitted. "You could maybe speak with Roberto."

"Roberto?" Kane asked.

"The harbormaster," the woman explained. "I'll go find him."

The woman disappeared through a door behind the counter, and while she was gone Grant and Kane spoke in hushed tones.

"According to Bry, the ship definitely came here," Grant grumbled.

"These records look pretty slapdash," Kane told him. "I'd venture anything could have snuck in here without being noticed, if the right palms were greased." Both Kane and Grant were used to the computerized data that Cerberus used, and prior to that the advanced systems of the Cobaltville Magistrates. To them, the harbor records in Tuxpan looked primitive.

At that point, the bespectacled woman returned accompanied by a man in his fifties. The man had a round belly and a vulpine face, his pointed nose sticking out between two close-set eyes. He wore a washed-out shirt that looked to be a size too small, with dark patches of sweat under the armpits. Roberto, Kane guessed.

"*Señor, señor,*" the round man enthused, "welcome, welcome. How may I help you today?"

"We're looking for a boat," Kane said, "name of *La Segunda Montaña*. A little fishing scow."

"Came down from the north," Grant added, "should have arrived sometime yesterday."

The harbormaster ran a hand over his jowls for a moment. "I don't recall such a boat," he admitted. "Have you checked the records?"

Kane nodded, then reached into his pants pocket and produced several gold credits. He counted them before putting two back. "Is there any way it might have come in and somehow been overlooked, not appearing on the official record? Or maybe the name got muddled up?"

The harbormaster's eyes twinkled as he eyed the gold in Kane's hand. "Slipups happen," he explained. "We're only human. I can perhaps look into it. Come, follow me."

"I'd appreciate that," Kane said, and he and Grant stepped through the gate in the counter and followed Roberto into his back-room office.

The office was a shambles, paperwork everywhere, including a pile of dog-eared skin mags on top of a filing cabinet that rose to shoulder height. Furthermore, it stank of tobacco and Mary Jane. There was a small black fan set into one window, eight inches in diameter and thick with dust and grime.

"Nice place," Grant rumbled as he sniffed at the rancid air.

"Have a seat, have a seat," the harbormaster said, gesturing vaguely to two chairs positioned before his desk. One of them had a stack of yellowing paperwork on it, and the other had the very clear imprint of a boot's sole on its seat.

Kane and Grant replied in unison, "I'll stand."

Roberto made a show of checking his records, including running through two filing drawers of paperwork, but came up with nothing. Kane gave him the bribe anyway, figuring it was good business to keep the man on side.

"You have any other ideas where the boat may have gone?" Kane asked.

"It would have traveled across the gulf," Roberto said. "There's been a few...ah...problems in that stretch, here to the west." He pointed to a fading map pinned to one wall. "Little freelancing going on, you catch my drift?"

"You mean pirates?" Kane checked the map, and the harbormaster nodded solemnly.

"I'm only speculating here, you understand, but some of the smaller ships they, er, don't fare so well sometimes."

"Yeah, I see," Kane said. "This boat had a cargo on it that we're trying to track. You have any idea where that kind of thing might turn up, if it was hit?"

"*Señor,* please," Roberto objected, "I'm just the boss of this little port, I don't control the seas."

"Does anyone?" Grant asked.

Roberto shrugged. "You need anything else, you let me know, yes?"

Kane thanked the man, then together he and Grant

left the office and made their way back to the exit. As they walked down the street through the busy docks, Grant turned to him.

"Well, that was a bust," the ex-Mag said.

"Yeah," Kane agreed, but he wasn't so sure. The pirate angle could be a wild-goose chase, but if *La Segunda Montaña* had been hit it was probable that pirates would have taken the cargo, even if they didn't understand what exactly it was. "I'll speak to Cerberus, tell them what we've found. They can use the satellites, maybe triangulate the boat's position. It's a long shot, but it might produce something."

BACK AT THE CERBERUS redoubt, astrophysicist Brewster Philboyd had taken over from Donald Bry as point of contact. Brewster was a tall man, oftentimes uncomfortably so in the seats of the ops room, with receding blond hair, black-framed glasses and the familiar pitting on his cheeks of acne scarring. Kane's summons came through via the headset he wore, and he answered it immediately, pausing the computer feed he had been checking over.

"What can I do for you, Kane?"

"Tuxpan dock turned out to be a dead end," Kane explained. "No record that the *Segunda Montaña* ever arrived."

Philboyd had been brought up to speed on the field mission as a matter of procedure, and he automatically called up the flight data from the Manta craft. "That's too bad," he replied. "So, what's the next move?"

"That's where we figure you might be able to help," Kane said. "Can you run a mapping program and see if you can trace the *Montaña*'s route? Harbormaster here reckons there're pirates active in the gulf. Might be it got snagged before reaching port."

"I'll run the data we have through our prediction software, Kane," Brewster assured him. "It'll take a few minutes. Please stand by."

"Acknowledged, Cerberus," Kane replied, cutting the contact.

"What's happening?" Grant asked as they trudged back to the Mantas.

"Brewster's bringing up the info now," Kane told him. "Looks like we're going fishing."

BRIGID HAD SLEPT, BUT it had been restless. Rosalia let her sleep in while she went down to breakfast with the other residents of the strange nunnery. When she came back with a plate of toast, she found Brigid had gone from the room, the covers of the bed pulled back in disarray.

Rosalia checked the wardrobe, confirming that Brigid's interphaser was still there. Then, after a moment's consideration, she placed the toast on the small writing desk and made her way down the corridor to the communal bathroom at its end. Brigid was there washing her face before the mirror, her hair pulled back in a loose ponytail. The mirror was steamed over.

"Everything okay?" Rosalia asked.

Brigid stared at the image in the misty mirror, looking at her emerald eyes as if seen through the fog. "Yes, I just needed a shower."

"Did you get to sleep in the end?"

"For a while. Thank you."

"I brought you some breakfast—toast. It's in the room."

"Thank you."

Rosalia stood in the open door, watching as Brigid stared at herself in the mirror. It was as if the red-haired woman couldn't quite recognize the face looking back at her. "Brigid, what you said last night," Rosalia said carefully. "That's between you and me, okay? You don't need to worry about it. I don't tell my secrets."

Brigid turned to face her, and Rosalia saw that she was smiling. "I've noticed. So, do you have anything planned for today?"

"We'll take it easy," Rosalia suggested. "Maybe sit in on a class."

"Sounds good," Brigid agreed.

IF THERE WAS EVER A MORE inaccurate usage of the term *take it easy,* Brigid was hard-pressed to recall it. The class in question was held in the courtyard and featured twenty girls in their mid-teens, each one wielding a long staff as they clashed in mock combat. The mock combat looked real enough to Brigid, and what was more, the nun running the class—one Sister Magdalene—insisted that both Rosalia and Brigid participate.

"The girls can learn something from you," she said, "and perhaps your experience will serve to inspire them."

Rosalia agreed without hesitation, enjoying being back in her home in the role of honored guest.

Brigid was less certain. "I don't really…" she began, shaking her head and waving away the staff that Rosalia brought for her.

"Come on," Rosalia said encouragingly, "it'll be fun. Good to get the heart pumping now and again, right?"

Reluctantly, Brigid took the shaft and entered the

marked area where she would spar with the other girls.
"Go easy on me," she told her first pupil, a spindly
girl with cocoa skin and hair in short black ringlets.
"I bruise easy."

The girl came at Brigid with a low sweep of the
staff, telegraphing her move so obviously that Brigid
leaped over it with ease. The follow-up brought the
blunt end of the six-foot staff up toward Brigid's face.
But already the redhead had dropped, bringing her
own weapon around in a forceful arc that clipped her
opponent behind the knees, dropping her to the ground.

The girl with the dark ringlets was disqualified
shortly thereafter, having suffered three sacks via Brigid's lightning-swift reactions. The whole time, Brigid
made it look easy.

Across the courtyard, Rosalia was making similar work of her own opponent, flicking the flexible
staff she held up so that it clipped the breastbone of
the brown-eyed girl who lunged for her, clacking her
teeth together even as she was knocked from her feet.

"Next?" Rosalia called, even as the other students
applauded her prowess.

Inevitably, Brigid and Rosalia were pitted against
each other before the sun reached its midday salutation.

Chapter 13

The phrase *needle in a haystack* came to mind as Kane and Grant swooped across the Gulf of Mexico in the Manta craft. Back at Cerberus, Brewster Philboyd had patched through a projected course that *La Segunda Montaña* might have taken, but they knew it was a long shot.

Thanks to innumerable man-hours of hard work, Cerberus had access to a Vela-class reconnaissance satellite through which they could monitor Earth, as well as the Keyhole Comsat for their communications. Tabulating data from that and the harbormasters' records from the East Coast, Brewster had done his best to put together a likely path that the boat's captain, Alfredo Stone, would have taken. Even so, despite the advances provided by Cerberus's prediction software, there was no escaping the fact that the odds were well-stacked against them.

"Boat coming up," Kane said over his Commtact link with Grant.

"I see it," Grant responded. "Is that a boat or a ship?"

"Not sure," Kane admitted as he urged more power into his aircraft's thrusters. "What's the difference?" The Manta swept low over the waves, kicking up trails of sea spray with its passage, flying alongside the vessel in question roughly fifty feet from its starboard bow. Kane glanced at it for a moment before turning back to his controls. It was a midsized trawler with red flanks, too large to be *La Segunda Montaña*.

The two Mantas continued their swoop of the area, with Brewster Philboyd monitoring their passage via the real-time satellite feed. Three hours later, both Kane and Grant were ready to admit defeat. If the little fishing boat was still out there, then they weren't going to find it. With a moment's discussion, they turned the Mantas around and rocketed back to the port of Tuxpan.

WHEN THEY RETURNED to the harbormaster's office in Tuxpan, Grant and Kane marched in without being introduced. Roberto was lounging back in his seat, a hand-rolled cigarillo clenched between his teeth. His secretary leaped up from where she had been kneeling by the desk as the two ex-Mags entered, her face blushing a brilliant red. She was no longer wearing her glasses; they rested on top of a pile of muddled papers on the man's desk.

"What is it, *señors?*" Roberto asked, spitting out his miniature cigar.

Her glasses back on the bridge of her nose, Roberto's secretary grabbed the burning cigarillo from the desk, patting out the embers where it had caught with some paperwork.

"We checked the gulf," Kane said. "There's nothing out there but water and a few boats. No sign of *La Segunda Montaña.*"

"So?" Roberto said. "What do you expect me to do about that? I'm just the harbormaster."

Kane jabbed a finger angrily in the fat man's face. "Exactly. Which means you're responsible for everything coming in and out of this port. And if something doesn't turn up, then you're obliged to check into it."

Roberto stretched his arms wide, smiling. "Ah, it's a nice dream, but you can't expect me to—"

Kane grabbed the man by his collar, pulling him out of his seat and dragging him close until he could smell the man's tobacco breath.

"Look, my friend," Kane gritted, "you're going to tell me everything you know about these pirates. Right now."

Behind the desk, the receptionist hunkered against the farthest wall, cowering away from what was happening.

Grant sidled around the desk, holding up his hands in reassurance. "It's okay," he said, "you just stay calm."

The woman moved as if to leave, but Grant glared at her. "Stay."

Then, Grant began searching through the drawers of the desk, breaking a lock with a sharp pull of his strong hand.

Roberto the harbormaster was sweating more, and his lip quavered as Kane glared at him. "I—I'm sorry about your friend or whatever, *señor,* but I don't know what happened to him. You have to believe me."

With both hands bunched in the chest of the man's shirt, Kane dragged the man over his desk, knocking aside the paperwork that had been piled there along with a glass ashtray that tumbled to the floor, spilling its contents.

"How long have you been in this job?" Kane asked.

"S-s-sixteen years," the fat man replied. "I was assistant for t-twelve of them."

Kane's expression was cold, emotionless. "So, tell me what you know about these pirates."

"Hey, I don't work with them," the harbormaster bleated. "I keep the hell out of their way. What do I know about pirates?"

"A man in your position knows enough," Kane said firmly.

"Okay, okay—th-there's a place they go to sometimes," Roberto babbled, "about twenty-five miles south. Locals call it El Cana."

"What is it? Like a club or something?"

"No, not a club, *señor*. A street in the middle of nowhere that can only be reached by boat." Roberto smiled, remembering. "Lots of sweet stuff goes on there, if you catch my drift. Girls, smokes, that kind of thing."

"That's great," Kane growled. "You got me a map to this El Cana place, Roberto?"

"No, *señor*," Roberto said, "but you give me five minutes…"

Kane violently let go of the man's shirt, tossing him back against the desk where he stumbled and fell, dropping to the floor on his well-padded posterior.

"Sure, five minutes," he said.

Standing behind the desk, Grant raised the revolver he had found, clutching its barrel between thumb and middle finger as if it were something diseased. "And hey, if you were thinking of surprising us with this little kicker, don't bother."

IT TOOK FOUR MINUTES in total for Roberto to provide directions to El Cana, and three of those had been spent rifling through his jumbled paperwork just trying to find a pocket map. Before they left, the man had tried to tap Kane for more money, much to Kane's and Grant's amusement.

"Scared," Grant said, laughing as they left the building, "but not scared enough not to want a bribe. We sure can pick 'em."

"Roberto said the only way to approach this place was by boat," Kane said, scouring the map as they walked through the busy dock. "It's got a strip of beach, probably too narrow to land the Mantas. You see anything?"

He passed the map to Grant, who looked at the unmarked area that the harbormaster had circled. "I guess Cerberus could take a look for us," he suggested, brow furrowed, "but nothing jumps out at me. We could go *here,* which is maybe a quarter-mile out."

Kane nodded.

"We could hoof it from there," Grant suggested.

BRIGID BAPTISTE AND ROSALIA stepped warily into the combat circle that had been marked in salt within the convent courtyard. Both women were armed with six-foot-long flexible staffs. Rosalia was just retying her dark hair in a ponytail that swished behind her nape. All around, the pupils of Sister Magdalene's class sat quietly to watch, with the robed sister herself standing close to the edge of the twelve-foot-wide circle.

Brigid glanced up at the sky, squinting against the bright sunlight. It was almost noon, and they had been out there now for more than two hours.

"How long are these lessons?" Brigid asked.

"Half a day, six days a week," Rosalia replied, rotating the bo staff in her two-handed grip. "Why? Are you tired?"

"Damn right, I'm tired," Brigid admitted. She had removed her outer garments and stood in just the figure-hugging shadow suit she habitually wore. As black as night, the suit clung to her sleek curves like a second skin.

Rosalia, too, had stripped down from what she had initially worn, leaving her in a sleeveless vest top and light skirt that brushed just above her ankles. Her feet were bare.

"A little exercise will do you good," she taunted. "Help you sleep."

Brigid gritted her teeth, eyes fixed on her opponent on the far side of the circle. "Fine."

Then Brigid took two paces forward, long steps that brought her close to the center of the circle.

Without warning, Rosalia flipped the staff in her grip and, still clinging with both hands, shot one end toward Brigid's midriff, jabbing at her like a hungry wolf. Brigid leaped back, dancing in place as the staff whizzed past her. Up to now, she had been fighting girls, well trained but still just learning the arts of combat. But Rosalia was in a different category entirely; the speed and deftness with which she brought her first attack was incredible.

As Brigid stepped back, Rosalia's staff changed angle, cutting across the circle in a long sweep. Brigid leaped, jumping over the flexible pole as if it were a girl's skipping game before landing on both feet, boot heels meeting with the dusty ground. Then she angled her body, bringing her own staff around and up in a sharp arc that ended at Rosalia's chin.

Or at least, it should have. Rosalia flipped backward, cartwheeling on one hand as she avoided Brigid's brutal attack. And then she was standing again, just feet away from Brigid, and before the red-haired Cerberus warrior could react, Rosalia's left leg snapped out, delivering a savage blow to the staff with the ball of her foot. Brigid felt the blow resound through the length of the staff, and it shuddered so hard in her hand that it threatened to drop.

Brigid clung on, shrieking savagely as her wrist was twisted with the transference of energy. Before she knew it, Rosalia brought her own staff around in a crosswise gesture, clipping Brigid across the back of her shoulders.

Brigid stumbled, staggering two steps forward, feeling herself falling toward the ground.

"No," she muttered, forcing herself to stay on her feet. Another step was all it took and, bringing herself low, she recovered, whipping her own staff around lightning quick and slamming it lengthwise against Rosalia's upper thighs. Impressively, the beautiful dark-haired woman held her ground, gasping as the staff slapped against her.

Brigid twisted the staff in her hand, using its own flexibility to make it snap back and strike her opponent again. This time Rosalia brought her own staff down sharply, blocking the blow as it struck the ground. Then, with Brigid's staff still touching it, Rosalia brought up her own weapon again, flicking Brigid's away and forcing the redhead back toward the edge of the circle.

Seeing her opening, Rosalia ran, crossing the small circle in less than two seconds, flipping her staff around in a one-handed grip that lined it up with her lower arm. As Brigid recovered, she saw Rosalia's right arm swing around, the pole trailing it in a bullet-fast arc.

Automatically, Brigid brought up her left arm in flinch response, crying out as the staff struck her. But she refused to yield. Ignoring the pain in her arm,

Brigid stepped forward and around, twirling so that her back was facing Rosalia as the dark-haired woman brought her staff around for another blow. Brigid stepped inside the arm, slamming her booted heel at Rosalia's bare toes.

Rosalia skipped back in an instant, avoiding the blow but losing her staff as she did so.

"Nasty," she stated, impressed by the savagery of Brigid's attack.

Brigid felt a pang of remorse then, recalling the ruthlessness of that other her, the one called Haight.

"I'm sorry," she said as she brought the staff to a horizontal position before her.

"Don't be," Rosalia said. "Show me what you've got."

For a moment Brigid stood there, absolutely still. She appeared to be watching her opponent, but her eyes were in fact fixed on a far distant point. The faces or the vase? Abruptly, she tossed the staff aside, letting it drop to the ground of the makeshift arena.

"I can't do this," she said.

Before anyone could say a word, Brigid turned, walking out of the circle and losing by default. Breathing hard, Rosalia watched her leave, both disappointed and concerned for this woman with whom she had become fast friends.

The class watched Brigid Baptiste leave, and none of them seemed to know what to make of it. The light whisper of hushed chatter buzzed between them for a moment until Sister Magdalene fixed them all with her steely stare, silencing them without a word.

Apologizing, Rosalia walked over to the holding pen, securing the combat staff in its mounts there. Then she trotted after Brigid, where the older woman had disappeared back into the building through the glass-and-wood doors. As she passed Sister Magdalene, she saw the unspoken question on the woman's lips and simply shook her head in reply. Then she was gone, calling after Brigid as she hurried into the building.

IN HER OFFICE OVERLOOKING the courtyard, Mother Superior Ungela had watched the whole scene and she shook her head at the way it finally played out. This woman, Brigid Baptiste, had come to her seeking help. But it was the sort of help that could only come from within, from the self.

Ungela turned away from the window, limping back to her desk where the seemingly endless paperwork for the school's fees waited.

KANE AND GRANT BROUGHT the Mantas around in a long swoop, following the shoreline down to El Cana with Brewster Philboyd tracking their movements via satellite. The journey itself was brief, just a matter of minutes from the Tuxpan docks. The two Cerberus men eased off the thrust as they approached the section that Roberto had marked on the map, surveying the stretch of shore from a little way out to sea.

A line of buildings ran just beyond the edge of the sea with two piers jutting into the waves. All of the buildings faced the sea, just six in all, and behind them lay nothing but the encroaching forest. It was like an old-time movie set, a line of buildings with nothing behind, not even a road in sight.

From his vantage point in the cloudless sky, Kane could see figures moving on one of the piers, and two small boats were docked there. A third boat was up on blocks by one of the piers, its underside turned to face the sky. Kane commanded the surveillance equipment in his heads-up display to magnify, and he focused in on the figures on the pier. They were just children, three of them in all, he saw, barefoot and running back and forth in some sort of chase game.

Behind the kids, a little stretch of beach, just a narrow sliver of golden sand, ran up to a path that followed the line of the buildings. Kane spotted another boat there, beached now and half-buried in the sand, leafy plants growing from its prow. Both ends of the beach ended abruptly in sharp rocks, stretched out into the sea like upturned needles, creating dangerous currents and blocking in the little settlement like a fortress. By boat, one could approach it either straight on or not at all, and nothing larger than a rowboat could navigate those treacherous rocks. Beyond the rocks on the south side lay a cove, dressed with another narrow strip of straw-colored sand.

"Looks quiet," Kane said over the Commtact. "Let's move in."

Acknowledging Kane with a single word, Grant followed his Manta as it streaked across the ocean and around the hidden settlement, flying on toward the south end of the beach. In a moment, the two craft were landing, coming down vertically to poise past the far edge of the beach, behind the jutting rocks.

There was not quite enough space for a Manta on the sliver of beach, so both craft came to rest half in the water, arranged nose to tail. They were durable transatmospheric craft with seagoing functionality; the seawater would do them no harm.

Kane removed his helmet as his engine powered down, propping it to the side of the pilot's seat before undogging the cockpit. The protective blister drew back and Kane clambered out of his seat, edging down the sloping wing of the Manta. Grant was just doing the same from his own craft, sneering at the water that lapped at his boots as he stepped down.

"Nice spot for a picnic," Grant said sarcastically.

Kane was busy checking his armament, and he nodded without looking up. Assuring himself that his Sin Eater was loaded and that the barrel was clean, Kane sent it back to its hiding place beneath his sleeve. He had a feeling he might need it—and it wasn't a feeling he liked.

Beside Kane, Grant was doing the same, checking not just his Sin Eater but also a Copperhead assault rifle he carried hidden in a sleevelike pocket of his duster coat.

"Let's not go in expecting trouble," Kane said as he led the way to the sharp rocks that hid this beach from the area dubbed El Cana. "Just be prepared for it, anyway."

"Always am," Grant assured him.

THE SPIT OF ROCKS PROVIDED a natural wall to El Cana, and it took Grant and Kane several minutes to clamber over them. The highest point was only perhaps twenty feet above sea level, but it gave a good view of the little settlement that waited beyond.

The buildings looked ramshackle and worn, and what paint existed had begun to peel away, the curse of living by the sea.

"A whole place dedicated to serving pirates and scoundrels," Grant said with a degree of admiration. "Tells you something, don't it?"

"This country was always a little more relaxed,"

Kane said. "I guess a crap hole like this is fine, as long as it doesn't do any harm to the rest of the populace."

"Yeah," Grant agreed sullenly. "And they called it El Cana. Spanish for *the cops*."

"Being ex-Magistrates, I choose to take that as a good omen," Kane said.

Grant chuckled. "'El Cana Kane.' Got a ring to it, huh?"

They reached the far side of the rocks and eased themselves down onto the beach. The kids were still playing along the beachfront, but when they saw Kane and Grant approach they turned and ran back up to the buildings, disappearing from view. The Cerberus men watched them go, vanishing into one of the tumble-down wooden shacks. The property had windows, and a door that had once been painted emerald, though the color had since faded in the fearsome sunlight to a kind of sickly sort of lime, so Kane assumed it was a house.

A few moments later, the lime-green door opened and a dark-haired woman appeared, a shotgun clutched in her hands. The woman looked to be around thirty, with wide hips and heavy breasts. Training the gun on Grant and Kane, she clacked the stock one-handed with practiced ease.

She called something in Spanish, clearly not extending a welcome.

"Please, *señorita*," Kane said. "In English, *por favor*."

"*En inglés*," Grant added hopefully.

The woman made no response other than to gesture with the gun she had trained on the two strangers, indicating they needed to get off the beach.

With their weapons hidden, Kane and Grant raised their hands, walking up to the path, sure to make no sudden moves. Two of the children they had seen playing on the pier reappeared in the doorway, peering from behind the woman's skirts. As Kane reached the pathway, the woman hissed something at the children, instructing them to move back.

The woman repeated her command in Spanish to Kane angrily, showing her teeth.

"Okay, slow down," Kane said, his hands held at shoulder height. The translation circuits of his Commtact had kicked in now and he could converse in her language in real time. "We're here looking for something," he explained in Spanish, tripping a little over the unfamiliar words. "A cargo that's become lost."

"How did you get here? No visitors," the woman hissed in her own language, jabbing the shotgun at Kane. The Commtacts fed the words in translation directly to Kane's and Grant's ear canals.

"Yeah, see, that ain't going to help," Kane said. "You think you could maybe lower the weapon…"

"Invitation only. No visitors," the woman repeated. "You fuck off back where you came from right now, and maybe I won't shoot you in the ass, pretty boy. Get it?"

"Now wait a minute," Kane said, taking another step toward the woman.

"Go," the woman said. "Now."

Moving the shotgun, the woman gestured at the rocks that Kane and his partner had just climbed to get there. As she did so, Kane leaped, seizing his chance—however slim—to disarm the woman. She saw him pounce, like some jungle cat, and she swung the shotgun around, squeezing the trigger and loosing a blinding burst of buckshot at the ex-Magistrate.

But Kane had already moved out of the line of fire, ignored the shot as it hurtled over his shoulder with an ear-splitting crack like thunder. Before the woman could get off her second shot, Kane had his left hand around the shotgun's barrel, driving it into the air as the woman clung on. At the same time, Kane's right fist drove forward like a jackhammer, dealing a resounding blow to the woman's jaw.

The woman sagged back as Kane's blow struck, her eyes rolling back into her head as she sank into unconsciousness. Still holding the barrel of the shotgun, Kane plucked it from her now-limp grip as she crashed to the floor.

"Sorry, lady," Kane said, wincing as her head struck the wooden sill of the door.

Behind Kane, Grant's voice rose in urgent warning. "Look alive, Kane, we have company."

Kane turned, still clutching the shotgun. Behind him on the road, more than a dozen men and women were watching, fierce expressions on their faces, eyes fixed on him and Grant. From his first impression, Kane would guess that every last one of them was armed and ready.

Chapter 14

In one of the Cerberus research laboratories, Mariah Falk sat on a high stool studying the contents of the strange crate that Kane's team had brought back from the Stone Widow's gathering. Lab assistant Gus Wilson had taken a moment away from his usual position in the back office to give her a hand. Both Mariah and Gus wore latex gloves as they handled the rocks, each one no bigger than a finger joint, retrieving them one at a time from the crate and placing each in the dish before Mariah. Once there, she trained a brilliant light on the rock for careful examination. The rock seemed normal upon first viewing, but even as she handled it she could feel something emanating from it, a sense of power that raised her hackles and made her wary.

"I'm imagining things," Mariah muttered, turning the rock over using a pair of metal tweezers.

Gus cocked his head at her words but decided to say nothing. A handsome young man barely into his twenties, Gus could be a little intimidated sometimes by the array of knowledge around him at Cerberus, preferring to keep to the stock checking and more solitary duties if he could. But he was a diligent worker and in Mariah he had found someone who wasn't forever speaking in formulas as if engaging in some private joke among the other science heads. He wore safety goggles, the elastic strap catching in the unruly locks of his russet-brown hair.

Despite her words of reassurance, Mariah couldn't shake the feeling that there was something different about the rocks. It was as if they were—well—*alive*.

Her lost love, Clem Bryant, had been killed because of these things, fighting against a whole squadron of acolytes who had pledged allegiance to Ullikummis and allowed him to place these same rocks inside their skulls. They had granted the stone god's acolytes an incredible special talent, allowing each of them to draw on his strength until their flesh hardened like granite.

As Cerberus's resident geologist, Mariah had studied a few of these stones over the past few months, most recently examining the one that had been buried and subsequently removed from Edwards's skull. But up until now she had never seen one *before* it had been placed inside a human host. Though inanimate, the rocks seemed to have the ability to grow and shift, the way a seed grew shoots that reached for the light.

Mariah turned the stone over once again in the dish. "Scalpel," she said, and Gus passed her a one-inch blade, handle first.

Warily Mariah brought the little blade down toward the rock in the dish, only to have the action interrupted by Gus.

"Mariah, your goggles," he said.

Mariah knew he was right. Who knew what might come spurting, leaping or rocketing out of the incongruous-looking stone when she cracked its surface?

Mariah pulled her safety goggles down over her eyes before bringing the scalpel blade down to touch the rock, putting enough pressure on it to cut a central indentation across the surface. With a push the two halves snapped apart, and Mariah stared at them. They seemed unremarkable, just two halves of a stone. There was nothing living in there that she could see.

Mariah plucked one half up with the tweezers, turning it over to examine it from all angles. Finally she placed it back in the dish. "Nada, zilch, just a rock," she confirmed.

Beside her, Gus made a record of her observation on the top sheet of the clipboard where a chart had been copied in which to log their findings. He glanced over at the crate that rested beside Mariah, his eyes glazed in thought.

Seeing him, Mariah smiled. "Could be a long day ahead," she said. "Sorry, geology can be a bit painstaking. Not many Frankenstein monsters being created by geologists, I'm afraid."

Gus smiled. "Thank goodness. That's what I'm here to avoid."

Mariah reached for the next stone, and she and Gus continued with their slow but necessary work.

AT A GLANCE, KANE REGISTERED a half-dozen Colts, two Taurus revolvers, a couple of what looked to be scratch-built emulation Browning machine guns and one very scuffed Ceiner Ultimate shotgun-rifle combo. They were all pointed in his direction as he slowly turned to face the locals. Very slowly Kane leaned down and placed the shotgun on the ground, keeping both arms well out to his sides as he did so. Meanwhile, standing on the edge of the strip of El Cana beach, Grant raised his empty hands once more over his head.

"All right, gentlemen," Kane said in Spanish, "let's all take a step back before we do anything hasty."

On the little strip of dirt road that ran between the

six ramshackle properties, the inhabitants of El Cana waited, their weapons trained on the two strangers in their midst, their expressions cruel and mistrustful. Like the buildings they inhabited, the locals were a mismatched bunch, though it struck Kane that none of them were much over fifty years old. The women who stood among the fifteen-strong group were young and dressed in shabby-chic, flimsy silks and nylons—brothelwear. The men were less populous, just five in all, including a broad-shouldered man in his fifties with thick jowls and two days' growth of beard. The man had an SAF submachine gun cradled in his hands, which he held steadily on Kane as he approached warily.

"You want to explain maybe what the fuck you think you're doing here, gringo?" the man with the SAF asked.

Hands still raised, Kane nodded. "That's a fair question," he said, "and we didn't come looking for trouble."

"Shana says different," one of the gaudily dressed women hissed, and Kane realized she was referring to the woman he had just knocked out, which was regrettable.

"I don't like having a gun pointed in my face any more than anyone else," Kane began slowly. "I simply…disarmed her."

"Bull!" the woman snarled, raising her revolver, a retrofitted Taurus 76 repainted in a leopard-skin design.

The man with the SAF machine pistol glanced at her, his eyes narrowed. "Okay, Mia, let's just hear the strangers out before we kill them.

"Well?" the man continued, raising an eyebrow at Kane.

"A boat's cargo went missing on the waters near here," Kane explained, "out in the gulf. We came looking for it."

"This isn't a port, *señor*," the heavily jowled man instructed. "We don't trade goods. Turn around and go back where you came from."

"I appreciate that," Kane said, "but I heard it might have passed through here, maybe even got stored here."

The man with the submachine gun looked intrigued, the hint of a smile curling his lip. "What sort of cargo are we talking about, *señor*? What kind of value?"

"It's not valuable," Kane began.

"Come now, you have traveled all this way," the man said, "broke in where you must have realized you weren't welcome. This cargo you're looking for must have some value."

"No, not really," Kane assured him. "What it is is dangerous. Very dangerous."

"What—a weapon? Something radioactive maybe?"

"Something along those lines, yes," Kane said, his arms still raised. "Not a weapon, though. More like livestock."

The man continued to watch Kane, the SAF submachine gun cradled in his arms. Behind him, the people of El Cana kept a wary eye on both Kane and Grant, ensuring neither man could make any sudden moves.

"Look," Kane said, "can my partner and I put our arms down yet? This really isn't the way I wanted to discuss this."

The man eyed Kane for a long moment, then glanced at where the bigger man stood at the edge of the sand.

"You're outnumbered and outgunned, *señor*," he warned. "No tricks, understand?"

Kane nodded. "Yeah."

With that, Kane lowered his hands slowly to his sides, with Grant doing likewise a few paces away from him.

Warily, the older man—who had assumed the role of spokesman—used his SAF submachine gun to gesture toward one of the weather-beaten buildings. "This way," he said, "and no tricks."

While Mia checked on Shana, the others spread out to surround Kane and Grant, hemming them in as they marched them toward the building in question.

"So you figured El Cana was lucky, huh?" Grant taunted under his breath.

Kane glared at him. "Well, we ain't dead yet."

Chapter 15

Back at the Cerberus redoubt, Mariah and Gus were still working with the crate of rocks. Mariah had tried heating them, initially to body temperature and then to a far greater heat, but there had been nothing notable about the rocks' reactions in either case. She had tried adding water to them, using a pipette to drip liquid on one of the stones, one tentative drop at a time. She had tried applying pressure, running them through various solutions, testing and altering their alkalinity and acidity. She had tried all manner of analysis, but other than the acid—which had eaten away at two of the rocks she had tested it on—the gamut of reactions crossed a very narrow spectrum of "no reaction" to "as predicted." In short, Mariah Falk, authority on rocks, had metaphorically hit a brick wall.

Reaching across the desk, Mariah took the clipboard where Gus had been logging the reactions and studied it. "There really is nothing here," she said with a sigh. She shook her head, scanning the tick boxes again. It was so frustrating; she had seen what these stones could do to people, so to be met with no unusual reactions was enough to make her want to scream.

Beside her, Gus saw the way Mariah's face had screwed up in annoyance, and he offered a word of consolation. "Maybe Kane's crew brought us a faulty batch?"

Mariah shook her head. "Their potency is dwindling with the loss of Ullikummis, but Grant assured me that these were the right stones. Domi's still in recovery after the way these things attacked her."

Gus didn't know what to say. "We can try the tests again," he suggested. "I could make us a drink first if you think that might help?"

When Mariah didn't answer, Gus got down from his stool and made his way over to the coffeemaker that waited in one corner of the lab. Like a lot of the nonessential equipment here, the coffeemaker was still covered in a spiderweb of stone veins from Ullikummis's attack, but it worked fine so the cleanup was deemed nonurgent. Opening the chute, Gus filled it with grounds and flicked the switch that heated the water.

Mariah's eyes were still on the top sheet of the clipboard when he came back with two cups of steaming java.

"Have you found something?" Gus asked, setting a cup before Mariah.

She nodded, pointing to the top line of the analysis. "They're magnetic," she said.

Gus read. The rocks had shown a little magnetism, nothing that would make them cling to anything, just an infinitesimal response to standard testing by a powerful electromagnet.

"Not very," he observed doubtfully.

"No, but it's something," Mariah said. "Oxygenated blood—human blood—contains iron. When levels drop, one can actually become weak. That's called anemia. These rocks attach themselves to humans, responding to living hosts to change their genetic makeup. I think they're doing it through the iron—

they're drawn to the ferrous material in the human bloodstream."

Gus nodded thoughtfully. "So, where does that put us?"

"Would the rocks react differently to someone with anemia?" Mariah posed. "Would they react at all? It's a medical question, and outside my knowledge sphere, but I wonder if that might give us the answer we're looking for."

"What do you suggest we do?" Gus asked.

Mariah looked at him thoughtfully for a moment with her smiling eyes. "Do we have any iron filings here?"

Gus nodded.

"Get them."

ENTERING THE WOODEN building behind the spokesman, Kane recognized that it was a bar, albeit a little worse for wear. The room stank of stale beer and Mary Jane, and the creamy paint of the walls had become discolored from cigarette smoke. The tables were scratched and stained, while the mismatched chairs showed a delicacy of carving, many of them featuring elaborate designs carved into their wooden backs showing ocelots, hawks and more fantastical creatures.

Two patrons sat at one of the tables, sipping at steeping cups of spiced tea, but there was no one else in the room, not even anyone serving. It seemed the afternoon lull was upon the business, though no one had bothered to use that time to clean the room. Judging by the smell, Kane suspected that no one had cleaned it in twenty years.

The spokesman with the SAF strode to a side booth that backed against a wall, instructing Kane and Grant to be seated there. Poorly lit, the booth wedged in the two Cerberus teammates, making a quick escape impossible. Gunmen took up positions beside the booth while another man brought over one of the chairs. This one featured intricate carvings running down its legs that made each leg look as if it were in the clutches of a striking serpent. The gunman turned the chair so that its back faced the booth, using it like a gate to block in Kane and Grant. Once that was done, the heavily jowled spokesman took up a position opposite Kane in the booth, with two of the armed women beside him, one to either side.

"Well, *señor,*" he began, "you have a story to tell, I think."

Kane nodded as his Commtact translated the man's words. "As I said before, we're looking for a missing cargo that came from a small fishing scow that got lost out in the gulf. The boat is called *La Segunda Montaña,* and it came way up along the East Coast. We think it was destined for Tuxpan but it never arrived."

"Never arrived?" the man repeated, scratching at his stubbly beard with grimy fingernails.

Kane nodded once more. "We believe that the boat got boarded, and that its cargo was probably stolen."

"What happened to the boat?"

"We haven't been able to find it," Kane admitted.

"So you have a missing boat," the spokesman said, "and no cargo. What makes you think that the people here would know anything about it?"

"We were directed here by someone," Kane said cagily. "He suggested there was a good chance that the boat was boarded by...some independent traders," Kane said, choosing his words carefully. "He suggested it would have been scuttled once the cargo was removed."

"Pirates!" the spokesman spit, a wide grin on his features. "You're talking about pirates. Is that right?"

"We're speculating," Kane said diplomatically.

Beside Kane, Grant eyed the guards, surreptitiously scanning the room for possible exits while his partner handled the negotiations. They might need to get out of there quickly, in which case Grant would be expected to take the lead.

"So, what is this cargo precisely?" the heavily jowled man asked.

"It's a box, a wooden crate about so big." As he spoke, Kane used his hands on the table to give an indication of the size, and he was conscious that everyone around him tensed as he did so, wary of a trick. "Full of stones or maybe half-full. Little pebbles."

"And what are these?" Kane's inquisitor asked. "Gems?"

"No," Kane said. "They're just stones. They look just like the kind you'd find washed up on the beach here. Only they're dangerous. Real dangerous."

"How can a stone be dangerous, *señor?*" the questioner asked, laughing. "Unless maybe I throw it at your head, eh?"

Kane fixed the man with his no-nonsense look, steely-gray eyes boring into his. "They're alive."

REBA DEFORE WAS WORKING up charts in the medical rooms of the Cerberus redoubt when her comm buzzed. She had Melanie the Stone Widow, Danny and the other three acolytes confined to a locked room where they could be monitored and move about freely without getting into trouble. Meanwhile, she had sent

Domi to her room, prescribing a minimum of two days' bed rest. While the widow's group had become less aggressive after their initial arrival, it didn't do to forget that they had met with Cerberus as enemies. Their faith in the false god Ullikummis meant they had to be considered a threat.

As the comm buzzed, DeFore stole a glance through the observation window, watching where Mel and the others sat and chatted. In their gowns with their aging skin and thinning hair, they looked for all the world like survivors of some terrible disease, another AIDS or the results of chemo treatment. They were the young-turned-old, the life sucked out of them by a vampiric stone seed.

"This is DeFore," Reba said as she toggled the switch on the squawk box.

"Reba, this is Lakesh. Mariah's upstairs in a lab. She thinks she's found something of interest, and she's asked that we attend at our earliest convenience."

DeFore nodded, despite the fact that Lakesh could not see her over the comm unit. As she did so, her eyes went to the observation window again, watching her patients for a few seconds. The woman with the dyed streaks in her hair was dancing in a ludicrous manner, pretending to be a puppet with strings connecting arms and legs. The others—her acolytes—laughed, enjoying the silliness of the show.

"Reba?"

The physician turned back to the comm unit. "Okay, I'll be there in a few minutes."

With that she cut the comm and gathered up her charts before exiting her office. As she paused at the threshold where two security officers stood guard, De-

Fore heard the laughter of her patients echoing from the sealed room. Dead people laughing, she thought.

"ALIVE, *SEÑOR?*" THE PORTLY spokesman mocked. "But how can this be?"

Kane stared at him across the table, ignoring the half-dozen blasters that were trained on himself and his partner in the seedy, foul-smelling barroom. "Contact with human flesh brings the stones to life," he said. "They bond with people's skin and take them over. You want a scientific explanation? Ask a scientist. All I know is these things are out here somewhere and they are dangerous as all get-out."

Something in Kane's tone struck a warning note with the people who were covering him, and it seemed that everyone around the table was holding their breath. Finally, after a very long ten seconds had passed, the portly man who acted as the group's spokesman, began—very tentatively—to laugh.

"You're joking with us, right?" he said. "Joking me. Huh? Big joke. You think you can play us for fools, is that it?" There was growing irritation in every word now, and the man was no longer watching Kane. Instead he was looking at the SAF submachine gun in his hands, raising it once more in a forceful thrust.

But before Kane could say another word, a new voice called out across the room. "It's no joke."

Kane, Grant and their captors all turned, seeking out the source of that voice. A man stood behind the bar, broad-shouldered and wearing a sweat-stained undershirt and slacks, with a five-o'clock shadow darkening his jaw. It was the saloon's owner, Sal, and he had returned to his usual post from his private rooms up above the bar.

"S-Sal?" one of the group guarding Kane and Grant stuttered. "What are you—?"

Sal held up a hand to halt the woman's words. "I don't know who these people are or what in the name of hell is going on here, but if I heard this gentleman right about the living rocks, then I can assure you he's telling the truth."

The tension was strong in the air, like a weight on the inhabitants of the grim saloon.

With some effort, Kane's interviewer pushed himself out from the booth and waddled across the room to speak more confidentially to Sal at the bar. Kane stilled his breathing to listen, and knew that beside him Grant was doing the same.

"These two no-goods arrived on the beach from nowhere," the portly spokesman explained in a hushed tone. "Little Ando saw them come clambering over the rocks at the south end."

"Shana's boy?"

The spokesman nodded. "Good kid. Their clothes, the way they carry themselves—they're not freelance, that's for sure. I figure them for port authority, doing a little undercover work. But they ain't asked for no bribes. Go figure."

Sal tapped one of his fingers on the scuffed surface of his bar, the fingernail striking it over and over with a sharp clicking sound. "Duena's sick," he said. "And I swear to you, it's what the white-skinned one described."

Kane watched surreptitiously from the corner of his eye as the two men stood in silence for a few moments, considering what to do with this new piece of knowledge. Finally, the portly spokesman waddled back to the booth and stopped before it, glaring at Kane.

"You have medical skills?" he snapped. "You know how to deal with this stone thing you're talking about?"

"I have some experience with it," Kane said evasively.

"My friend's daughter—Duendecito—she has a problem," the portly figure explained.

Kane pushed himself up from the benchlike seat with Grant following suit. "We'll look," Kane said.

The portly spokesman brought the muzzle of his SAF submachine gun around and jabbed it at Grant, indicating he should sit back down. "Your friend will stay down here with my friends. You understand, gringo?"

Kane nodded. Collateral, to ensure neither of them tried anything.

LAKESH AND DEFORE had joined Mariah Falk in the lab as she went through her findings concerning the living rocks.

"We don't have much to go on," Mariah explained, "but it's clear that the stones have a magnetic charge, which means they can be affected by a magnetic field."

Lakesh nodded, encouraging Mariah to continue.

"We think that they came from Ullikummis himself, budding from his body in a similar manner to the seeds of a plant," Mariah said as she consulted her notes. "We've seen them bond with the human nervous system, forming a symbiotic relationship with the subject. What we haven't really known, up till now, is how they have formed that bond.

"I ran the sample stones through a number of tests," Mariah continued, "and the most striking aspect is how they react to magnetic phenomena. In very simple terms, they are attracted by a magnetic field—it's

what brings them to life. Although our tests are rudi-
mentary at this stage, we've found that these stones are
especially responsive to iron, and it seems that this factor would be crucial in their response to a human subject. Oxygenated blood contains iron, and that's likely
acting as the draw for the stones, as well as providing
them with fuel. Look."

On that instruction, Mariah's assistant Gus tipped a
tiny spoonful of iron filings on one of the stones that
rested in a high-sided glass dish. The dish was twelve
inches across and its walls were almost six inches in
height, with a thick base. As soon as Gus had added
the metal filings, he stepped well back from the container, nervously rechecking that his safety goggles
were in place.

Ten feet away, Mariah, Lakesh and Reba watched as
the stone responded to the iron filings. At first it seemed
to shake with excitement, rattling against the thick base
of the container, drumming louder and louder with each
passing second. The iron filings that had fallen on the
stone itself clung to its sides like sprinkled icing sugar
on a cake, but something strange seemed to be happening to the other filings that had been dropped into the
container. Lakesh took a step forward, getting just a
little closer so that he could see more clearly.

"Be careful, Dr. Singh," Gus warned.

Within its dish, the stone turned in a stuttering,
start-stop manner, as if moved by some hidden hand.
Around it, the iron filings stood on end, waggling in
place as they pointed toward the stone in their center.

"Now Gus will add some water," Mariah explained.

Lakesh and DeFore watched as the laboratory assistant approached the high-sided dish, a beaker of
tepid water in his hand. Holding the beaker at arm's

length, Gus tipped its contents into the dish, letting just a little water into the bowl where it splashed on the stone therein. The water created a little pool in the dish that was roughly a quarter-inch deep. The metal filings floated on its surface like insects, swirling a little with the motion of the water.

Then a remarkable thing happened. Still covered in iron filings, the stone in the center of the dish began to rock in place, and points emerged from its sides. The points became longer and longer, snaking across the bowl in squirming tendrils like the reaching arms of an octopus. With the stone at its center, the reaching tendrils, each no thicker than the lead of a pencil, spread across the bowl, sprawling through the liquid and plucking at the iron filings that clung to those reaching, flailing limbs.

"What is that?" DeFore whispered, astonished.

In the dish, the stone continued to vibrate, its eerie limbs flailing in the water.

"They don't last long in our tests," Mariah said, "but we can speculate that if the liquid were blood instead of water, then the stone might become more vibrant."

"Of course," Lakesh agreed.

The lab fell into a foreboding silence as all four people continued to watch in awe as the stone's tendrils continued to claw through the water in the dish.

KANE FOLLOWED THE GRIZZLED bartender through the bar and up a narrow staircase with several of the armed women closely following. The stairs were bare wood that creaked with every step, and the ceiling above them was low enough that Kane and the bartender had to stoop before they reached the landing.

Lit by an overhead bulb in a lacy lampshade, the

landing was carpeted with a green rug, its tassels
grubby with ground-in dirt. Several rooms led off from
the landing, and Kane followed Sal past the open door
of a bathroom and on to another door. The drapes were
drawn within, and it took Kane a moment to take in
what he saw there.

A woman sat in a straight-backed chair that had
been placed beside the head of the bed. She was curva-
ceous beneath her simple clothes, with long dark hair
that had a slight kink to it, and Kane pegged her for
perhaps forty years of age. Beside her was a single bed,
and the woman leaned forward, stroking the forehead
of the figure who lay within, pushing the occupant's
hair back. Tucked beneath the blanket, the figure in
the bed had long dark hair that matched the woman's.

"My wife, Janie," Sal explained miserably, "and our
daughter, Duendecito."

The room was overdecorated, the small bedside
table covered in knickknacks, the walls smothered
with pictures, magazine clippings, old photographs
and a book cover torn from its source. The drapes were
closed, and Kane saw they had thick bands of ribbon
across their midpoints in a horizontal line, tied into
matching bows.

"Can we get some light in here?" Kane asked.

Janie muttered a greeting to Kane before switch-
ing on the bedside light. It turned the room a pinkish-
orange with its dull glow.

Then Kane approached the bed, his eyes fixed on its
occupant. She was a young woman, he saw, most likely
still in her teens, with long dark hair that matched her
mother's. She lay on her back, rocking slightly, her lips
pursed in pain, and as he approached Kane could hear
the wheezing of her breath.

Janie had stepped up from her seat, leaving it for Kane as she took up a position at the edge of the bed. As he sat, the woman reached for the bedcovers and drew them back, speaking soothing words to her daughter as she did so.

Kane watched, his heart drumming faster against his chest as the covers were pulled away.

LAKESH, MARIAH AND DEFORE had taken up positions around a table in the open-plan laboratory, where they sat discussing Mariah's findings.

"It seems, then, that the combination of liquid and iron is what powers these stones, allowing them to meld with the human nervous system and take control of a person's metabolism," Lakesh summarized. "And also their mind," he added after a moment's consideration, recalling the horrors they had all seen under Ullikummis's brief reign.

"Liquid seems to be the trigger," Mariah confirmed. "I'd guess that once placed in the human body the tendrils continue to reach out, solidifying over time to create something akin to the hard rock sections we found inside Edwards's skull, as well as having the ability to be drawn to the surface of the flesh on command, creating a sort of hidden armor just beneath the subject's skin."

Lakesh nodded. "The stonelike flesh of the firewalkers."

"The longer the stone is connected, the more complicated its web becomes," Mariah said.

At a nearby bench, the bowl with the stone in it continued to fill with the writhing, snaking tendrils of the rock wrapping in on themselves in the iron-dappled water. Gus Wilson had placed a glass lid over the open top of the bowl and sat watching it from a safe distance to ensure nothing untoward happened. He appreciated they were on a whole different scale of "untoward" to begin with, and did his best to work within the newly defined parameters.

DeFore voiced her agreement to Mariah's observation. "Like most symbiotic relationships, the bonds become stronger over time," she said, "until the division between the two organisms is blurred. At that point, they become almost impossible to separate without endangering the life of one or both participants in what is now a mutually beneficial relationship."

"Where does that leave us with regards to Melanie and the others that Kane's team brought in?" Lakesh inquired.

"With the level of bonding that we see in the sample group here," DeFore said, indicating the glass bowl, "I'd say it doesn't look good. These things may be rotten, but they're still strong enough to intertwine with the human nervous system. Unlacing that connection would require major surgery, and the recuperation time would be staggering."

"But we saved Edwards," Mariah blurted.

DeFore looked sorrowfully at her longtime colleagues. "Edwards's stone was still 'alive' when we excised it," she reminded them. "His had come directly from Ullikummis, was placed there by him, directly into Edwards's skull.

"We may never map all the different types of stones that Ullikummis employed to create his army of followers," the physician continued. "Suffice to say that Edwards was, relatively speaking, one of the lucky ones."

"Relatively speaking," Lakesh repeated. Then he turned to Mariah, eyebrows raised to encourage her.

Mariah shrugged. "Living rocks are a little outside my field," she explained. "We're at the very outside perimeter of my discipline. I can tell you about their properties until I'm blue in the face, but I can't tell you how to fix the people who have them inside. That's a medical question."

"I don't think they can be fixed," DeFore said.

Lakesh gazed at the stone in its glass prison for a few seconds, puzzling over everything in his mind. "Then we cannot do anything for Mel, Danny and the others?" he concluded.

"I have all five under observation right now," Reba said. "But I think the best we can do is help them live out the rest of their days in comfort. They don't have that many."

KANE STARED AT THE FIGURE in the bed, feeling the frustration well inside him. She had been a pretty girl once; of that he had no doubt, her slender body just brushed with the first flush of womanhood. He suspected she had had a pretty smile, too, but now that had changed. Beneath her bottom lip, her face was caked with a web of splintered rock, and as the woman drew the blanket back farther Kane saw that the rocky growths worsened, becoming a thick collar that covered the girl's throat, neck and reached down over the top of her rib cage.

The weight of the barman's words hit Kane like a hammer as he spoke. "You can help my daughter, *señor?*"

Chapter 16

Kane studied the rocking figure in the bed for a moment longer before turning back to Sal. "Let me speak to someone," he said, his voice low.

Without further explanation, Kane held his hand to his ear and engaged his Commtact, patching through to Cerberus and, a moment later, to Reba DeFore. He didn't need to hold his hand to his ear; he simply found it served to make the people around him quiet and give him privacy. Standing at the doorway, the two female guards watched suspiciously for a trick. With curt professionalism, Kane swiftly described Duendecito's condition. "She looks like she has a rash," Kane concluded, "only it's chitinous, like stone."

"How far has this rash extended?" DeFore asked, her words piped directly to Kane's mastoid bone so that only he could hear her as he stood in the room above the bar.

"Her whole neck's covered, including the throat," Kane said, examining the girl as her father and mother watched. "Her breathing is shallow. I'd guess the stone extends to the inside of her trachea."

Sympathetically, DeFore explained about the experiments that Mariah had been conducting, bringing Kane up to speed on their conclusions. "The stones appear to be bonding with the iron in our blood," she said. "Once bonded, I can't see any possible way to remove them without killing the subject. The synthesis is too chaotic."

"What about ultrasonics?" Kane suggested, recalling how this process had been used on several of the Cerberus personnel during the latter stages of the war with Ullikummis.

"I've forecast that to be workable in certain circumstances only," DeFore said. "In essence, while Ullikummis was alive we might have stood a chance. But the properties of the stones have changed now that he's gone. I'm sorry, Kane, but your patient is not going to recover," she finished.

Kane clucked his tongue thoughtfully. "Thanks, Reba," he said, closing off the conversation. Then he turned back to Sal where the big man stood in the doorway and gently shook his head, just once. "I'm sorry" was all he said.

Sal stood there, just inside the doorway. He was a large man, imposing when he needed to be. His bar, out of the way in this semilegal stretch of dirt, was doubtless tribute to just how well he could handle himself. Kane watched as Sal's shoulders slumped, and he stood there, shaking silently as tears rolled from his eyes.

Kane took a makeup pencil from the cluttered bedside table, held it by the end and prodded it against the armorlike growth that covered the girl's chest and neck. It was hard like metal, with no sense of give to it.

"I'm not a medic," Kane explained gently. "We came here to find the things that made her like this—a crate of stones. You know where we can find that, Sal?"

"*Señor,* my daughter is very precious to me," Sal said. He was shaking his head as he spoke, and behind him Kane could hear Janie, the mother, crying also. "I don't know…" He stopped, sobbing once more, swiping at his tears as if they were insects crawling over his face.

"When did this happen?" Kane asked.

"Last night," Sal said. "Duendecito went out for some… She was serving with me, and I took my eye off her for a moment. You understand? Just seconds, a minute maybe. She's…of that age. A free spirit. You understand me?"

Standing, Kane reached for Sal, steadying him with his firm grip. "Sal, I'm not blaming you. I just need to know what happened."

"We get a lot of visitors here, *señor*," Sal said. "Some regulars, others not so much. There's a crew that comes here, led by a man named Black John. Not a nice man."

"Are we talking about pirates here?" Kane asked.

"Yes," Sal confirmed, nodding. "Handful of them came here last night. They were plenty raucous. One beat up one of the girls in the bathroom downstairs after he'd… Well."

"What about Duendecito?" Kane asked. "What happened to her?"

"She went off with one of them. I didn't see," Sal explained regretfully. "I found her on the beach, her clothes were torn, she'd been…."

Behind Kane, the girl's mother burst into great retching sobs, making some plea to the heavens, the words coming out so distorted that his Commtact could not make sense of them.

"Go on," Kane said, his eyes fixed on Sal.

"Kids…girls…they get in trouble, you know?" Sal explained. "Always drawn to the wrong kind of man. She went off with one of Black John's crew. I don't know his name. I found her on the beach later. There was blood and she couldn't move. She was like this, like you see her now."

Kane eyed the girl again, his gaze drawn to the terrible growth that marred her chest and neck. It looked like the sand-encrusted shell of some kind of sea life, hard like a crab's shell.

"You have any idea how?" Kane asked. "It's different to what I've seen before. I can recognize the pattern, but it's different."

"When he found her, she could still speak," Janie said. It was the first time she had spoken, and her voice was timid, quiet, as if she was afraid of the words she was using. "She told me the man had held her down and that when she cried out he had forced something in her mouth to quiet her. A stone. It became lodged in her throat, but he wouldn't let her move. She couldn't spit it out." Janie was crying again by the time she finished her explanation, and her eyes were fixed not on her daughter or Kane but on her husband, as if fearful of his reaction.

"I have medical people looking into this phenomenon right now," Kane said, "but I don't want to raise your hopes unnecessarily. In the meantime, the crew has more. We need to find these stones before they can do any more damage."

Sal nodded in understanding, his brow furrowed in emotional torment.

"You know where I can find this Black John and his crew?" Kane asked. "You said they were regulars."

Sal nodded once more, humbled. "There's a series of caverns a little way down south," he explained. "About three miles from here, right on the seafront. They have a place there, as well as some properties inland."

"Right on the seafront, you say?" Kane confirmed. "How will I recognize these caves?"

"You won't miss them," Sal said. "Their boat will be docked there, big thing, looks like someone took a rocket and dunked it in the ocean. *La Discordia*."

"Discord," Kane translated. "Thanks, we'll look."

"If you find them, what will you do?" Janie asked.

Kane turned to her, seeing the haunted look in her eyes. "We'll get the stones out of circulation," he promised. "Beyond that—we'll see."

"You find the man who did this to my daughter," Janie said, "and you kill him for me, *señor*. Kill him like a rabid dog because that is all he is."

Kane said nothing in response, knowing it was the woman's grief speaking. Whether he would have to kill the person in question, he couldn't say.

DOWN IN THE SALOON, Grant had remained in the booth where Kane had left him surrounded by the gun-toting group of locals. In Kane's absence, a Latina with terribly dyed blond hair had taken to asking Grant solicitous questions that rapidly descended into jibes at his sexuality when he chose not to respond. Dressed in a sheer silk dress the green color of unripe tomatoes, she waved a snub-nosed Colt as she spoke, weaving it through the air as if it were a toy.

When Kane reappeared, fifteen minutes after he had gone with Sal to examine the man's daughter, Dyejob was outright haranguing Grant with a nonstop series of racial slurs and sexual epithets as the others laughed. The rotund spokesman of the group had extricated himself and now sat at the bar, working his way through a bottle of whisky. Grant sat there staring straight ahead as her friends egged on the harridan, ignoring her as the group cheered with the production of each new and more vulgar name to describe the stoic ex-Magistrate.

"I'll bet you can't even get it up for little boys," she shrieked, tossing her head triumphantly as her colleagues cheered. "Huh? Is that your problem? Little dinky thing there in your pants, doesn't wake up when you want it to?"

Grant stared ahead as the crowd cheered, no trace of emotion on his face.

"That's right," the woman continued, "I've seen your sort before, come in my room all swagger and shit. What turns you on is animals, right? Chicken-fucker, that's what you are."

Kane strode across the room with Sal following from the stairwell that ran up behind the bar. The two guards who had been posted on Kane followed in a relaxed manner, trusting Sal's opinion of the man.

"Made some friends?" Kane asked as he caught Grant's eye.

Grant looked sour. "Not exactly."

Kane smiled. "We have a lead."

"Then we're leaving?" Grant asked, and Kane nodded.

Sal hurried to speak with the portly spokesman who had brought Kane and Grant to the bar and, after a moment, the spokesman gave orders in Spanish and the people around the booth parted.

"You are free to leave, *señors,*" the spokesman said. "Sal has vouched for you. That's good enough for me."

Edging to the end of the bench, Grant extricated himself from the booth and stood.

"Going so soon, little boy?" the blonde teased, pressing close to Grant, her body touching his. "Maybe you have more success with the gnat-catchers, yes?" As she spoke, she played her free hand down his body and along inner thighs, running it up to grasp for his groin.

Then, in a flurry of movement, Grant snagged the woman's right hand in his, clamping his fingers over her hand and the little Colt revolver she had there, crushing tighter. The woman shrank back, letting out a little whimper as Grant squeezed her hand, gun and all.

"You behave," Grant warned.

"You've got…" the woman began, but then she shrieked as the pain in her hand became greater. "Let me…free…"

The other members of the group were watching the scene openmouthed, but it didn't take them more than a few seconds to react, drawing their blasters and eyeing Grant and the woman. Then Grant let her go, and the woman toppled backward into one of the chairs as she continued to pull away from the grip even as it was released.

"Stupid chicken-fucker," she muttered as she struggled up from the floor. Her lip was bleeding.

"Yeah, I'll miss you, too," Grant growled as he and Kane left the sweat-smelling barroom.

Outside, the late-afternoon sun was beating down, and the sand and the lone dirt-track road radiated the heat they had absorbed through the day. As the two men made their way to the outcropping that bordered the strip of beach, Kane explained about Sal's daughter and the information he had gained.

Ten minutes later they were back in the cockpits of the Mantas, ready to do a surveillance sweep of the indicated caves. Kane used his Commtact to file a sitrep with Cerberus, bringing Brewster Philboyd there up to speed.

"Glad you're making progress, Kane," Philboyd responded.

"Playing detective doesn't sit well with me," Kane grumbled. "Too many variables, too many people with vested interests."

"At least you're getting answers," Philboyd consoled.

"Yeah," Kane grumbled, "but never ones I like."

As they spoke, the shining Mantas took to the air swiftly.

ROSALIA WAS PREPARED to search the whole of the compound for Brigid Baptiste, but there was no need. The red-haired Cerberus warrior had returned to the upstairs dorm room that they shared, and she was kneeling by the open doors of the wardrobe when Rosalia located her.

"Brigid? What are you doing?"

"Leaving," Brigid said without looking up.

Rosalia watched as Brigid brought the carrying case containing the interphaser from its hiding place inside the wardrobe. "Where will you go?" she asked.

For the first time, Brigid turned and met Rosalia's gaze with her own, and in that instant Rosalia could see that she had been crying. "Just away. Does it matter?"

"You fight well, Brigid Baptiste," Rosalia said. "And it is you, not her. You don't need to be afraid of letting go."

Brigid held the other woman's gaze a moment longer before turning back to her task, opening the locks on the carrying case and powering up the interphaser. After a moment, its control board flashed with lights at the base of the pyramid, and Brigid eyed the screen there as data coalesced.

"Please, thank the mother superior for her hospitality," she said in a voice drained of emotion. "I'll be out of your hair in a few minutes."

"Brigid," Rosalia began, "you're not running from me or from this place, you're running from something you think is inside you. And that's something no interphaser jump will get you away from, no matter how many times you try it."

Brigid's voice was heavy with weariness. "My head won't stop spinning," she said, "and I keep wondering who I am. I don't think I know anymore."

Rosalia took a step into the room, conscious of the evidence all around her of childhood and innocence. It seemed right somehow, the way it represented young girls becoming women, finding their identities for the first time.

"Brigid, you're safe here," she said. "I promise."

"I just want to forget," Brigid muttered, "and I can't."

"You think that forgetting will make it all not have happened?" Rosalia challenged. "Is that what you think?"

Brigid didn't look up.

"It happened, and you have to find a way to live with it," Rosalia continued. "Running away won't change what happened. This isn't some failed relationship, some lover you can run away from, change the locks. This is you, Brigid—this is the part of you that got molded by that…that satanic thing, that monster. You need to see that."

"Vase or faces," Brigid said, "I see it all. I can't stop seeing it. What she'd do. What I'd do."

"Brigid…"

"I just want to forget," Brigid said. "Why is that so hard to understand?"

Rosalia was standing over her now, and very gently she placed one hand on the woman's shoulder. "Stay," she said. "Until you have somewhere to go, at least."

Brigid looked up at Rosalia with red-rimmed eyes, tears on her cheeks. Behind her, the interphaser continued its automated powering-up sequence.

THE AFTERNOON SUN played across the Mantas' wings as they cut through the skies in line with the shore.

"That looks like the place below," Kane observed, and Grant's acknowledgment came back to him a moment later over his Commtact.

To the starboard side of the Mantas, a stretch of foreboding land edged against the roiling sea, whose crashing waves hammered against it like the last gasp of a punch-drunk pugilist. Rocky crags jutted from the sea like blackened teeth, the spume running from them like saliva. Beyond them, a sheer cliff towered more than forty feet, looming over the sea in an inward angled crescent like the outstretched arms of some awful giant of myth. The black cliff face was dotted with cave mouths as if riddled with woodworm, each mouth barely discernible amid the darkness of its surrounds.

"Taking a closer look in three," Kane said, "two, one…"

Then Kane veered his Manta craft closer, dipping the starboard wing as he swooped over the cliff's edge even as Grant veered away to his port.

The scanning equipment of the Manta analyzed the data it was being fed in an instant, picking out two rowboats, as well as three warm bodies hidden among

the dark crags of the surface. The people were picked
up as illuminated shadows across Kane's heads-up
display, a chirrup of sound accompanying each new
discovery: plink, plink, plink. Two of the people were
together, tucked just inside one of those wormhole
mouths, while a third waited in a recess near the top
of the cliffs. With a command as quick as thought to
the Manta's scanning units, Kane zoomed in on the
higher man, picking out a rope ladder that dangled
down from where he waited.

"Got company," Kane advised his partner over the
secure Commtacts as his Manta shot high over the
cliffs and onward inland.

"Found something here," came Grant's response.
His Manta was traveling farther down the shore at a
restrained speed, but even at that slower pace he had
almost missed the ship hiding among the jagged teeth
of rocks.

Shaped like a needle, the ship was painted the green
of the sea. Only its shadow against the rocks gave it
away, the sun sparkling on its hull in the same rhythm
as the ocean.

La Discordia.

She had been left two hundred yards from the cliffs,
woven between the fearsome array of jutting rocks
with the precision of a seamstress. As Grant's Manta
hurtled by overhead, he scanned the craft bobbing
at anchor, his displays picking out crucial detail and
searching in infrared for the warm glows that would
mark the crew. It showed that the crew had been kept
to a minimum, just two men patrolling across the deck.
The scan showed, too, that the engines were warm,
kept at a lulled readiness in case there came the need
for swift escape.

"I've got two men here," Grant stated, bringing his aircraft around for a second pass, keeping to a high course.

"Three," Kane responded professionally.

Kane's Manta was set on a low course over the sloping land beyond the cliffs, where stubborn scrub clung by its straining roots and emaciated trees bent toward the drop as if with the onset of osteoporosis.

The cliffs were still moving, it seemed, losing a battle with the sea, inch by agonizing inch, year by agonizing year. The land beyond looked hard and unmanageable, sun-yellowed grass dappling it in a sickly patchwork, skeletal bushes springing like the unsightly clumps of hair from an old man's nostrils.

A half mile inland, Kane spied a thicket of thorny bushes wrapped on themselves like barbed wire, creating a natural fence around a two-story cottage. The cottage was built of stone, large enough to house three generations of family comfortably, with a gravel drive leading to the roads beyond. Several automobiles hunched against the path, one of them up on blocks in a state of disrepair. A wide outhouse hunkered beside the cottage, the wooden lines of its roof patterned with weather stains as if an old fighter showing off his scars.

Kane rolled his Manta, pulling it up and away from the cottage. "Got a house out here," he told Grant. "Looks occupied—may be trouble."

"Roger that," Grant acknowledged.

The two fast-moving craft met again inside six seconds, swooping in formation a little way farther up the coast where a spit of beach nestled against the cliffs. Just six feet wide, the sandy spit jutted into the ocean like a withered finger, parts of it washed over by the rolling waves. The Cerberus pilots brought their craft down, landing beside the spit with the grace of swans. The bronze-hued alien craft were incredibly adaptable, and could be used in an ocean environment as well as they could navigate the atmosphere. They churned up the waters as they came to a halt, kicking up sea spray.

A moment later the two craft had settled, their wings resting on the ocean's surface, their bellies sunk beneath the waves. Kane toggled a switch on the dashboard and removed his all-encompassing bronze helmet, casting it aside. The cockpit pulled back smoothly on its runners at Kane's command, and he was out of his seat and trotting across the craft's sleek wing in a matter of seconds. Fifteen feet behind him, Grant was doing likewise, the flapping tails of his long duster catching in the wind as he made his way across the sloping wing.

Stepping onto the spit of sand, Kane glanced up toward the crescent-shaped bowl where the pirate caves were hidden. They were just a few hundred yards away, neatly hidden in the blind spot of the crescent, using the pirates' own defenses against them.

"Not much shore here," Grant observed as he joined Kane on the sandy strut.

Kane eyed the shore along the cliff's edge. A rough and narrow line ran along that edge, irregular shapes carved into the stone by the sea over millions of years. Walking along it would be like navigating the open drawers of a dressing table, like—appropriately enough—the children's perennial favourite game of Pirates.

"We'll manage somehow," Kane assured his partner, and together the two men approached the towering rock, leaving their Manta craft bobbing behind them on the undulating surface of the sea.

It took forty minutes to navigate the cliff's edge, moving swiftly but carefully across its ragged form as they made their way to the hidden alcoves where the pirates had made their hideaway. Both fine physical specimens in the peak of fitness, Kane and Grant made short work of the climb, negotiating each jutting crag and razorlike rock with an effortless professionalism that made the feat look easy. In actuality, few men could have managed that path without falling, and fewer still could have done so and remained calm, exhibiting not so much as a hint of breathlessness from their actions. Even with the afternoon sun beating lazily on their backs, neither Kane nor Grant showed any signs of exhaustion or tiredness, arriving at the cove with all the sweaty evidence of a sunbather who'd spent a relaxing afternoon by the pool.

With both men clad in the dark colors of their shadow suits and jackets, they were sufficiently camouflaged to escape casual notice as they nudged around the corner and into the pirate bay. Kane pointed out the three guards to Grant, raising concerns about the man at the high point who would have the best perspective on their approach. With the jutting, uneven walls here, they could remain almost entirely hidden from the other two who waited in the cave's mouth, their movements masked amid the furious lashing of the waves.

The ship itself, *La Discordia,* was too far away to pose a threat, kept as it was several hundred yards downwind from the bay, presumably because of the difficulty in navigating a larger vessel through the needlelike shards of stone that littered these waters.

So it was that the two Cerberus operatives approached the pirate stronghold with relative ease, a testament to their physical superiority that allowed them to navigate the seemingly impossible approach. They were just eight feet from the cave mouth where the two pirates were hidden when they were finally spotted. The two guards there had been sitting playing cards, and it was only by chance that one of them—a grizzled-looking man with a vicious scar running from brow to chin—glanced up as he took his turn to deal.

"What the—?" the man exclaimed.

By then it was too late. Freeing his grip from the rock face, Kane bounded across the last few feet to the opening, running his right palm along the rock as he effortlessly kept his balance. At the same time, Grant secured himself to the rock by his left hand, kicking out to swing himself up higher on the ragged cliff face, climbing it spider-fashion.

Neither of the cardplayers had much time to react, and it was to their credit that they managed to bring weapons to bear at all as Kane dived through the yawning mouth of the cave. The grizzled man had snatched up what appeared to be a rebuilt Ruger MP-9 that rested by his leg. His partner, a dark-eyed man with olive complexion and a greasy red bandanna across his head, produced a chrome-hued Taurus blowback pistol from somewhere within the folds of his shirt.

But already they were too late. Kane came hurtling into the cave like a thrown rock, one long leg snapping up and flicking the MP-9 aside with an outstretched toe, even as its wielder's finger squeezed against the trigger. The shots went high, 9 mm Parabellum bullets reverberating loudly in the enclosed space as they struck the rocky ceiling overhead.

Beside the grizzled pirate, his partner brought his own blaster in line, snapping off a shot directly at

Kane's face. Kane dropped as his outstretched foot came back down hard on the floor of the cave, and the bullet zipped by just inches over his head, speeding wildly out the cave's mouth and over the ocean beyond.

Still moving, Kane bounded back up from the cavern floor, tucking his head down as he slammed into the bandanna-wearing pirate, striking his breastbone with the top of his head.

The noise of spewing bullets had alerted the watcher hidden in the higher recess, and he shouted a query as he stood and brought his own blaster—a bolt-action rifle with a scope—out to scan the area beyond. As he did so, Grant's hand snapped out from below and to the right of the recess, snagging the muzzle of the weapon and yanking it out of the gunman's hands. The pirate stumbled forward as the gun was pulled free, spitting an oath as he barely refrained from toppling over the sheer drop and into the sea in the same way that his rifle was doing.

Grant was on him in a flash, clambering up the last few rungs of the swaying rope ladder and powering a sledgehammer fist into the pirate's gut. The man tumbled back, slipping on the straw that acted as bedding in the recess before cracking his skull against the wall behind. When he looked up, the pirate saw Grant standing before him, the sunlight behind painting him in silhouette like some grim specter of death.

"Who the f—?" the man screeched, but that was all he said. Already Grant had blurred into motion, driving another of those sledgehammer punches into the man's face, smacking him back with incredible force so that he slammed against the unforgiving wall once more.

Grant smiled in grim satisfaction as he saw the

shabbily dressed pirate sag against the wall, overcome by unconsciousness.

"All clear here," Grant called before reaching down to check the man and the little recess for other weapons and radio equipment.

Thirty feet below, Kane was making similarly short work of the two cardplaying pirates whose game he had interrupted. The man with the bandanna fell to a vicious elbow to the back of his head, crashing against the hard floor like a sack of potatoes, while his scarred partner finally struggled back to his feet from Kane's first attack. He lunged for Kane, but the ex-Magistrate was already in the zone, channeling that incredible point-man sense he exhibited to avoid the attack and counteract before his attacker even realized what had happened. Ducking beneath the blow, Kane charged at the pirate, sacking him with such force that the man went head over heels before finally landing half in the water, his chin striking the jagged rock edge of the cave with a crimson utterance of spilling blood.

A moment later, the two ex-Mags regrouped, using the pirates' own belts to tie them before making their way deeper into the network of caves. The pirates would sleep for a while now.

Chapter 17

Moving with admirable rapidity, Kane and Grant checked the handful of other cave entries before returning to the one where the defeated pirates lay. Several of the caverns stretched a long way back into the rock, but none of them appeared occupied, and the vast majority hit a wall around the same time as they hit shadow.

Assured that no one else was about to raise the alarm, the two ex-Magistrates placed smoked glasses over their eyes before they entered the main cavern. Though they looked like sunglasses, these specs featured electrochemical polymer lenses that gathered all available light to give Kane and Grant a limited form of night vision, providing them with a crucial advantage as they hurried into the network of tunnel-like caves. They made their way along the lone cavern that burrowed into the rock, pacing warily along its length as swiftly and quietly as they were able. The conversation they made was kept to a hushed whisper, and the pair would frequently stop when Kane detected something, raising his hand to indicate that his point-man sense was unsettled.

The tunnel stretched on an almost straight path through solid rock, a little taller than six feet and changing in width every twenty feet or so. Now and then it would branch, a little offshoot leading nowhere and often not even worth the time it took to explore. In several of these nowhere offshoots, Kane found evidence of habitation: discarded cigarette butts, a handful of dropped coins, one time a damp-stained paperback book with its lurid cover hanging by a few strands of the worn-through binding.

At times, the dark rock walls were wide enough apart for Kane and Grant to walk abreast with ease, while at other times they marched single file.

"Must be a drag bringing booty through here," Grant grumbled, and Kane shook his head.

"Which suggests they have another route inside," Kane said thoughtfully. "We'd better stay alert."

Mostly blank, the cave walls were made of a dark rock that looked like schist or slate under the faint sketch granted by the night lenses. Here and there markings had been etched into the rock, occasionally an arrow of direction when they reached a fork in the uneven tunnels.

Underground, the tunnels themselves were warm, and Kane brushed his damp hair from his face, grateful for the self-regulating temperature of his shadow suit. In the cave, the echoes came from the walls in strange arrays, unnatural-sounding yet doubtless the same way they had sounded for hundreds of thousands of years. Water or ice had drilled these tunnels millions of years ago, creating this hidden pathway inland. Occasionally the two Cerberus warriors would find signs that man had helped nature along: a sheet of wood covered a gaping crevasse in the main path; a small run of steps had been carved into the rock where that same path seemed to jump four feet upward. Another sheet of plywood rested against the wall by the crude steps, standing on its end to be used to cover them if something heavy or wheeled was transported through this hidden route under the soil. In places, water swished by their feet at the edges of the path, glistening in the false refraction of their night lenses.

They had traveled for more than ten minutes without meeting anyone, nor did they come across any great treasure horde in the manner of a children's story. The path had sloped gently upward over time, and Kane wondered how much higher they were than when they had started. Now there was soil above them, and the bent evidence of plant roots poked here and there through the packed earth. A mouse skittered along the tunnel, followed by two more, their bodies fleeting and tiny. Kane watched them dash past as if in a marathon, the race of life driving them on to the finish line.

Though they found no great evidence of treasure besides the odd discarded coin or poker chip, ultimately what Kane and Grant did reach was a wider cavern where two wheeled handcarts had been stored by the wall. The cavern was almost square in shape with a wooden ceiling and wooden ladder running up to a trapdoor in its center. The foundations of a building sank down all around them, stone columns and metal rivets. There were boxes stacked against the rock wall, and when the two men peered inside they found plenty of unused ammunition along with firearms and two smaller boxes that contained jewelry—necklaces, rings and bracelets—much of it broken. Kane sifted through the jewelry with his hand, feeling a pang of despair as he saw a small ring with the shape of a teddy bear carved into its love heart feature. It was something a child might wear, or a young girl still caught up in the throes of innocence. Taken with force, it had found its way here to the home of these men of dishonor.

Opening a larger crate, Grant found it filled with papers and photographs, many of them explicit in nature. "Seems like a cheery bunch," he groused miserably.

Kane placed the girl's ring back in the box. "Let's go find what we came for," he said.

With Kane behind him, Grant ascended the ladder in the center of the chamber. It was clear to both men that this was some kind of subbasement, and they were most likely beneath the cottage that Kane had spied on his flyby.

As Grant climbed, Kane twitched his right hand nervously, bringing the Sin Eater pistol into the cup of his hand and raising it to target the trapdoor that waited like a mystery above his partner's head.

Silently Grant counted down on his fingers before pushing on the trapdoor. The door opened with ease on its well-oiled hinges, and Kane and Grant held their breath as they waited to see what might react up above. Thirty seconds passed, ticking tensely across the face of some imaginary clock. By then, both men felt certain no one was coming to check out the movement. Grant pushed the door high and peered through the gap, his head pressed to the door, ear first.

Grant eyed the area, assuring himself that it was empty. The room was in darkness, but the electrochemical polymer lenses provided an adequate view. It was a cellar, with stone walls blotched with mold, and freestanding shelving units that leaned at uncomfortable angles like distressed acrobats.

Confident that the room was unoccupied, Grant signaled to Kane once more before pushing the trapdoor fully open and clambering through. Grant was a strong man, and he made opening the door seem effortless.

He stood in the cellar basement, checking all around as Kane climbed up to join him.

The first thing they noticed was the noise, muffled whoops and cheers that sounded like the throwback from a bawdy barroom or strip joint. The sound was coming from above them, filtering through the low ceiling or prying at the crack beneath the wooden door at the top of the stairs, a low thrumming beat cutting through it with the repetition of music. Besides the sloping shelving units, there were a number of mismatched crates in the room, constructed of plastics and flimsy wood, along with several cardboard boxes that showed evidence where rodents had gnawed at their edges. As Grant turned, he saw the dark blob of a mouse scuttle across the room, no doubt sensing his presence.

Light spilled from beneath the door located at the top of a rickety wood staircase, its faint glow made bright by the polymer lenses, like a rapier catching the sun's rays. Grant pointed to it, and Kane nodded. They would go that way if they needed to, but first they would check the contents of the room itself.

They split up and checked the contents of the boxes that lined the room. There were more than thirty in total, and some were stacked in piles high enough to brush the low ceiling. Kane looked first for something that matched the boxes they had found with the Stone Widow before moving his attention to opening the other boxes he could reach, judging some by weight alone and assuring himself from their sound and feel that they did not contain what he was looking for. Grant, too, followed a similar process, pulling several likely candidate boxes from the listing shelves, rifling through each one's contents in a matter of seconds.

Within two minutes, they had checked everything they could.

Indicating the staircase once more, Grant kept his voice to a low whisper. "Guess we're going up," he said.

Kane nodded, brushing a finger to his nose in the old one-percent salute that the two would often employ to acknowledge the long odds they often faced.

Despite his bulk, Grant moved up the stairs in almost complete silence, creaking boards complaining just twice as he reached the top. Kane followed, keeping a few steps behind his partner, listening intently to the sounds coming from above.

Once he had reached the top stair, Grant gripped the brass door handle and gently twisted, confirming that the door was unlocked. Then, with another quick hand gesture, he counted down for Kane before opening the door. It swung toward him, and Grant ducked before inching into the corridor beyond.

The cellar door was located in a recess under the building's main staircase, neatly hiding Grant from wary eyes. It was louder out in the open, and Grant felt strangely exposed as he heard the bawdy laughter coming from the far end of the corridor along with the music. The corridor itself had been wallpapered once, decades earlier. Now it looked sickly, its vibrancy gone, like some old man peering with rheumy eyes from his deathbed, his sheets stained with sweat, his mouth rimmed with saliva. While the walls themselves were shabby, ostentatious light fixtures and statuary were dotted along them, the spoils of the pirate lifestyle. Several boxes were piled in the recess beneath the stairs, though none was the one they sought. There was a smell, too, of brewing and of hashish, the latter's sweet scent ingrained in the drapes and the thick, peeling wallpaper.

With his back pressed to the wall and body hunkered down, Grant made his way to the edge of the recess while Kane waited in the open doorway of the cellar, his Sin Eater in hand.

Grant found himself in the main corridor of the house and he guessed he was close to the rear, the front door waiting at the farthest end of the passageway. The door had been draped with a heavy curtain, cutting out all but the slimmest of light, hiding the activities that were occurring within. Naively, Grant realized, he had expected the pirates to live in the caves at the sea. In actuality they lived here in relative comfort, easily accessible by sea and perhaps one of many bases they had established along the coast.

Silently, Grant made his way along the corridor, his polymer lenses providing a clear view of everything despite the thick shadows. Kane glanced behind him before following, that old instinct coming into play once more, aware that there was an open entry behind them in the form of the trapdoor.

Up ahead, Grant could hear voices, could see the lit open doorway of a room, and beyond that came the whoops and cheers of a party, discordant music playing like a chained thunderstorm pulling at its leash. Crouching, Grant edged toward the first open door, listened to the voices of two men as they bickered contentedly, their friendship clear beneath their outward hostility.

"Two pair, nines and jacks," one said with a *fwap* of cards on the table between them.

"No way, man," the other growled. "You dealing drunk again."

"Not me, brother," the first man insisted. "Your luck's just not on today. How much you lost now?"

Grant heard the other's response, an expressive and defeated sigh. "Deal again, let's do it."

The first pirate laughed. "You have a gambling problem, man."

"Hey, it's not my money so what's the problem?"

At that, both men laughed, and Grant heard another laughing with them. Three then, likely sitting around a table. The echoes came off hard surfaces, which meant no carpeting, and that usually meant either kitchen or bathroom. He listened, waiting for the cards to be shuffled and dealt, timing his movements for when the three men would be looking at their cards. When he judged the time was right, Grant hurried past the open door in a crouch-walk, watching the room as he raced past. As he'd guessed, three men sat around a Formica-topped table located under a simple orange chandelier, several stacks of poker chips and some jewelry strewed across the table. A pot steamed on the stove behind them. Intent on their game, none bothered to look up as Grant crossed the door and continued down the corridor.

Behind Grant, Kane did likewise, waiting for the right moment before crossing past the open door to follow his partner deeper into the house. They needed to get a clear idea of how many people were there before they launched any kind of assault. Ideally they could keep any casualties to a minimum and simply talk things through with the pirate crew. Sure, Kane thought caustically, like that's gonna happen. Outlaws like these were seldom renowned for listening to reason.

Once they had both passed the open door, the Cer-

berus men made their way to what should be the main
room of the house. That was where the shouting and
party noises were coming from, the boisterous whoops
and cheers. It made Grant faintly uncomfortable, since
the sounds seemed closer to animals than men.

Carefully Grant edged forward, while Kane double-
checked the kitchen behind them, confirming they
were not being followed. With a practiced flinch of
his wrist tendons, Grant commanded his Sin Eater
into his hand and edged around the doorway, peering
inside. Within, a handful of men—the pirate crew—
were swigging from bottles as a dark-haired woman
with pendulous breasts danced topless upon a table.
Music blared from a sound system, its speakers vibrating angrily to the heavy bass, a set of flashing lights
pulsing over and over, splashing distracting patterns
across the night-vision lenses that Grant wore while
the woman gyrated to the beat. He blinked against the
lights, momentarily dazzled through the night lenses.

Their backs to him, Grant speculated that he and
Kane might be able to take the whole crew before they
could reach for their weapons, forcing them to surrender at the business end of their Sin Eaters, just like
in the old days when they had been the Magistrate
authority. But even as the thought crossed his mind,
something snarled and barked from the corner of the
room, and Grant saw a blur of motion as a beast on
the end of a long chain came charging at him through
the flashing lights.

"Rrrrrr!"

Through the dazzling effect of the lights on his polymer lenses Grant could have sworn that it was—*a girl!*

Chapter 18

On the second floor of the pirate property, in a richly appointed reception room, three men were arguing, unaware of the strangers who had infiltrated their base. The room was decorated with tasteful statuary set on tables and potted plants to either side of the grand doorway. Contrary to the popular idea, pirates didn't live in squalor. Why would they? They stole whatever they wanted to and didn't pay taxes.

In the farthest corner of the vast room, Fern Salt was sitting on a replica Louis XVI chair with velvet covers. Opposite him, Mr. Six ate an apple as he rested on a chaise longue, cutting it into slices with a small paring knife. Xia sat in the matching chair to Salt's, smoking a clay pipe, which he tapped now and then against the bowl-like ashtray that perched on his knee.

"I tell ya," Salt snarled, "I'm taking control o' *La Discordia*. Sailing to greater heights, fresh booty. Ye'll see."

"Ain't no fresh booty, you numbskull," Six said between bites of his apple.

"Always something out there to steal," Salt insisted, and Xia added his agreement.

"So you want to challenge for captainship now that Black John's dead—is that it?" Six asked.

Salt smiled, a nasty slash of yellowed teeth appearing across his ugly face. "No challenge, Mr. Six," he said. "You'll still be my first mate, same as ever was."

"You'll run us aground 'fore we know it," Six said, digging his knife into the apple to carve out another wedge. "What the men need now is stability, not a coup. He may have been a bastard, but Black John held this crew together. You need to remember that."

"He ain't coming back now," Xia said, wisps of sweet-smelling smoke trailing from his nostrils.

Six glared at him. "I ain't saying he didn't deserve to die," he growled. "Shit, there weren't no one deserved it more, if you want to know the truth. But the crew's still figuring out how things are going to work now, which means it ain't the time to start bickering. We'll follow the chain-of-command protocol for now and—"

"Which puts you in charge," Salt observed. "Mighty convenient that."

Six took another bite of his apple. "For now."

ONE FLOOR BELOW, THE SOUND of their movements masked by the thundering bass of the music system, seven crewmen reacted in astonishment as the feral girl barked and ran at the stranger in the doorway.

There was no time for Grant to react with anything more than instinct. Seeing a naked girl lunging across the floor on all fours toward him, barking like an animal, he adopted a defensive stance, assuring himself that his Sin Eater was out of her immediate trajectory. Grant was a trained soldier, and he would kill if necessary—but only if necessary—he was not in the business of executing defenseless women, no matter how viciously they approached him.

He braced himself as the girl hit.

HER NAME WAS AMY LITTLE, and she had been kept in chains so long that she had turned into a dog. Not literally, of course, but mentally. Mr. Six had kidnapped her three years earlier during a pirate raid, when she was just thirteen years old. He hadn't had the heart to execute her, and Black John had given him that fiery look when he realized what he had done, the look that meant that something had to change or someone was going to lose a hand.

Black John had told Six, in no uncertain terms, that the girl could never be freed. "You will beat the language out of her," he snarled, "until she can no longer make sense even if she did escape." Which she wouldn't.

Six had placed a chain around her neck, welded it closed and bolted it to the wall. The girl had cried at the heat of the welding and the coolness of the collar against her skin, and Black John had simply watched, emotionless, as empty a vessel as the ones he left floating out in the gulf. Amy Little had complained only twice, and the first time Black John had beaten her with a bottle and the second time he had violated her with the same. After that, she had said little or nothing, just waiting at the end of her chain in the corner of the old cottage's main room.

She had never been pretty, but now she had become something feral. Her unwashed hair had turned to rats' tails and tangled about her head in a clump, its dark tresses touching the base of her spine. She was naked, and the lower parts of her body were caked with dried blood. She had come of age while in the custody of the pirates, and she hadn't known what to do with the blood, so she had ended up scooping it out of her body and smearing it over herself in monthly ritual, the closest thing she had to makeup or clothing.

She was always ill, feverish, the deep cold grasping inside her body like a clawed thing unable to find its way free, plucking at her insides like a psychotic mole. For the past three years she had never once left this room where the chain was cinched to the wall, its eight-foot length giving her the run of the room but no more. She had adopted a corner behind the benchlike sofa, hiding there as a matter of course after one too many drunken encounters with the morally bankrupt crewmen of *La Discordia*. By fourteen she had known more men than she could remember, their faces blurring in her fracturing memory into some all-encompassing face of snarling, drunken savagery.

If she had ever spoken, and she couldn't remember a time when she had anymore, she had lost those words now, complicit in her torture, yipping and barking like a dog when she was instructed to. What she had taken thirteen years to learn she had forgotten in nine months, dehumanized to a point where she could no longer follow anything beyond the present, her past a forgotten dream, her future unknowable. She couldn't remember her parents, but after what had happened to them that was probably for the best.

They would leave her for days, with only scraps in a bowl to feed her, or sometimes nothing at all. The gnawing at her stomach would make her whimper, and she would ache from cold and fear. One time, it had been ten days until the ship's crew returned, and she was woken abruptly to find a man molesting her, laughing right in her face as she woke up screaming and hissing and spitting at him. He was one of the crew, and the others had watched and laughed as she bit a great chunk out of his nose in her desperation to get away.

Whatever she had once been, now she was a feral thing, permanently locked in a cycle of fear and violence. If Six had thought to rescue that innocent girl he had taken pity on aboard the boat, then he had failed, and the knowledge of his failure had informed him never to try again.

THE GIRL BARKED AGAIN, her feet striking the bare boards of the floor as she caromed into Grant amid a clatter of her metal chains. With the swiftness of second-nature muscle memory, Grant brought his left arm up to defend himself, feeling the naked girl impact there with the savagery of a wild animal. She stank, and her body was smeared with blood and feces, her hair tangled like an untamed briar. Despite his weight, Grant stumbled back with the force of the strike, falling as the girl piled onto him, her ragged-nailed hands clawing for his face.

"Get the—" Grant barked.

Behind her, the other occupants of the room turned, several blasters materializing as they realized that there were strangers among them, their shouts sounding over the music.

Outside, Kane ducked back behind the door frame, willing himself not to be seen. He had caught just a glimpse of the interior of the room, but his trap-quick mind was already filtering through the information to tell him everything he needed to know. Eight people were in the room, including the dancing girl on the table, plus the feral wolflike thing that had leaped onto his partner. Even now, Kane could hear the feral thing's screeching as it struck at Grant, but he had to trust that

his partner could handle it alone. That left him with
seven pirates, presumably all of them armed, and odds
were that the dancer was armed, too. If it came to it,
he only needed one of them alive to tell him where the
sentient stones were.

Back in the music room, Grant was struggling with
the messed-up-looking girl who had pounced on him
with that weird battle cry. But it was she who acciden-
tally saved him from the pirates' initial volley of shots,
her body blocking each bullet's path as four blasters lit
the room with explosive bursts of propellant.

The nude girl's body rocked in place as chunks of
bloody flesh were torn from her shoulders and back,
spattering the room with gouts of crimson. Reeling
under the impact of the strikes and the girl's vicious
lunge, Grant struggled still farther back, striking the
door frame behind him with a loud thump. Another
bullet sailed by close to his face, smashing wood from
the frame in a splintering of wood.

Grant turned his head, ducking and shoving the
wounded girl away. She rolled from him, leaving a
bloody trail in the air for just a moment before the
drops of blood washed across the dirt-streaked floor
in a wet splatter.

A few paces behind Grant, Kane was standing with
his back flush to the wall, and he winced as the second
hail of bullets came blasting from the room.

"Intruders," came a frantic voice over the sounds
of the girl's barking. "We're under attack."

Kane muttered something about only being there to
talk, but he already knew he couldn't be heard over the
cacophony. Down the corridor, the three cardplaying
crewmen came hurrying out of the kitchen, each man
brandishing a weapon. Kane felled all three with three

sharp shots, cutting their legs out from under them in a trio of perfectly placed 9 mm slugs. The men fell to the floor in agony, while Kane wasn't even breathing hard.

In the main room, Grant scampered across the floor, his head down as bullets cut the air all around him. He grunted as he felt them strike his coat, rebounding from the Kevlar plating with the force of hammer blows.

The girl who had attacked him lay on the floor, sniffling to herself as she clawed at the bloody wounds on her shoulders and back. She was nude and painted in grime, and beneath that Grant could see she was emaciated, with bird-thin limbs and the bones of her rib cage pressing against her skin like the roots of an ancient tree. He leaped over her, deftly stepping past the thick steel chain that tied her by a neck collar to the far wall.

His gun was already up as he leaped past the girl, drawing a bead on the first of the pirates as the seven men strived to keep pace with him in the enclosed space of the room. While the pirates got in one another's way, Grant's Sin Eater spit, sending a cone of steel-skinned death at a wide-eyed man in a black shirt. The man's jaw exploded in a pop of blood, and he fell back into his nearest colleague, much to the latter man's irritation. The second man had a prosthetic in place of his left leg, a graceful curve of molded fiberglass that flared from an attachment on his stump knee, turned backward like the legs of a cricket. Grant's second blast took the prosthetics wearer in the gut, gouging an expanding red hole in the right-hand side of his shirt.

"We just came here to talk," Grant was shouting, but the pirates had their own theories as they tracked him with their spitting blasters.

"Fuckers are after our spoils," one of them screamed, and his heavy-gauge blaster boomed, lighting up the room with its discharge.

Grant's palm slapped the floor as he ducked beneath the violent discharge. His Sin Eater blasted again, launching a bullet across the room and directly into the music system, where it embedded in a shower of sparks that abruptly halted the loud, bass-distorted music. The dancer screamed, whatever passed for tranquillity ruined in this moment of abject chaos.

Though the room was large, there were too many of them in the enclosed space, and they were getting in one another's way as Grant whirled through the room. Grant's Sin Eater spit in deadly reply to every attempt that was made on his life, even as his Kevlar and shadow suit protected him from the shots that threatened to fell him.

Where are you, Kane? he wondered as he ducked past a chair.

His gun blasted again as he leaped the comfy armchair, the flickering colors of the lighting rig turning the rocketing projectile green then red then yellow before it found its target, ripping into the shoulder of another of the room's lawless occupants.

IN THE UPSTAIRS RECEPTION room, Six, Xia and Salt stopped in middiscussion and listened. The music had ceased, and they had taken that to be someone changing tracks, ignoring it for the first few seconds of silence. But then came another noise, equally familiar to all three men.

"Hear that?" Xia said. "Gunshots."

"What the fuck?" Six growled, already on his feet and marching to the broad door of the room. "Can't we leave those idiots alone for five minutes without them taking potshots at each other?"

Salt was on his feet, too, hurrying after Six as he stormed across the room. "Sounds like a fucking jungle down there," he growled.

But as they reached the door, both men stopped. Some extra sense, honed from years of experience, seemed to kick in as they both realized there may be another reason for the shots.

"Someone's here," Six said.

"But how'd they get here?" Salt wanted to know.

Behind them in the room, Xia had left his seat to stand before a drinks cabinet, knocking three bottles of spirits aside. Then he flipped a switch hidden from view in a cabinet, and with that engaged the cameras. Embedded in the cabinet, a screen flashed to life behind the remaining wall of half-full bottles, bringing up split-screen views of the cottage property from a variety of locations. One of the images turned from black to gray as something parted before it, and then the image started to rise, as if the camera was poised on an insect or bird.

Six and Salt joined Xia at the cabinet.

"Send it in," Six said. "Let's see what we're dealing with."

DOWNSTAIRS IN THE CORRIDOR, Kane cursed as another burst of gunfire peppered the door frame, forcing him to retreat. Stepping back, he became aware of something flying toward him down the darkened corridor, and he turned to face it instinctively. Through the night-vision lenses, the thing looked like a bird, wings spread like the arms of a boomerang as it cut through the air in his direction. As it rushed at him,

Kane saw that it resembled a parrot but glinted with a metal sheen, and he could hear the whirring motors that powered it within, straining to keep its impossible body in flight. He reached forward, punching at the air with the Sin Eater still in his grip, snapping off a shot even as the fluttering faux-creature reared away in mockery of the life it tried to imitate.

Kane's first shot went wide, drilling a single bullet into the banister beyond the robot parrot, but he followed through with a second burst of fire, snagging the automaton even as it wheeled in place in the space above his head.

There was a burst of sparks and Kane darted aside as the wounded would-be bird fell, crashing to the floor in a jumble of ruined parts. He glanced at it for only a moment, recognizing it then for what it really was—a spy eye, painted to look like a parrot, a simple remote-controlled device used by the Magistrates on covert missions to scope out areas where it might be too imprudent to enter.

The spy eyes were often an elusive presence, a childhood bogeyman that still occasionally haunted Kane in his dreams. He felt a pang of irritation then, as if he had been betrayed. The spy eye felt like his own technology being used against him, the very stuff he had come to rely on while he served as a Magistrate in the protection of Cobaltville. Back in those simpler days, he had never really thought of how the same tech might be acquired, bootlegged and used against him. It seemed that the arms race was ongoing even here in the backwaters of Central America, far away from the perceived safety of the villes.

The pirates were tracking him, trying to pin him down before they swarmed at him from some unknown angle.

"FUCKER, WHO IS THAT?" Xia cursed as the screen went dead.

"Navy maybe?" Six pondered.

Beside him, Salt pulled the Llama Comanche free from the shoulder rig that lay on a table by the chaise longue. "Let's go find out," he growled.

STANDING AT THE FAR wall of the room behind the wrecked speaker, the pirate called Tuska was staring in horror at Amy's shuddering form where she lay in her own pooling blood. Tuska had been with Six when he had brought the girl here, and despite Black John's best efforts, Tuska had never quite let that bond between them go. He felt a tie of responsibility to the feral girl that seemed humiliating now as she lay wounded. "Everybody cease fire," he called, trying to get the situation under control.

Bullets continued to spray; no one had heard Tuska over the cacophony of death. He watched as the figure in the black coat struck out with powerful fist, the knuckles cracking against the nose of a crewman called Drake. Drake's nose and jaw seemed to explode in a spatter of blood, and he went crashing to the floor as this sharpshooting shadow brushed past him, finished with him already, lunging at the next man in the room.

From the doorway, a second intruder peered into the room, leveling what Tuska recognized as a Magistrate blaster in a professional, two-handed grip. Tuska ducked as the weapon spit, and the wall behind his head exploded in a burst of plaster.

Tuska dived into an alcove behind the speaker, an alcove so small, in fact, that he could barely fit his huge frame inside. As he did so, the table on which the woman had been dancing came skidding toward him as Grant kicked its side with astonishing force. Still screaming as if she might never stop, the woman went tumbling from the hurtling table, and Grant held out his free arm to catch her while training his Sin Eater on the man trapped in the alcove.

Tuska peered past the huge man in the black duster, out at the wreckage of the room. All of his colleagues lay wounded or unconscious—perhaps dead—bloody smears across the walls and furniture, groans emanating from the few who were still alive. The stranger's partner came striding into the room, a matching Sin Eater blaster in his hand. Between them, these two men had overpowered the pirate crew in less than three minutes.

"All right, man, all right," Tuska said, raising his empty hands high above his head. "Just don't shoot."

Grant nodded. "Good boy."

Kane surveyed his surroundings for a moment before addressing the dark-skinned pirate. "Now, me and my partner here are looking for something," he began.

Before Kane could say another word, a blast came from the doorway accompanied by an angry shout. "And you've found something—your funeral!"

Grant turned as Kane collapsed to the floor in a heap.

Chapter 19

Grant ducked, bringing the dancer down with him as he dropped to the floor. His Sin Eater bucked in his hand, blasting two quick shots into the figure in the doorway with economic brutality.

Fern Salt lurched backward, screaming as twin bullets struck him in the head and chest, his skull blooming into redness as he tumbled to the floor.

"Whoever else is out there, drop your weapons right now," Grant called, making his voice loud over the hoarse sobbing of the woman in his arms.

For a moment, nothing happened. Through the night-vision lenses, Grant could see two figures standing at the foot of the staircase. Both were armed, and they seemed uncertain of what to do. They thought that the darkness of the staircase hid them, unaware that the lenses Grant wore picked them out as clear as day.

"I can see you at the foot of the stairs," Grant said. "Both of you. Put your weapons down and come here."

The two men discussed the situation for a moment more before edging tentatively down the stairs.

"What do you want, *señor?*" one asked in Spanish. It was Six, his voice trembling just a little. "We have done nothing."

"Put your blasters down," Grant replied, glancing just for a moment at Kane where his partner lay facedown on the floor. Kane had taken a hit, Grant knew, but he couldn't be sure how serious that was. In the back of his mind, the thought came to him that Kane might be dead or losing a lot of blood even as this exchange continued.

Seeing neither man move from the stairwell, Grant snapped off a single shot from his Sin Eater, drilling a 9 mm bullet between the two of them in a shower of ruined plasterboard. "Hurry it up, gentlemen," he growled. "My patience is wearing thin." Beside him, the dancer sobbed loudly, her wails annoyingly close to his ear.

Behind Grant, the broad-shouldered pirate called Tuska was trying to move the table aside from where it had wedged him in the alcove. His body was so large that he didn't have the room to get leverage, nor the space to climb over it. As Tuska struggled in vain, Grant heard the whispered voices of the two men on the stairs as they weighed their options.

Finally, the two figures placed their weapons on the bottom step before walking into the room, arms raised above their heads. They stepped over Fern Salt's fallen corpse, and Six couldn't resist smiling for just a second; that solved the problem of who would captain *La Discordia,* at least. "Okay, *señor,*" he said as he stepped through the open door. "No need to get rough."

Grant was still crouched on the floor, half-hidden by the bullet-pocked sofa. "Anyone else up there?" he demanded.

"Just us, *señor,*" Six assured him, and Xia nodded furiously in agreement. "What is it you want? You're trespassing, you know."

Letting go of the sobbing woman, Grant warily pushed himself to his feet, his blaster still trained on the two pirates who now stood before the door, just inside the room.

"We didn't come here looking for trouble," he said.

"Just seemed to work out that way, huh?" Xia replied sarcastically.

Grant ignored him. "We're looking for some plunder," he said, "something they're saying you folks might have picked up."

"You did all this for a robbery?" Six spit, staring at the wreckage of the room. *"This?"*

"Not a robbery," Grant told him. "Not really, anyway. The cargo in question came from a little trawler called *La Segunda Montaña.* It traveled down from the north with what we think was a group of refugees. But among them there was a box, a little crate that contained some ordinary-looking stones."

"And what makes you think we've seen this boat or that we would have such a cargo?" Six challenged.

"Call it a hunch," Grant said. "But since I'm the one holding the blaster, you can assume it's a serious one, my friend. Now, these stones don't look like much but they are dangerous as hell. They're artifacts from a weapons program. Bio-ware, they bond with the human body and ultimately kill it. In the wrong hands, that's going to lead to a lot of problems."

"I see your dilemma, *señor,*" Six said. "But once again, I must ask, what makes you believe we would have such things?"

Without warning, Grant squeezed the trigger of the Sin Eater, sending a bullet into Six's right knee. The mustached pirate's leg buckled, tossing him to the floor. Six screamed in agony, rocking back and forth as he clutched at his ruined knee, while behind him Xia began to tremble in fear.

"My friend is lying wounded," Grant said. "You keep asking dumb questions like that, you'll end up trying my patience."

Muttering a curse under his breath, Six looked up to the towering ex-Magistrate who stood just a few feet away. "Name of a name! You didn't need to—"

"The stones," Grant interrupted. "Where are they?"

Six glared defiantly at him, his face pulsing color beneath the flashing lights. Then he saw a smile break across Grant's face, and it was a hideous, ugly thing.

"You realize I only need one of you alive to tell me," Grant said, bringing the muzzle of his weapon to Six's temple.

"Okay, okay," Six blurted. "Let's not get stupid. The stones, yes, I remember them. Came from that scow, Xia and me picked up the box."

Still standing in the doorway, Xia nodded. "I got a weird feeling from that crate," he said. "I told you that, didn't I?"

"Where are they now?" Grant asked.

"Upstairs, I think," Six explained. "We were going to divvy them up along with some other stuff. I don't think anyone really knew what to do with them. They seemed like ballast. But, hey—any port in a storm, right?"

Grant stared at the bleeding pirate through the electropolymer lenses. "I'm going to tend to my friend, and after that you are going to take me to the stones. Okay?"

"My leg, *señor*," Six pleaded. "I can't…"

"Your friend can look at it, patch you up," Grant said. "Any tricks and I will shoot you. Make no mistake on that."

"Thank you, *señor*," Six said. "Thank you."

As Grant went to check on Kane, Xia crouched and tended to Six, tearing a strip from the man's shirt to bind the wound until they could clean it properly.

Grant nudged Kane, keeping his voice low. "Kane? You alive in there?"

Kane rolled over slowly, a strained hiss emanating from between clenched teeth. "Something hit me," he muttered, bewildered.

"You were pretty out of it," Grant told him. "Careful now, let me take a look."

When he pulled back Kane's scuffed jacket, he saw that the Comanche's bullet had winged him, skipping across his shoulder close to his neck, missing the back of his head by no more than three inches.

"You'll be okay, soldier," Grant assured him. "You've been through worse."

Across the room, the dancer had finally stopped sobbing, and she was glumly strapping her impressive breasts back into her skimpy top. Her makeup had been ruined, dark streaks of black and silver running down below her eyes like flashing blades. Grant eyed her for a moment before turning his vigilant gaze back to the two pirates. The Asian was crouching over the mustached one, wrapping his shot leg in a torn strip of shirt. Already grimy, the pale material was turning red even as it was looped over the wound. The Asian whispered something to his partner, so low that Grant couldn't catch it.

"All right, you two," Grant warned. "That'll do."

"But, señor," Six whined, "my leg is…"

Even before Six had finished the words, Grant saw the flicker of movement from his partner as the other pirate threw something toward him. The projectile was made of metal and tapered to a point like a dart.

Grant's arm shot up and the tossed item struck his left forearm, embedding itself in the thick Kevlar sleeve. It was a paring knife, used to peel fruit.

Before Xia could follow through with his attack, both Grant and Kane had commanded their Sin Eaters into the palms of their hands, clenching the guardless triggers automatically. Xia went from bounding toward Grant to rattling in place as a dozen 9 mm bullets struck his torso and face, turning his features into a bloody ruin. The hulking pirate crashed to the bloodstained floor, slamming into it like a spent shell. His body spasmed for a moment as the life drained out of it.

"You...shot him," Six muttered. "He's..."

"Yeah," Grant said, his tone ominous. "Now, let's go find these stones. And no more tricks."

GRANT AND KANE FOLLOWED the limping Six into the hallway, leaving Tuska trapped behind the table. The three cardplayers remained sprawled a little way farther down the corridor, and they could see that one of them was waking up, dozy and unsure of himself. Six stopped to speak with the man for a moment, instructing him in some patois slang that the Commtacts had trouble making sense of. Kane and Grant had their Sin Eaters poised on the proxy pirate leader, and they knew they were forced to trust he would not betray them through fear of the consequences. They did not have many other options, other than securing all the remaining pirates and searching the property themselves, and that could take hours, with no guarantee of finding what they came for.

After that, all three men made their way up the stairs and into the richly appointed second story of the property. Kane was not surprised to see how rich the surroundings were. It reminded him a little of the beachfront villa of Billy-boy Porpoise, a Florida-based arms smuggler whose operation had been shut down more than a year before by Cerberus. That was back before Ullikummis had come and changed everything, driving the secret doubts between himself and Baptiste.

"Down here," Six said, leading the way along the wide, carpeted hallway. He was dragging his foot just a little where he had been shot, and grunted an audible huff of air through his nostrils with each step.

The air of the second story became sweeter as they approached the doors to a reception room, and both Kane and Grant recognized the smell as marijuana.

"Were you guys having a little party up here when we arrived?" Kane asked sarcastically, making a show of sniffing the air.

"Always a party, *señor*," Six replied, his contempt for the man clear in his voice.

As Six stepped through the wide doorway of the reception room, Kane heard a shuffling noise coming from behind him, that old point-man sense kicking in. He spun on his heel, brows furrowed as he scanned the corridor.

Grant frowned at him. "Everything okay? Kane?"

Kane held up one hand for silence, making his way warily down the corridor, the Sin Eater extended in his other hand.

"What is your friend—?" Six began, but Grant placed his hand over the man's mouth, silencing him.

Kane was now standing before a rich mahogany door that had been left ajar. Soft light was streaming from the door, and the shuffling noise was coming from inside, a kind of scuffing like boot heels against a wooden floor. Kane placed one hand against the door and, without offering any warning, pushed the door wider, the Sin Eater thrust before him. Within, Kane saw a neat bedroom centered around a double bed covered in rich fabrics. The walls were papered in dark colors, and a single bedside light offered its warm glow, enriching the coziness of the room. A figure lay on the bed, semiclad and rocking a little in place. It was a man with a narrow frame, his chest and feet bare though he was still wearing tan leather pants. The man made no reaction as Kane entered, and after a moment Kane padded closer.

To Kane he was still a boy—maybe nineteen or twenty years old with a patchy tuft of beard on his chin—a wanna-be gangsta in a hard world. There was a thin line of dried blood running along one arm from palm to elbow, leading to a pinprick from a syringe. The needle itself lay forgotten on the bedside table beside the other accoutrements of the lad's addiction. Strips of stone surrounded the pinprick in his skin, like islands on his young flesh. Kane could see the stone beneath the skin, running up in thin trails to his collarbone where it pierced the skin once more along that delicate line that stretched ear to throat, sharp cones of rock jutting through the pink flesh. The lad's eyes were open, but they had that distant look as he stared at the ceiling, as if he was no longer seeing the room at all. The boy was shaking a little in place, his movements creating the shuffling noise as his twitching shoulders butted against the silk covers.

Once again, the misery had spread.

Behind him, Kane heard Grant and the pirate come to the doorway, waiting just at the edge of the room.

"Enrique?" Six asked. "Is that...?"

"Dying," Kane said, making no effort to pull that

emotional punch. "Seems the kid found your stash before we did, got one of those rocks inside him."

"Thought you said there was no one else up here," Grant added.

Six limped a hurried few steps into the room before Grant grabbed his shoulders, and he stretched forward, trying to see in the dull light. The pirate muttered an oath under his breath, his eyes wide as he looked at the young man.

"This is what it does?" he asked, fixing Kane with a look. "Your bio-ware?"

Kane nodded. Even in this light he could see that the pirate had turned pale.

"Why would anyone—?" Six muttered, shaking his head, unable to finish the sentence.

"Now do you see?" Grant probed.

"We're going to need all of them," Kane reminded the pirate. "Everything you found."

Six nodded, swaying a little on his feet. For a moment Kane thought the man might faint, but he held himself upright, leaning on Grant a little for support. "How do we cure this?" he asked.

"There's no cure," Kane said.

"But with a biological weapon of this nature…" Six started.

"Put it out of your mind, and thank your stars it didn't get to you, too," Grant advised from over his shoulder. "Far as we can work out, this shit is irreversible."

"Yeah," Kane said. "There's a girl in El Cana who got infected with this thanks to your men. Pretty girl, barman's daughter, maybe you remember her."

Six nodded heavily with shame. "Duendecito. I know her."

"Where her face was, it looks like a statue now," Kane told him. "Her breathing's screwed up, her throat is clogging and her lungs are filling with stone flecks."

Six looked at the lad on the bed, and his mouth opened and closed as if he wanted to say something more, but he couldn't find the words.

"I wouldn't go back there for a while," Kane said. "Maybe ever. She's going to die, just like your pal here."

"Can it spread?" Six inquired.

"Not as far as we know," Kane told him. "You might want to burn the body just to be sure."

"Yes," Six agreed, looking wistful. "*Señors,* for what it is worth—we didn't realize. We thought the rocks were probably valueless, took them on a whim. If we had known—"

"You didn't," Grant said. "No point beating yourself up on that score."

Six nodded, accepting that.

"But you still scuttled a boat and executed the crew and passengers in cold blood," Grant continued. "That doesn't sit well with karma, you realize."

"We all have to eat," Six reasoned. "We lost our captain that day. Without him, things here will change. I personally guarantee it."

Kane glared at him. "Just get us the rocks."

SIX LOCATED THE BOX of living stones and handed it over to the Cerberus team with a resigned sigh.

"If we had known, *señor*..." he began, but Kane stopped him.

"You have any tape?" he asked. "String? Something we could seal this shut with?" Kane was talking about the box; its card lid was open, the two leaves woven into one another but still with some space between them at the center.

Six nodded, limping his way across the wide reception room where he, Salt and Xia had been discussing who would run the crew now that Black John was dead. Under Kane's scrutiny, the pirate pulled a medical kit from one of the cupboards and found a roll of bandage. "This do?" he asked, and Kane nodded.

After that, the Cerberus men made their way back down the stairs, wary of a possible attack. Grant lugged the box, using both hands to carry it, while Kane sent Six ahead to ensure any ambush placed the pirate in the immediate line of fire.

Despite the strewed bodies, no attack came. A few of the pirates had awakened and were nursing their wounds, and the hulking figure of Tuska had finally been freed from the alcove where he had become wedged. But on Six's instructions, no man attacked Kane or Grant, all of them accepting the first mate's assurance that these people were here to help.

"Some help," Drake muttered as he taped gauze across the feral girl's belly, but his proved the only voice of dissent.

Six led them to the back door of the stone cottage and operated the locks.

"Take the stones and go," Six said as he worked the last of the bolts and opened the door.

Out there, the skies were ominous with clouds and the grass and trees shuddered. The wind was picking up; a storm was brewing.

Kane looked at Six for a moment, fixing him with his no-nonsense stare. "So, what's to stop you shooting us in the back?" he asked.

Six looked innocent. "The thought never crossed my mind," he insisted.

"Sure, it didn't," Kane mocked, his tone dripping with sarcasm. "We didn't come here to perform a mass execution, and we don't want to have to do that just to stay alive. So you listen close. I'm going to let you live, tempted though I am to burn this whole sorry pesthole to the ground. Don't make me regret that decision. We have friends who know precisely where we are right now, which means they know precisely where *you* are. You want to risk it, rest assured you'll lose everything."

Six nodded. In truth, he was grateful to be rid of the intruders before they decided to take more of his crew's assets. Losing a box of stones, even ones that had proved to be dangerous bio-ware, was a small price to pay given the professionalism with which the two men had taken out his crew. But if they ever crossed paths again, he vowed to himself that things would be different.

"You take care, *señor*" was all he said. "Get rid of those wicked things and don't ever come back to my door."

"I understand," Kane said.

Without another word, Six closed the door and Kane and Grant stood there beneath the narrow porch, listening to the clicks and shunts as the locks were put back in place, securing the pirate base from the outside world.

"So, I guess it's back to Cerberus," Grant said, hefting the stones with tautly muscled arms.

For a moment, Kane didn't respond. His eyes were fixed on the sky, watching the dark clouds marching toward them. He had noticed the wind as soon as they stepped from the building. It was strong and churning, blowing from everywhere all at once.

As Grant waited on the sill behind Kane, the box of stones clutched under his arm, he watched his partner staring into the skies. He followed, spying the thick clouds that loomed there, dark and brooding.

"What is it?" he asked. "Looks like a storm."

Kane was still watching the skies. The clouds formed a broad, circular pattern that seemed to congregate at a point a little way out to sea. "Not like any storm I've ever seen before," he said slowly. "The air doesn't smell right."

Grant drew a deep breath, tasting the air. It had a tang to it, like smoke. "The hell is that?"

"Look," Kane said, pointing to the center point of the clouds.

As he watched, Grant saw that the clouds were moving. And though there was nothing unusual in that, it was uncanny the way they seemed to rotate on themselves, following a wide path around their fixed point even as their numbers swelled and expanded. Then Grant saw something flash in the center of those swirling clouds, wondered for a moment if it was an aircraft of some sort. Then it flashed again and he saw it was lightning, but not like any lightning he had ever seen before. This lightning was dark, colored the deep blue-green of a person's veins.

Chapter 20

The dark lightning reminded Kane a little of when the interphaser was engaged, cutting a gateway through the quantum ether.

"What is that?" Grant asked from the porch step beside him.

Kane shrugged. "You want my best guess? It's the storm from hell. Let's go take a closer look."

Swiftly but not quite running, Kane and Grant made their way across the open fields behind the cottage, clambering past the dead hedge barricade and onward to the shore. As they moved, Kane radioed Cerberus via his Commtact, asking if they could bring satellite surveillance to bear.

"We've got a storm brewing here, Donald," he explained, "but it's like no storm you ever saw. There's something uncanny about what's going on. I need you to give me a data feed on whatever you can bring up."

At the other end of the Commtact link, back in the Cerberus operations room, Donald Bry assured Kane he would bring up the data as soon as possible, and he set about repositioning the satellite's cameras to track the growing storm.

And "growing" was right—already the storm clouds had expanded to claw overhead, casting the shore in darkness as Kane and Grant reached the edge. Above them, the clouds spun like some slow, unstoppable wheel, revolving and growing larger with every pass-ing minute, painting dark trails across the sky.

The rain hit a moment later. It was like walking into a thick curtain, the raindrops so hard they stung the skin.

Kane brushed wet hair from his face as he hurried ahead, clambering down the cliff face toward where he and Grant had left their Mantas.

"You ever seen rain like this?" Grant shouted, strug-gling to be heard over the storm.

"Never," Kane said, working swiftly down the rock face despite the slippery stones.

Above them, the skies darkened even more, and the gray clouds seemed to be tinted with red. The Mantas were bobbing in the water, the waves getting higher as they clung to the spit of sand.

By the time Kane and Grant reached the sand spit, the clouds above were dark-lit in red, their darkest shadows turned the rich wine of blood. If there had been any doubt in their minds up until that point, it was gone now; whatever was happening was more than a freak weather phenomenon.

THEY HAD SPOKEN FOR a while, Rosalia and Brigid, but it seemed like the same conversation running over and over, a circle without end. Finally Brigid had closed her eyes and the room had fallen to silence, with only the sounds of students hurrying to and from their rooms on the floor, and the occasional noises from the nun-nery's kitchens as they geared up for dinner, break-ing the spell.

Outside, the sun was dropping toward the horizon, visible in all its peachy-orange glory through the sin-gle window of the room. Sitting on one of the beds,

Rosalia watched it for a while, recalling a more innocent time when this—or a room very much like this one—had made up the entirety of her life. Brigid remained sitting on the floor, head tilted, eyes closed. She looked small somehow, Rosalia thought, where once she had seemed almost too large—a legend come to life. It was her posture, of course; she had lost her confidence, her nerve, and without it Brigid Baptiste was only—regrettably—human.

At some point, as the minutes ganged up into hours, Ungela came to the room, standing quietly in the doorway to survey the scene. In Spanish she asked Rosalia if their guest was okay, and the concern was clear in her motherly eyes.

Rosalia nodded. "I hope so," she said, smiling her dazzling white smile.

Sister Ungela stood there a moment longer, her concern for Brigid palpable. "When she needs to eat—or when you do—you call," she said in Spanish. "Food is the great healer for misery."

Rosalia nodded gratefully once more, and Ungela turned and left. Rosalia listened to her familiar gait, the shuffle of her feet as she limped down the corridors of the nunnery.

After a while, Rosalia stood and made her way to the dresser that rested against one wall, a neat pile of schoolbooks piled to one side. She did that simply to stretch her muscles, for she was patient enough to remain at Brigid's side for as long as the woman needed her. Rosalia was nothing if not patient. The nuns had taught her that discipline when she was a girl, and she had used it to unsettle people, hurrying them to error while remaining on the cusp of readiness herself.

There was no mirror at the dresser—the girls were

not allowed such things in their rooms, since the ones in the bathrooms would suffice, they were told—but there was a hairbrush there, turned up so that its bristles pointed toward her like a porcupine's quills. Rosalia took the brush and returned to the bed, running it through her long, flowing locks, tugging at the kinks and knots that had formed during the earlier combat session.

As if from nowhere, the window began to rattle, and when Rosalia looked she saw that it had started raining, hard. In fact, it was raining harder than anytime she could ever remember in Mexico. As she went to look, Rosalia heard the shrieking of the girls in the dorms, their excited cries and chatter as they saw the meteorological onslaught explode from the heavens. Doubtless some were still in the courtyard, finishing their exercises when they got caught in the sudden downpour. Peering through the window, Rosalia saw it was thick, hard rain, the kind of monsoon one associated with rain forests. Girls were running in from the storm, hands over their heads, hefting exercise equipment as Sisters Magdalene and Annette encouraged them to get inside. The lancing droplets were turned orange by the late-afternoon sunlight, peeking through a tiny gap in the thickening clouds.

Shaking her head, Rosalia made her way over to the bed once more, the brush clutched in her hand. As she padded across the room, something caught Rosalia's eye as it flashed across the interphaser's display. She halted, leaning down to examine it more closely. She had used the interphaser on several occasions, and while she was no expert, she could see that something did not look right. The unit's display was a small bar that ran across the base of the interphaser, beneath the silver pyramid that dominated its form.

But now, the display flickered through a sequence of coordinates as if the parallax points were altering, shifting across an ever-changing surface. Rosalia reached for the display, then, thinking better of it, pulled her hand away and called for Brigid's attention.

"Brigid? Look at this."

Slowly, with the weariness of one who had not been asleep but had fallen into the trancelike thought process that often preceded it, Brigid opened her emerald eyes. "What is it?" she asked in a quiet voice.

"Look," Rosalia said, moving a little way back from where the quantum interphase inducer sat on the floor.

Brigid saw the flashing numbers hurtling across the readout display like comets, and she frowned, reaching forward to deactivate the unit. "It must have become confused."

"It's a machine," Rosalia chided, "it doesn't get stir-crazy."

Brigid toggled the switch on the control board, powering down the interphaser, and its display turned to darkness as the illuminated panel was shut off. It felt warm to the touch, not hot but still discernibly warmer than it normally was.

Brigid left the device for a slow ten count in her head, saying nothing but turning over what she had just seen in her mind's eye. Outside, the rain continued to lash against the window, rattling the glass in its aging wooden frame like some torturous cat-o'-nine-tails striking over and over against its glassy skin.

Deftly Brigid's fingers played across the control panel of the interphaser, bringing it back to illuminated life.

"You think there's something wrong with it?" Rosalia asked.

"Not sure," Brigid said, engaging the miraculous machine in its swift boot-up sequence. After a moment, the lights coalesced and numbers again began flickering on the tiny screen.

Chapter 21

Grant placed the box of stones in the back of the Manta as he positioned himself in the pilot's seat. The box was sealed, so he ran no risk of the stones escaping and causing the sort of mayhem they had in El Cana and Luikkerville. Along the spit from Grant, Kane was clambering into the cockpit of his Manta and strapping himself in, fitting the all-encompassing tactical helmet over his head. As Kane looked in his direction, Grant smiled, brushing his finger to his nose once more in that private gesture they shared.

The starcrafts' seats were wet as soon as each man pulled open the cockpit, for the rain was so heavy. The rainwater itself remained clear, despite the red tint to the clouds above. Over a century before, North America had been recovering from the nuclear exchange that had threatened to destroy civilization forever. During that period, the skies could open with toxic rain, and the clouds would take on the colors of their pollutants, cotton-candy blurs of red or green or yellow. But now, two centuries after that nuclear exchange had done so much damage, the sight of such clouds was just a memory, something only grandparents or great-grandparents recalled.

The rain came with a stink, an acrid taste that lashed at the mouth like sulfur from a burning match. Brimstone, they had called it, in the days when people expected Revelation to come to judge them.

Donald Bry's report buzzed through as the two Cerberus warriors powered up the Mantas and prepared to take off. He had pinpointed the clouds, but could offer few insights.

"From above it just looks like a weather pattern," he told Kane, "albeit a forceful one. This kind of cloud pattern isn't unusual in, say, hurricane situations."

"Keep monitoring it, Donald," Kane requested. "We're going to take the Mantas up for a closer look."

"Be careful, Kane," Bry said. "Those Mantas may be designed for transatmospheric travel, but they can still get damaged by lightning."

"When have you ever known me to be reckless?" Kane teased before cutting the communication feed.

A moment later, he and Grant were in the air, a vertical takeoff pulling them up above the lip of the cliff.

BACK AT THE NUNNERY, Brigid and Rosalia sat on the floor staring at the cycling through of the interphaser display screen.

"What does it mean?" Rosalia asked, narrowing her eyes as the illuminated points swam across the screen.

"I'm not sure," Brigid said vaguely. The parallax points were fixed locations on Earth's surface that were used as way stations for an interphase jump. Significantly, these points never moved.

Brigid engaged her Commtact and called upon the resources of the Cerberus headquarters. "Cerberus, it's Brigid. I need you to do something for me."

With Donald Bry engaged in monitoring the satellite feed, it was Brewster Philboyd's familiar voice that replied, channeled through Brigid's mastoid bone by the hidden mechanics of the Commtact.

"Hi, Brigid, we thought you'd forgotten us. What's happening?"

"Do you still have one of the interphasers there with you?" Brigid asked, ignoring the man's joviality.

"Sure do," Philboyd confirmed.

"Go get it," Brigid said. "And get Lakesh. I need you to fire the interphaser up and then use the mainframe to search for parallax points. See if you detect any anomalies."

"We have a computer simulation," Brewster pointed out reasonably. "Where are you looking to travel?"

"No, Brewster," Brigid said, tamping down the edge of alarm that threatened to overcome her voice. "It has to be the interphaser itself. I need someone to power it up and let it run through its start-up protocols."

There was a pause of a few moments as Brewster spoke to someone beside him in the Cerberus ops room, and then he came back to Brigid over the Commtact. "Roger, Brigid—we're just getting it now. Stand by."

IT TOOK JUST THREE MINUTES to get the interphaser and run it through its start-up sequence in the operations center of the Cerberus base. In that time, Lakesh was called from his vigil at Domi's bedside in their rooms. She was trying to sleep when he left, and his weary body language suggested that was something he needed to do also.

"Mr. Philboyd, what is occurring here?" Lakesh asked as he stepped through the ops-room doors, stifling a yawn.

"Brigid's on the comm," Brewster explained as Farrell worked the interphaser in the mat-trans chamber. "She's asked us to power up the interphaser and run a diagnostic." Brewster wore an earpiece that linked him to the Commtact communicators, and he handed a similar device to Lakesh as they met.

Lakesh was an expert in the theoretical science of teleportation, having been a part of the development team of the mat-trans, and the first man to have his atoms discorporated in the very first mat-trans jump. What Lakesh didn't know about the physics behind teleportation wasn't worth knowing, or hadn't yet been theorized.

"Brigid, this is Lakesh," he said as he hooked the Commtact receiver over his ear. "How is Mexico, my dear?"

"Lakesh, my interphaser's going haywire," came Brigid's urgent response. She sounded worried.

"Does this mean that you were planning on returning to us shortly?" Lakesh asked in a friendly manner.

Brigid stopped him with her tone. "Lakesh, I need you to check your interphaser there. What does it show?"

By this time, Lakesh and Philboyd had joined Farrell in the mat-trans chamber, its brown-tinted armaglass walls shielding the room from the ops center beyond. The interphaser rested on the floor with Farrell kneeling before it, its pyramid shape glistening beneath the harsh lights of the compact, hexagonal room. Lakesh peered at its readout screen with a frown. "The unit is running fine," he explained over the Commtact. "There doesn't seem to be anything untoward—"

Lakesh stopped, watching as the display changed. Numbers were moving across the display almost too fast for the eye to detect. From his position on the floor,

Farrell peered up at the Cerberus leader, his bearded mouth slack. "Dr. Singh?" he asked.

"Brigid, dear," Lakesh said slowly, "the interphaser's display is wonky. It must be a fault in our reading somehow. I'm going to reboot it and see—"

"No," Brigid replied. "I'm getting the same thing here. I think that something is happening to the structures of Earth, something that the interphaser is reacting to."

"Do you have any idea—?" Lakesh began, and stopped. Brigid, typically, had cut their communication. He hoped she was all right.

THE MANTAS TREMBLED as they took to the air, and Kane felt his hands slip on the controls as he tried to tighten his grip. Whether that was sweat or rainwater, he couldn't be sure, but he eased his grip on the yoke, wiping his palms on the legs of his pants while the vehicle continued to rise.

Beside Kane, Grant's craft followed in a shadowing pattern, vertically rising from the sandy spit, straying no farther than fifteen feet from Kane's wingtips. Above, the clouds were massing and turning, dancing their slow-step Terpsichore through the reddening sky. Lightning flashed across Kane's view, and he counted the seconds to the accompanying thunderclap, estimating the source was just six miles distant.

"We're going to have to get closer," Kane said, engaging his Commtact.

"Closer to what?" Grant snapped. "Are we going to chase a storm?"

"There's more to it than that," Kane insisted. "Just look at the clouds."

Secure in his own cockpit, Grant scanned the im-

mediate area. When they had left the pirate base a little more than fifteen minutes earlier, the edge of the
scarlet clouds had still been visible, the storm front
churning overhead. Now, the front was distant, the
clouds covering the whole sky like a blanket, obscuring the sun. Below them, it was dark, the world recast
in shadow. But surely no cloud moved that fast, expanded that fast.

Grant tapped the yoke, urging power to the Manta's
engines as he pulled his craft around to follow Kane's.
"You have any idea what we're going to do once we
reach—what is it—the eye of the storm?" Grant asked.

"One thing at a time," Kane replied. It was a mad-
deningly typical response from a man who lived by
his instincts.

Grant followed him into the depths of the storm,
their Mantas racing over the waves, dipping as the
lightning flashed between cloud troughs above them.
From below, the clouds looked like stalactites, a dark
ceiling on the world.

A DOZEN OR SO MILES AWAY in the port of Tuxpan, Roberto the harbormaster was just leaving work. Mad-
elyn, his secretary, had already left for the day,
declining the offer of a ride in his electricity-powered
automobile.

He whistled happily to himself as he locked the office door and, still holding the jangling bunch of keys,
marched outside to secure the outer door.

Outside, hard rain had begun to fall, lashing against
the tarmac roads and the metal plating all around the
docks in imitation of a thousand jumbled drumbeats,
each one striving to be heard, a battle of the bands.
Rain lashed against Roberto's back as he hunkered be-

neath the porch, working through his bunch of keys. He needed fewer keys, he reminded himself, the way he reminded himself every time he went through this ritual when it rained. He still had a key to the apartment that he and Dee had left three years earlier, still had his daughter's door key from the apartment she had left five years earlier.

Standing outside the port authority building, Roberto automatically pulled up his jacket's collar against the rising wind, felt it tug at the bundle of keys as he sought the pair that worked the two locks of the door. As he inserted the first, his grease-slicked hair pulled at his scalp as if clutched in a man's hand, and he pushed it back into place without complaint, the whistled tune still emanating merrily from his pursed lips. The wind had really picked up, he realized, glancing at the skies through the sheets of rain.

What he saw there made the cheerily whistled tune die on his lips. The sky was heavy with clouds, and they were dark clouds, as dark as smoke filtering across the midnight moon. The clouds were visibly moving, not in one direction as if with the wind, but rotating, turning as if on some unseen axis, like an eerie, sky-bound merry-go-round. And within them, Roberto could see the redness, a red like blood, like something cut.

Roberto turned at a crashing sound, saw one of the great container ships that bobbed at anchor begin to pitch toward the waves, the stacked crates on its deck flying free as a rope snapped.

"What is this?" he muttered. "What the hell is this?"

ALL ACROSS MEXICO, PEOPLE were being struck dumb by the phenomenon, hurrying to gather billowing clothes from their washing lines as the rain started, cursing the roads as their automobiles swerved to avoid falling branches torn from the trees.

The clouds loomed in red, the smell of sulfur filtering through the air.

"IT'S NOT A LOCALIZED phenomenon," Brigid told Rosalia, her eyes still fixed on the readout screen on the interphaser. "Something's happening that's affecting the unit at Cerberus, too."

"Then what are we going to do?" Rosalia wondered.

"It's either the interphasers or—" She stopped, turning to watch the vicious rain as it struck against the window.

"Brigid?" Rosalia prompted.

As Rosalia watched, Brigid pushed up from the floor and stalked across the room to the window, her eyes fixed on the vista beyond. The rain was coming down with the force of bullets, driving against the ground in a murderous cacophony of violence, rattling everything it touched. The skies above were black and red, the swirling crimson of blood pouring down a drain, turning on some distant axis point, moving like the unrelenting second hand of some vast clock. As Brigid watched, a bolt of lightning raced through the scarlet clouds, its color a sickly blue-green like veins beneath the skin. The lightning churned across the surface of the clouds, zapping to and fro in a series of jagged patterns that went to and from the distant central axis in echo-and-response configurations.

"What's happening out there?" Brigid whispered, while on the floor of the dorm room the interphaser's display continued to alter in flashing bursts of illumination.

Rosalia stood beside Brigid now, searching the incredible skies with awe. "I don't know" was all she could think to say, but when she turned to Brigid she could see the faraway look in the woman's emerald eyes. Brigid wasn't speaking to her anymore—it was the Commtact, come to life in her ear to report.

"THE SKIES ARE GOING nuts, Baptiste," Kane explained as the Manta raced through the incredible storm. Below him, the Gulf of Mexico was churning with twenty-foot-high waves, each one cresting like the grasping paws of an attacking bear. Fishing vessels were being overturned in the high seas. "Can you see it?"

"Red skies here," Brigid said, "and lightning. Green lightning. It doesn't appear to be striking the earth, Kane."

Kane swerved the Manta, making it stand on one wing as a blue-green fork of lightning cut down from the sky toward his craft.

"It will," Kane told her ominously. "Right now, that lightning's playing tag with Grant and me."

"Where are you?" Brigid asked, intense concern in her voice.

"Inside the Manta, flying toward the source," Kane said. "At least, it looks like the source from where I'm sitting. The whole sky's turning on a spindle above a point in the gulf."

"Kane!" Brigid spit over the Commtact. "It's the thunderstorm from hell and you're sitting in a metal capsule rushing toward its center! Do you know how stupid that is?"

"I've done stupider," Kane growled. "Let's just figure out what the heck it is all about, shall we?"

Behind Kane, Grant flopped his own aircraft close

to the colossal cresting waves, skipping over them like a skimming stone as lightning battered down all around him like a giant flyswatter.

"WHERE ARE YOU NOW, Kane?" Brigid asked. She was still gazing out the window of the dorm room as if she could somehow see him, hundreds of miles away.

"We followed the coast down from Tuxpan," Kane said. "I don't know the name of our exact location, but I can triangulate coordinates... Shit!"

MANY MILES SOUTH, KANE dropped the Manta down low as a bolt of blue-tinted lightning exploded from the sky, lashing toward him and Grant in a vicious trident of electricity. The blast snagged the Manta's starboard wing, striking with a flare of flames and running electrical fingers across the surface of the craft.

Kane looked up through the helmet display, gazing past the glowing alarms to see whether he could outrace the next lightning strike. What he saw there made his heart skip a beat, and he felt the breath catch in his throat. The clouds were dark, their shadowed clefts turned red as he had observed before. But within those scarlet shadows, things seemed to be turning—giant cogs and chains, clockwork things.

"Grant, look at the clouds," Kane instructed.

"Can hardly...keep...my eyes off them," Grant insisted as he fought with his controls, rolling the Manta out of the path of another flash of lightning.

"Look into the reds," Kane continued, wrestling with his own controls as the wind batted against his craft's sloping wings. "Do you see something there? Like machinery?"

There was a momentary pause as Grant assessed

the clouds before he responded. "I'd call you nuts if I hadn't seen it myself," Grant said, "but yes, there's some kind of machinery in the clouds. Looks like a ghost image to me."

"Me, too," Kane confirmed. Grant was right—the cogs or whatever they were looked as if they were seen through plate glass, as if they lay beneath the crimson surface of the clouds.

Kane angled his Manta in a sweeping arc, nosing close to the underside of clouds as another burst of lightning lit the air, the high wind battering his flanks.

"Kane, be careful," Grant instructed.

But Kane ignored him, driving his aircraft ever closer to get a clear look at the machinery within the clouds. His heads-up display glowed and flashed, bringing up conflicting information as it scanned the surrounding area.

Behind him, Grant clenched his teeth as another burst of lightning zipped through the sky, striking Kane's Manta with a brilliant hammer blow. The Manta wavered, its wings dipped and it began rushing toward the sea.

"Kane?" Grant demanded. "Kane? You okay?" Grant powered his Manta into a lunging dive, following Kane's craft, struggling to keep it in sight through the driving rain that assaulted both their vehicles. "Kane?"

Suddenly Kane's diving Manta lifted, skimming the crashing waves by mere feet.

"I'm okay," Kane's voice assured Grant over the Commtact. "Shaken, but okay."

"Great, let's get out of here," Grant decided.

"No way," Kane responded, and Grant could see

him angling his craft toward the whirring center of the clouds.

Secure in his cockpit as lightning crackled all around him, Grant muttered a curse as he followed Kane through the sheet rain. "I hope you know what you're doing."

An eighth of a mile ahead of Grant, Kane had spied what he was looking for. Above him, the clouds rotated on their apex, darkening the skies with that grisly red light. Below, Kane could see a ghostly trail of smoke pouring upward to feed them. The trail emanated from a speck of an island, visible through the thick cover of the trees.

"That's what we're looking for," Kane said, reengaging his Commtact. "I'm sure of it."

FIVE HUNDRED MILES to the north, Brigid was hanging on Kane's every word as they were piped directly to her ear.

"Kane?" she demanded. "What is it, Kane?"

"An island," Kane explained. "So small you wouldn't even notice it from a mile out."

"Be careful," Brigid insisted. Her heart was racing despite her best efforts to keep calm. She knew how Kane could be.

"There's something down there," Kane replied, and Brigid recognized that familiar note of reckless bravado in his voice. "It's coming from the jungle. I'm going in."

Brigid held her breath, waiting for Kane's next frantic report.

Chapter 22

The Temple of Dreams had waited ten thousand years for someone to make it work.

The structure had stood unnoticed for most of the intervening time since then, gradually becoming overgrown by a forest that had little interest in the paltry dreams of modern man. The building itself was small, not really a pyramid or anything that might rival one, just a modest temple from an earlier age. A temple to the old dreams, and the dreamers who dreamed them, it predated the local Mayan civilization by at least six thousand years. While it bore some surface similarities to the pyramid of El Castillo—and perhaps might be mistaken for being the same—the actualities of the design were too different for that to be anything but coincidence. Perhaps one had inspired the other, perhaps not. Dreams had a way of reaching out, snagging more people as they washed onto the shores of subconsciousness, plans drawn in their trailing spume.

The design had been inspired by a dream, though the name of the dreamer or dreamers had never been recorded. This was a primitive society, where the import of dreams was still recognized and the use of hallucinogens was encouraged. The difference between the sleeping and waking worlds was less clear than it was to modern man; dream structures moved freely between the two worlds. The finished design reached up to the heavens before delving lower than ground level, clawing into a vast basement built to specific and esoteric measurements. Like everything else, those measurements had come from the dream, precise and oblique all at once, lines congregating to form dream patterns.

Though they might be mistaken for such, the designs on the walls were not writing. They had been carved there by engravers high on peyote, drawing the great shining shapes that they saw in their minds, trying to fix them to the walls with hammer and spike the way a butterfly collector would pin his most beautiful acquisitions. They had been trying to nail down the impossible, to affix it to the walls.

The process had lasted 360 days, like the splinters of a circle. The stone construct had been warm inside then, buried within the earth, its people working relentlessly to see their designs completed on the walls, ghost writing, ghost pictures. Smoke and incense filled the air from burning sconces, its heady stench mixing with the smell of sweat in the underground lair. The group who toiled there never complained; they just continued working at their designs, dragging dreams into the real world and carving them onto the stone walls, marking them there for eternity.

The floor was also made of stone, great, heavy slabs placed end to end in a vast circular design. Each stone featured a carving, the patterns linking one to the other to create a huge network of channels.

In the place where Black John Jefferson had lain down to die there had once been dancers, trained men and women who would use the sound of their steps to call forth the new age. They had danced barefoot, the hardened soles of their feet sweeping against the stones in intricate patterns that followed the instructions from those carvings, from those dreams. In a way, their steps sounded like raindrops, creating a distinctive pitter-patter. For rain had always refreshed, and in its wake it brought new life, so the makers of the stone structure had hoped that its imitation would also bring the new life, the new world.

Their perception of that new world came from dreams, too, visions of a future so unutterably alien that it had the power to enlighten.

And to horrify.

Yet despite all the work that had gone into constructing it, the building had never been set to its purpose. Instead it had been abandoned and forgotten.

It was the Omniforge, and it had waited ten thousand years to finally be activated. All it took was human rain—*blood*. Blood and the burning need for vengeance; the burning desire to change things forever; to spoil them and clear the way for something better.

A day before, Black John Jefferson had lain on the floor of the incredible Omniforge beneath the temple, choking on his own blood, feeling the awful warmth running down and into his lungs even as his chest bled onto the carved floor where the dancers had danced their rain steps. He had been beyond thought, no longer conscious in any sense that mattered. All he could cling to was the hate he had felt. Hate that he had nurtured all his wicked life. Hate that poured into the dream patterns on the floor through the rich red rain that flowed from the man's veins.

The Omniforge had listened to that song of rage, its hidden gears shifting and turning beneath the earth, bringing a prophecy to life, a prophecy that had been known by just a dozen people and had been forgotten thousands of years ago.

Around Black John, a bloody light had torn the air, flames of crimson charging across his body. Black John had been too close to death by then to notice. His vision was ruined, as his brain had been starved of oxygen too long, and all he knew was the slightest heat that those flames brought. It was the heat of dreams, the heat of imagination coming to life in a virtuoso of awful sparks.

Like any forge, this one required heat. The burning came from the things it had been fed: a dying pirate, a circle of dreams, anger at the world.

Whether Black John ever had an inkling of what he had let loose was unlikely. He had sucked in his final breath as the Omniforge lit to its fullest, burning out through multilinear space from our world.

The imago universe was following, and the allotrope of man would come with it, replacing all that had come before. But first came the clouds and the rain, to wash away the world that was. To wash away the known world.

Chapter 23

"There's a building down there," Kane said as he brought the Manta close to the cover of the trees. "Looks like a—I don't know—a pyramid maybe."

Behind him, Grant kept his distance, warily eyeing the churning clouds above as that dark lightning flickered across their surface. "You see anyone?" he asked.

"Negative," Kane replied. "Looks like it's on fire, kind of. Like there's a chimney at the top. It's from there that the smoke's coming, and I think that's what's making the clouds."

"What are we talking about here?" Brigid's voice kicked in over the shared Commtact frequency. "A weather-making machine?"

"Hard to say," Kane admitted. "I'm going to go in, take a proper look around."

"The hell you are," Grant spit, and Brigid said something similar. "We can bomb this baby, take it out in an air strike."

"It's generating its own weather," Kane pointed out incredulously. "You don't bomb something like that out of existence."

"We could try," Grant insisted.

"But if we did that we'd never know what it was," Kane said, and his teammates could hear that little smile in his tone. "Besides, aren't you guys at all curious?"

"DIDN'T YOU HEAR WHAT happened to the curious cat?" Brigid reminded Kane over the Commtact as she sat before the flickering display of the interphaser. "It went and got itself killed, Kane."

But she was smiling now, too. Something about all this, the promise of adventure, of a problem bigger than their own, had lit the old fire within her.

Despite herself, Rosalia nodded as she watched Brigid work. It seemed that all of Brigid's self-loathing and introspection had evaporated in that moment, to be replaced by the personality she had known from before the dark days of Brigid Haight. Like lovers reunited, Brigid Baptiste had slipped back into familiar patterns with the promise of adventure stretching out before her.

"Kane," Brigid said, unable to disguise the urgency in her voice. "Be careful. I almost… You almost died before. When—"

"Baptiste," Kane interrupted, "whatever it is you think you're saying, don't. It doesn't matter anymore. You're there if I need you. You always were. I never doubted that. Now, let me concentrate."

In his Manta, Kane was swooping around in a second flyby of the tiny island. It was located close to the shore, but it was so small it seemed to be almost nonexistent. His onboard scanners informed him it was less than a half mile square, and it was lush with greenery, even through the heavy rain. The trees had grown tall and wild, clustered in thick clumps that covered almost the whole island. Which was a problem, of course, as it left Kane with nowhere to land the Manta.

Kane swooped around a second time, pulling the Manta hard to starboard as another jagged finger of lightning jabbed down from the heavens, which were as dark as a bruise.

Behind Kane, Grant was weaving through the lightning strikes, too. The airborne electricity was shaking his Manta to the core with each strike.

"Kane, we need to get out of this storm," Grant insisted. "The Mantas weren't designed for this kind of punishment."

Kane agreed. "Follow me," he said, bringing his craft around once more toward the tiny fringe of beach that ran around the western edge of the island. He could see nowhere else to land; they would just have to hoof it from there.

WITH LAKESH GONE FROM her side, Domi had left her bed and snuck outside, still dressed in the cotton examination gown that Reba had given her. She loved Lakesh dearly, and his concern for her was absolute. But she was a child of the Outlands, and being cooped up indoors for too long made her anxious. She made her way through the Cerberus complex on bare feet, reaching a side exit where work dismantling the web of stone had only just finished, huge bins containing chippings and rock dust waiting by the walls to be cleared away.

After punching in the code to open the door, Domi stepped out onto the plateau fronting the redoubt. Out there, away from the recycled air of the redoubt, things felt different. But there was a strange tang in the air. Domi sniffed, her pale nose twitching. "Smells wrong," she muttered.

Sensitive to changes in air pressure, Domi knew right away that a storm was brewing, but it was more than that. The dark clouds above were furious, thick things like the hairy caterpillars of a child's nightmare. And within their depths, Domi saw the redness of blood.

Something had cut the sky.

DOMI APPEARED IN THE Cerberus ops center just three minutes later. She had run all the way and, while she was not out of breath, her chest was rising and falling rapidly. She burst through the doors beneath the Mercator map with little delicacy, calling for Lakesh even as she entered the room. The personnel there looked up in surprise, and Lakesh turned away from the interphaser and hurried across to her.

"What is it, my love?" he asked.

"Outside," Domi panted. "Death in the sky. Saw it, smelled it."

"It's okay, calm yourself," Lakesh said, placing his hands on Domi's shuddering shoulders. Then, still holding her steady, he turned to one of the personnel in the ops room and asked him to bring up the monitoring feeds for the redoubt.

Returning to his desk, Farrell nodded, his fingers already racing across the computer keyboard. Twinned screens there showed a number of exterior views of the redoubt and its surrounds, split in multiples across each screen.

"Nothing special," Farrell said as Lakesh came to join him, his arm around Domi's waist. "Cloudy out there, looks like rain."

"More than that," Domi insisted.

Farrell looked at her a moment. The albino girl was standing there in a light cotton nightgown that barely reached her hips, her legs and feet bare. Curiously, this was probably the most clothing—or at the least the most modest clothing—that Farrell had ever seen her in.

"Air pressure is pretty high, but there's no sign of attack," Farrell related. "If that's what we're looking for."

As the three of them watched, rain began to fall, sluicing across the monitor feeds like thrown javelins.

A few desks across from them, Donald Bry's fingers blurred across the keyboard of his computer, bringing up a live feed from the satellite in geosynchronous orbit over the equator. "I think you guys should see this," he said, beckoning them.

Lakesh strode across the room between the twin aisles of computer monitors where several other personnel worked at their own tasks, the ghostly figure of Domi padding along beside him. He stopped before Bry's terminal, blanching a little as he leaned closer to examine the display.

"Oh, my word," he gasped.

The view from the satellite was like nothing he had ever seen before and, if it was accurate, it was pretty bleak.

"Donald, I need you to check this immediately," Lakesh instructed. "Confirm we don't have a glitch and that it's not something obscuring the lens."

Bry nodded. The flickering screen before him showed an overhead view of the continent of America. Marring the familiar coastline, a colossal cloud blotted out almost all of North and South America. The cloud slowly rotated as if on the eye of a hurricane, its lunging arms windmilling farther outward, stretching across the oceans to Africa to the east and halfway to Japan in the west. Flickers of lightning could be seen in that cloud, tiny bursts of dark electricity rushing across its surface like fleas on a dog. As they watched, the cloud could be seen visibly turning, its spreading arms reaching farther and farther outward, darkening the skies over West Africa, casting the Sahara Desert in shadow.

LANDING IN THE THUNDERSTORM proved a relief. The Mantas were designed for vertical takeoff and landing, and Kane and Grant brought them down hard and fast, meeting the beach with all the grace of a boxer's punch.

Kane had his helmet off in a second, and he leaped out of the cockpit and scampered down the sloping wing as lightning shook the sky, the rain slamming against his body.

Grant joined him on the beach a moment later, the rain bouncing off his shaved head in an almost comical manner. He still carried the box of stones with him, and Kane gave him a look.

"These things have caused enough trouble already," Grant reasoned. "I'm not letting them out of my sight until I'm sure they're decommissioned."

Kane nodded. He knew caution could prove its own reward in times like this, and the natural instinct to tackle the next problem should not compromise dealing with the first.

"You know where we're going?" Grant asked.

"There's a structure inland," Kane said, leading the way to where the sodden beach met the dripping jungle. "Looks man-made, some kind of pyramid. Can't be certain but it sure looks like the source of the thunderstorm."

Grant nodded. "Let's check it out."

It took ten minutes to locate the Temple of Dreams, with Kane and Grant struggling through the rain-heavy foliage that barred their path. Grant managed to wedge the box of stones under one arm while Kane led the way through the jungle. The foliage was so thick it acted as cover from the torrent, and it was not long before they stood in the small clearing before the stone monument itself.

Grant whistled when he saw it. "How old do you think it is?" he asked.

Kane shook his head. "Old. Hard to imagine who built it or how they got the stone here. Probably had to bring it across the sea, block by block."

"Anyone who did that did so for a reason," Grant said.

Kane agreed. "A calling. The urge to worship something."

Both men had spent the past few years looking at ancient temples and other sacred sites, much of it relating to the alien overlords called the Annunaki. Finding another temple hidden for millennia was of little surprise to them although they might have balked had they realized its age. As Kane put it when he began to search the building, it was "just another day in the office."

Together Kane and Grant hurried around the rain-lashed stones as the thunder rumbled overhead. Before they reached the summit, Lakesh's voice piped through to both of them via the Commtact link.

"We have an additional development," Lakesh began, concern clear in his voice.

"Go ahead, Lakesh, we're listening," Kane instructed. As they spoke, he and Grant made their way around the stone structure, eyeballing it from all angles, searching for a way in.

"Your weather system has grown," Lakesh said. "We're looking at it now."

"How big?" Kane asked.

"I repeat, we are looking at it now."

"You mean it's *there*?" Kane queried, unable to hide the surprise in his voice.

"That's correct, Kane," Lakesh confirmed. "The storm has reached us with no sign of abating. Satellite scan shows it's moving at an unbelievable rate—far greater than the winds would indicate—literally expanding to cover the surface of the globe. The strange cloud formation has already covered much of South America and it's reached us here in Montana. It's expanding in a circular pattern, which means it's also masking some of the Atlantic and North Pacific Ocean. We can't even see the Gulf of Mexico through the cloud cover now—it's like a thick blanket covering the sky."

Kane cursed. "Keep us apprised, Cerberus," he instructed. "We're going to take a closer look at what we've found here. I think it may be the source."

"Roger, Kane," Lakesh acknowledged.

By that point, Kane and Grant had walked around the whole of the pyramid-like construction, batting foliage out of the way here and there as they eyed the mysterious carvings on the temple's surface. Now they found themselves back at the lone flight of sandy-colored external steps.

"Looks like the only way in," Grant grumbled, and Kane agreed, the rain dripping from his hair as he nodded.

Lightning crackled overhead. Thunder banged. The storm from hell was continuing without pause, lighting the sky with its scarlet trails and forking veins.

Together, Kane and Grant began to ascend the stone steps, feeling trepidation but not fear. They had faced many challenges over their careers, from their days as Magistrates in Cobaltville through to their battles with madmen and faux gods across the globe in the company of Cerberus. To balk at this, no matter how huge it seemed, was simply not in their nature. Around them as they ascended, the strange smoke continued to churn from the ancient building, oozing from the covered area at the apex of the pyramid in a continuous stream, belching from the sides in irregular puffs.

AT THE CERBERUS OPS CENTER, Donald Bry was looking more worried than ever, his tousled copper curls even more disheveled than usual.

"We've lost all visual on them," he explained as he heard Lakesh break contact with Kane. "No satellite built by man could pierce this cloud cover."

"What about infrared?" Lakesh suggested. "Ultraviolet?"

Bry shook his head. "The cloud—and it is just one cloud now—is so thick it's like a wall. We may as well try peering through rock."

"We still have the transponders, Donald," Lakesh reminded him. "We can utilize those to triangulate the team's position."

Bry huffed with impotence. "And what if they need our help?"

"Then we shall provide it as we always have," Lakesh reasoned. "To the best of our abilities, no matter the obstacles placed in our way."

Bry turned back to his computer monitor and continued to track the progress of the ever-expanding cloud.

In Mexico, Kane and Grant had reached the top of the pyramid-like structure, where the stone portico resided. The flight of sand-colored steps ended abruptly here, and the roof covered a second set leading down and into the heart of the temple itself. The underside of the roof was coned, Kane saw now, so that it flared the belching smoke around it in four winding columns. The columns of blackness wended their way up past the roof before reknitting a dozen feet above the temple's zenith. Rain drummed against the stone roof so that it sounded like a booted, marching army.

With the outpouring smoke, it was hard to see into the pyramid itself. The steps were painted in darkness, occluded by that billowing blackness that came forth in a torrent. This close, the smoke stank of sulfur, its acrid tang so strong it almost felt like a physical jabbing inside the nostrils. Automatically, Kane and Grant drew their polymer lenses from their pockets, placing them over their eyes. The lenses would provide some form of vision even in the smoky gloom, and what's more, they should help keep the sting of smoke out of their eyes. Then they added kerchiefs to cover their mouths and nostrils, protecting them from the worst of the smoke.

Kane took a deep breath through the material and then, gritting his teeth, made his way down the steps with Grant following just two steps behind him. It was like walking through fog with that smoke billowing around them. The walls to either side were all but lost to the smoke, hidden as if behind a curtain. However, the carvings there showed even through the black smoke, glowing in the same eerie scarlet that tinted through the sky above, a bleeding wound on the face of the stone. If the outside had been glowing they had not seen it in the light, but here in darkness the glow was unmistakable.

Warily, Kane reached out, pressing the side of his hand to those glowing carvings. Like blood, they felt warm, the esoteric symbols carved not just in red but in heat.

"Warm," he said.

"Let's keep going," Grant said, biting back on the urge to gag against the sulfur stench, even through his kerchief.

Above them, the rain continued to fall, drumming against the roof like something punching the stone over and over, the power of a monsoon. The ancients who had built this temple knew the power of rain, that within the water were the seeds for new life. The rain was opening the space between the worlds, bringing the new and fusing it to the place that was.

Kane and Grant were relieved to find the smoke thinning as they reached the bottom of the stone staircase. It was still there, its snaky tails trailing all around them. But where it had thinned they saw the redness within the black, the tint of shadows turned to blood.

Belowground, the temple was silent. The rain still brushed the stone roof overhead, and the thunder cracked, but they were away from it now, well below its heavenly might. The two ex-Mags stood in a corridor, its walls carved from stone with more of those intricate designs hammered within it. The tunnel featured a low ceiling, and Kane and Grant found they were stooping without thinking about it, despite there being enough room for them both.

Removing their kerchiefs, they paced along the corridor warily, with Kane leading the way. He had recalled the Sin Eater to the palm of his hand, held it in a steady grip before him. The two men followed the corridor for at least a hundred feet past those inexplicable red carvings, until they suspected that they were no longer beneath the temple. Everything here was stone, even the floor on which more of the unusual carvings had been driven. Grant hefted the box of stone buds under one arm, trusting Kane to lead the way.

A series of steps had been carved at the end of the corridor, and as Kane reached them he saw that they spread wider than the tunnel's mouth, working in semicircles that led into a lower room. Shaped like a perfect circle, the room was vast, with jutting flanges at regular intervals around its edge where fires had once been lit. There were no fires now. In fact, without the polymer lenses, Kane and Grant would have barely been able to make out anything here other than the strange drawings that covered the stone walls, glowing crimson in the darkness.

The stone steps were the same ones that the dancers had danced upon ten thousand years ago, their bare feet slapping against them in the rhythm of rain, the rain that brought the change. It had taken ten thousand years to reach this point, ten thousand years for the catalyst to be engaged, for the world fusion to begin.

With his booted foot on the rain steps, Kane stepped forward, eyeing the shadowy walls of the temple, their crazy patterns and alien script. He had fought gods and he had triumphed. First in the physical plane, where gods seemed little more than men in silly disguises; and ultimately in superstring space, where action and reaction blurred and switched places, and where a man's sanity was just another weapon that could run out of ammunition.

He had been pushed to his limits and beyond, past

the very edge of human endurance, physical and mental. But through it all, Kane had retained one thing—his abiding sense of justice.

For this temple to change that, for the world fusion to change who he was, what he stood for, to change his very core—that could never be. Kane would stand firm, even as the world disintegrated about him.

And to Kane's left stood Grant, as he always had—the bedrock on which their adventures had been built.

"We can take this," Grant said. "Just tell me how."

Kane held his right hand high, the Sin Eater waiting in his palm, scanning the room through the smoky air, the dark mist drawing shadows across the night-vision lenses he wore. Then his heart seemed to jump, his eyes registering the thing before he was even conscious of it.

"There's someone in here," he said.

Chapter 24

"There," Kane indicated, "in the center."

Grant looked, peering through the smoky, bloodred glow of the room, the dream sigils all about him. There was a figure, just as Kane had said, slumped on the carved stone floor, unmoving.

"He dead?" Grant asked.

Kane didn't know. He called to the figure, asking him to respond. When he didn't, Kane stepped closer, eyeing the fallen man warily, his gun poised on his unmoving form. The red light seemed to emanate from him, a bleeding wound come to life, a cut tearing through the shadows of the world, touching everything and changing everything it touched. Here was the source of that red glow that lit the walls, the same glow that rippled through the clouds outside.

Once he got close, Kane toed the figure gently, still with his Sin Eater targeted on him.

"Hey, you asleep?" Kane asked. "Wake up."

The figure did not respond. It just lay slumped there, exactly as it had fallen, traces of red misting across its static body. Kane had seen enough dead bodies to recognize a corpse when he saw one. He didn't know who the man was, but he was sure now that he was dead. Point of fact, he could smell the tangy mixture of sweat and blood over the figure of the dead pirate, that odorous mix that accompanied violent death.

"Guy's dead," Kane confirmed, crouching to take a closer look.

Grant peered around the room, making sure no one else was hiding and that no one had followed them. Then he placed the heavy box of stones on the floor, leaving them just inside the doorway to the room before entering. As he paced down the little flight of steps, Grant watched Kane reach for the slumped figure in the center of the room. All around them, the dream writing throbbed and glowed a fearsome shade of red, like the crimson fires of hell. Kane pulled at the fallen man by the back of his shirt. The shirt was stiff, caked with dried blood. With care, Kane rolled the man onto his back, the red mist pouring from his every fleck of skin.

The man slumped over onto his back, and his head dropped back, knocking against the stone beneath. As it did so, the figure's eyelids widened—the eyes had been open already in death, but the movement had caused them to open farther. Kane saw the redness glowing there, as if a scarlet bulb had been placed inside the man's skull on a dimmer switch, turning brighter and darker, brighter and darker.

Kane felt that red glow overwhelm him, searing through the protective lenses of his night-vision goggles and burning directly into the lobes of his brain.

Grant cried out as Kane toppled over as if his knees had simply given way, dropping to the flagstones of the Temple of Dreams.

"Kane!"

But it was too late. Already, Kane's mind had been pulled into the Omniforge like a hooked fish, drawn into the star stuff from which worlds were created.

THE OMNIFORGE WAS A DREAM structure whose purpose was to change the world, its design dragged out of dreams and into reality. Once lit, it had begun the fateful turning that would twist the world in the heavens, moving it fractionally, just enough to change everything and to bring about the new epoch.

Kane saw it from the inside now, the structures that underpinned worlds, the way in which new universes were strung together. It was like the inside of a clock, each piece brushing against another, striking its fellow to generate the perfect movement that made the world. Everything was painted red here, even the air itself, as if Kane's eyes had been veneered with blood. It was huge, too, a structure so large it went farther than Kane could see. It created the disconcerting feeling of being both indoors and outside all at once, such was its immense scale.

Kane looked about him, scanning his surrounds, trying to make sense of wherever it was that he had been suddenly placed. He was no longer underground; that was for sure. Gigantic cogs turned, their massive teeth shunting from one stuttered movement to the next. Huge wheels spun, first one way and then the other, gathering energy then dissipating it in a shower of sparks.

There was a sound, too, a relentless pumping throb that seemed tinged with the sound of grinding metal—*buh-dmm-buh-dmm-tsssssk, buh-dmm-buh-dmm-tsssssk*. Accompanying that noise came the smell, a sharp, chemical stink of gas, both repulsive and strangely addictive at the same time.

"Where am I?" Kane asked.

For a moment, no answer came, and Kane was left

searching the unfathomable mechanism, trying to see
where—or even if—it ended.

"WHERE AM I?" GRANT heard Kane murmur as he
scrambled across the sacred space to his side. He
sounded like a man possessed, the voice barely his
own.

"It's okay, buddy," Grant said. "I'm right here, right
next to you. You fell."

"His eyes," Kane said. "Don't look in his eyes."

Kane was lying on his back with Grant crouched
over him, and his moving mouth was the only indication that he was in any sense conscious. Perhaps he
wasn't, Grant thought. He had the disturbing feeling
that he was conversing with a dreaming man.

Without turning, Grant pushed his empty left hand
against the dead pirate's face, turning the man's head
away. As he did so he scanned the underground room
again, searching those glowing scarlet glyphs all
around him for some sense of meaning.

"Kane, what's going on?" Grant asked. "You hurt?
Able to get up?"

Kane spoke as if from far away, and his words
seemed to cause him pain.

"This thing's some kind of machine," he said.
"Don't ask me how, but I think that dead guy there—
I think he tapped into it. And now it's sucked me in,
too."

"A machine?" Grant asked. "What kind of machine?"

"I think it's building the world," Kane said. "Or
maybe rebuilding it. The crazy weather, the things we
saw in the clouds—it's all a part of it."

"And what about you?"

Kane's voice was hoarse when he spoke again, as if he was having trouble being heard.

"Get Baptiste," he said. "She'll know what to do."

Grant shook his head in frustration. "Yeah," he muttered, "Brigid will know what to do. Always does. No one ever asks Grant what he'd do, do they?" He stood, glaring at the strangely glowing walls all around him as Kane and the dead pirate lay slumped on the floor.

"Okay, so maybe on this occasion, Brigid will have a better idea. But dammit, just once he could ask me first."

BRIGID WAS STILL RUNNING over the boot-up protocols on the interphaser when Grant's voice came to her over the Commtact. Though she had resigned herself to the fact that its internal detection system was altering at an incredible rate, Brigid could not help but try to reset it. The logical side of her demanded an answer to the mystery, and the anxious part insisted she be doing something. As the numbers flared across the screen once more, Grant's voice spoke in her ear.

"Brigid, we're going to need your input here."

"Everything okay?" Brigid asked, cursing herself for such an asinine question the very second the words left her lips.

"Define *okay*," Grant replied. "We're inside what appears to be some kind of temple, and there's a dead body in here. What's more, Kane is down. He's still conscious, but I don't think he can move. He says he's been snared by some kind of machine, and it's operating through the temple structure itself. He may be hallucinating, but I think we're talking about some other level, a different plane of being."

Brigid whistled. "That's a lot to take in all in one

go," she said as Rosalia gave her a quizzical look. "Anything else?"

"The temple's generating the crazy weather we're all experiencing," Grant said. "At least, we think it is. Lakesh says this storm is covering a good chunk of the Atlantic and Pacific already, and he's got it up there in Montana."

Brigid gazed out the window at the torrential storm. "Wow, it never rains but it pours, huh?" she muttered.

"So, come on, Brigid," Grant urged. "You're the brains of the outfit. What do you prescribe?"

"I need to be there," Brigid announced, gritting her teeth in frustration. The interphaser might be able to get her close if only it was operating properly. Instead, its boot-up sequence completed once more, the backlit screen danced with running dots.

Sitting on the edge of the bed, still staring at the interphaser, Rosalia called for her. "Brigid, something's happening to the interphaser. Look."

Brigid watched as the rhythm on the screen fluttered, then stabilized as if its proper function had been restored.

"Grant? Where did you say you were?" Brigid inquired.

Grant's voice came over the Commtact, reverberating along her mastoid bone and into her ear canal as if he was in the room. "A little way south of Tuxpan, maybe six miles out to sea. I don't think this place has a name."

"It's the Bay of Campeche," Brigid assured him. "Part of the Gulf of Mexico. Hurricane central."

"What's that?" Grant asked.

"Nothing," Brigid told him. "Not important. I'm

going to confirm your coordinates with Cerberus ops, just to be sure."

In the temple, Grant waited, not sure whether to curse or punch the air in excitement. If there was one thing that was frustrating about working with Brigid, it was her tendency to think three steps ahead of anyone else.

"Damn eidetic memory," he muttered, looking around the glowing walls.

There were occasions when it led to nothing but waiting around.

"THE BAY OF CAMPECHE is right," Donald Bry confirmed as Brigid's inquiry came through. "Their transponder signals show both Kane and Grant are there now, just a few miles from the westerly hook."

"That's great, Donald," Brigid said. "Do you still have the interphaser functioning there?"

Bry told her they did, and on her instruction he went to check its status. The readout was no longer flashing with trauma. Instead, it appeared dark.

"This is something I've never seen before," Bry explained as Lakesh came to join him.

"There must be some fault in the equipment," Lakesh said, taking over the communication with Brigid. "On the mainframe we have all of the parallax points showing in one region."

"Overlay Kane's location," Brigid instructed.

Bry consulted his computer monitor. "They look like the same spot," he confirmed, and Lakesh agreed.

"Brigid, my dear," Lakesh inquired over the Commtact, "do you have the slightest idea what is happening?"

IN THE DORM ROOM, where rain streaked across the window with the violence of a viral infection, Brigid's mind worked overtime. She answered Lakesh's question hesitantly.

"Maybe," she said. "Something's opened up the hidden structures of the planet. Something in the Bay of Campeche that's been there for a heck of a long time. Long enough to generate hurricanes for hundreds of years. Like some kind of...Well of the World."

Lakesh was surprised. "A well?"

Brigid toggled a switch on the side of her interphaser, powering it into full life.

"A wishing well, maybe. I'm going to find out."

Rosalia was staring at the woman, her brows raised in surprise as the interphaser came to life.

"Brigid, what do you think you're doing?"

Brigid fixed her with her stare.

"I'm going to help Kane."

Beside her, the interphaser was rumbling, the familiar cones emanating from its heart, one flickering and growing above the summit of the pyramid, a second burrowing impossibly through the floor.

"Surely you don't mean to use that thing?" Rosalia chided, shaking her head. "It's nuts—there's no way of knowing where you'll end up. You're stepping into the unknown."

"I've spent my whole life stepping into the unknown," Brigid told her. "And this vacation's over."

Outside the window, the world was changing, the weather patterns turned psychotic, the skies rent with bloody streaks. The interphaser had changed, too. Formerly a direct, if esoteric, means of traveling across vast distances following the hidden network of ley lines, now it was forced to tap the new reality, drawn to a single point like water to a drain. Web lines of haunted color poured forth as it reached full activation, their messy splinters like a compass needle twisted beneath the pull of a powerful magnetic field. The cones of crackling energy looked different from before, and Rosalia and Brigid recognized something that had once been subliminal—that it was humming a different tone to the one it had always produced.

Brigid stepped back as the unit powered up, watching the quantum energies burst free from the pyramidal shape. Its once familiar cone-burst of color etched with lightning had become something new and monstrous, and Brigid watched as it formed and re-formed before her, a scream of bloody darkness scored not with lightning but with the black lines of a shattered mirror.

"Brigid," Rosalia warned, "you don't have to do this."

Brigid stared into those dark flames and flexed her fingers, trying to dissipate the tension she felt. "Yes, I do," she said. "It's what I've always done. It's what *we've* always done."

"You need me to go with?" Rosalia asked.

But before Brigid could answer, the whirring energies of the interphaser seemed to expand, sucking the red-haired Cerberus warrior through a quantum window in space and time. Rosalia turned hastily away as the red light threatened to dazzle her, expanding and contracting like something alive. A moment later, Brigid and the interphaser were gone, sucked into the quantum tear.

"Good luck, Brigid," Rosalia said to the empty room. "Godspeed."

Chapter 25

In the operations room within the hidden Cerberus redoubt, Lakesh was pacing back and forth, trying to process every monitor screen as they bombarded different information about what was rapidly becoming a world event. An alert had gone around the mountain base, summoning all personnel. Whatever was happening, Lakesh was determined to be on top of it or, failing that, to be the last man standing when the world ended.

"No sign of the rain easing up out there," Farrell told him.

"We're registering that same series of parallax points, all of them clustered on the Bay of Campeche," Donald Bry confirmed.

"Weather system is growing exponentially," Brewster Philboyd said dourly as he studied the live satellite feed. "It's reached Europe and shows no indication of stopping."

"And what about Kane, Grant and Brigid?" Lakesh asked, turning his attention to another monitoring terminal to the far right of the room where physician Reba DeFore had just taken her seat.

"Grant's transponder is regular," she explained, "while Kane's shows the standard biological waveforms I'd associate with the REM state. As if he's dreaming," she said.

"And Brigid?" Lakesh pressed.

"Her transponder's been dead ever since Ullikummis attacked," Reba reminded him. "We simply have no ability to track her right now. I'm sorry."

Lakesh shook his head with annoyance, clenching his fist and looking around for something to punch and so vent his frustration. Domi caught up to him before he could do so, brushing her fingers gently along his sleeve.

"You always tell me to keep a cold head, lover," she urged.

"A *cool* head," Lakesh corrected. After a moment, he laughed, the smile breaking his solemn expression. "You're right, of course. Panicking won't fix this situation. The absolute best thing we can do for now is to stay calm and keep monitoring."

If anyone else in the ops room heard, they paid Lakesh no mind. Professionals all, not one of them had any intention of leaving his or her post during this time of crisis.

BRIGID'S INTERPHASER should not have even worked that way. The whole system was predicated on fixed-point travel, accessing only specific quantum paths whose gateways were locked at specific locations. Brigid recognized that for the interphaser to suddenly open a gateway within the Mexican nunnery went against every principle of its operation.

But this was no ordinary gateway. It had opened in a manner far different from the usual sequence, and it functioned not to provide access to the quantum roads that formed a hidden web beneath the structures of the world, but to channel any user to one point and one point only. That point was located in the center of what was now the location of every parallax point that had ever existed. The nearest equivalent that Brigid could think of was a funnel, where no matter which part of the wide mouth a substance fell it was always filtered down the narrow tube that sent it on its way with pinpoint accuracy.

She gritted her teeth, narrowing her eyes against the wealth of color—the wealth of information that was coming her way as color—that bombarded her. She was in nowhere now, in no-time. She traveled between the structure of the fixed world like some sailor cast adrift by fate, hurtling toward destiny itself.

GRANT SPUN AS A HOLE in space ripped open right there in the circular room beneath the temple. A fugue of color blossomed in the air, cut through with thick, dark lines. And then the interphaser materialized and beside it Brigid Baptiste. Her red mane billowed about her and she looked a little breathless by the journey, but otherwise she looked just as Grant remembered.

"Brigid, how did you—?" Grant asked.

"Interphaser's gone crazy," she said as if that explained everything. "Now tell me again what happened. Is that Kane?"

Already Brigid was running across the room, and she slid down on one knee as she reached Kane, touching his sweating face.

"Kane? It's me, Brigid. Are you okay?"

KANE WAS IN A MYSTICAL otherworld when he heard Brigid call his name. The world was layered in scarlet and carmine and coral and crimson, salmon and wine and vermilion and maroon.

Before him, huge cogs, each one as large as a building, turned, click-clacking into place as their teeth caught another slot of the grand mechanism, another rotation closer to the end of the world. Behind the machine, Kane could perceive the star field, familiar constellations winking at him from the sky as they caught his eye, all of them viewed as if through that same red filter.

Figures were moving within the redness, coming to life as their shapes coalesced, solidifying from the nothingness. They were tall and svelte, with long, rangy limbs and swanlike, graceful necks. Their backs arched as they walked erect, their faces still blank, waiting to find form. There had to have been a million of them, each perfect, climbing forth like a plant emerging from the soil. Kane looked at them as they began to march, crossing the star field and down to the rebuilt structures of Earth, the vein-dark lightning crackling through the air, the rain washing away the foundations of the old world.

"Kane? It's me, Brigid. Are you okay?"

"Baptiste?" Kane said, bewildered. "Z'at you?"

"Yes, Kane, I'm here," Brigid said. Somehow he knew this wasn't the Commtact link. Brigid sounded instead as if she was beside him, as if she was really there.

"I looked in the dead man's eyes," Kane explained. "He's a part of the world machine, the thing that's doing all this. Don't look at him, or you'll get pulled in, too...." His voice trailed off. "Save yourself," he finished.

Brigid was looking at him, a crease appearing down the center of her brow with concentration. "How are we going to do that?" she muttered, speaking to herself. "The world's ending, and you want me to save myself. I'm only human."

In that moment, Brigid regretted going there unarmed. It seemed that the blaster would have been reassuring against her hip, even though she had no clue what it was she was going to shoot. She stared at the walls, her gaze sweeping over the whole room in just a few seconds. In her urgency to see Kane, she had hardly noticed it before.

"Grant, what's that writing?" Brigid asked, indicating the glowing bloodred inscriptions that lined every wall of the temple.

"Damned if I know," Grant admitted. "Thought you might be able to tell us."

Pushing herself up from the floor, Brigid stalked across the room to the nearest wall and ran the fingers of her left hand along one of the inscriptions. It felt hot and wet, and when she drew her hand away she saw that some of the writing had come away with her fingertips. She examined the redness on her fingers for a moment, sniffing and then tasting it. "Blood," she concluded. "The walls are leaking blood."

"You got all that from just one drop?" Grant said, incredulous.

"Warm red liquid," Brigid told him, "hence, reasonable assumption. When you hear hooves, you shouldn't think zebras, right?"

"Right." Grant nodded, smiling broadly. If nothing else, seeing her in action served to remind him of how much they had been missing during Brigid's absence. "So what do we do?"

"With any wound you staunch the flow," Brigid said, "which means figuring out where it's all coming from."

"Dead pirate." Grant pointed, indicating the figure sprawled beside Kane. "He was here before we were. Don't ask me how, but Kane figures he set things off."

"How did he die?" Brigid wondered as she approached the body. She did so warily, recalling Kane's warning about the man's eyes.

Grant shrugged. "He was dead when we got here."

"But not by much," Brigid realized, prodding at the exposed skin on Black John's arms and belly. "No signs of decomposition yet, but rigor mortis has set in."

Rigor mortis, the stiffening that the dead succumbed to, only lasted about seventy-two hours. Grant recalled that fact from his training as a Magistrate many years before.

Still crouching beside the pirate, Brigid eyed his belly wound and glanced over his head wound, then eyed the room once more. "No one body creates this much blood," she said. "If this is the oil that greases the machine, then it's self-replicating, in just the same way that blood is in the human body. Once it has some, it can culture and reproduce it in the vast quantities it needs."

"We saw blood in the clouds out there," Grant informed her.

"Yeah, me, too," Brigid said. "Five hundred miles away, no less. This is huge."

Grant paced the room, glancing over the glowing sigils with a muttered curse. "So, what are we going to do? You said something about staunching the flow."

"We could bind this guy up, but I think it's too late for that," Brigid told Grant. "Horses or zebras. If we assume this is the center of the disturbance, then we might presume that by shutting down this—what is it, a temple?—then we can turn back the blood tide. But that's a very big 'if.'"

Grant fixed Brigid with a resigned look. "Not many other options presenting themselves just now," he said. "But that storm out there is too much to bring artillery here, even if we do have time. I told Kane we should have bombed this pesthole out of existence while we had the chance."

Brigid looked around the room once more, her eyes fixing on the small flight of stairs and the dark, smoke-filled corridor that ran beyond. "Where are we?" she asked.

"Some island in the Gulf of Mexico," Grant answered. "Don't know its name."

"No." Brigid shook her head. "I mean where? Where does that tunnel lead?"

"Up top," Grant told her, realizing that in traveling here via interphase jump, Brigid hadn't seen this structure from the outside. "We must be a little way underground, about a dozen yards clear of the entrance."

"Underground," Brigid pondered. "Like a bunker. Do you really think you could bomb that?"

"Good point," Grant said. "Further proof we got worries mounting up." As he spoke, a light bulb seemed to switch on in his mind, and Grant snapped his fingers. "Wait, I've got something with me that eats up blood. Stones from Ullikummis. They thrive on the stuff."

"Where did you—?" Brigid began.

"Long story," Grant said, hurrying over to where he had left the box of stones at the top of the flight of semicircular steps. "You've been out of the loop for a while now. Guess you didn't know about the Stone Widow and what we all found in Luikkerville, huh?"

Brigid's red tresses swayed to and fro as she shook her head. "Tell me about it later," she said. "If these stones can stem the flow, then we may be able to halt whatever is going on in its tracks. But we still need a way to shut it down. It's moved parallax points, for pity's sake. This device, whatever it is, works at an apocalypse level."

Grant was unpacking the box, using a hastily gloved hand to reach for the rattling stones inside. "I figure I'll distribute these around the room, sic 'em on the bloody walls and let them feed. Vampiric bastards, let them gorge until they're sick."

Brigid nodded. "But we'll need to destroy this thing internally, as well," she said. "Kane warned me not to look in the dead man's eyes, right?"

Grant looked at her, his expression dour. "Oh, no, Brigid, you can't mean—"

"Kane's my *anam-chara,* my soul friend," she said, plucking Kane's electrochemical polymer shades from the bridge of his nose. Beneath, Kane's eyes were wide-open and a single color—a bright bloody-red. "Time we connected."

With that, Brigid looked in Kane's eyes, her mind sinking into those whirling scarlet pools as she was drawn into the Omniforge.

Grant watched as Brigid's lifeless body slumped to the floor. "Crap, why does this *anam-chara* shit always have to come up?" he muttered.

Chapter 26

Of course, Brigid didn't feel her body slump in the underground chamber. In meeting with Kane's eyes, her field of perception was altered, sucked down into the machinery that the temple fed, like the nine-tenths of the iceberg that lurked beneath the surface.

It was red here, a red like blood. Brigid rocketed through it, struggling to make sense of the multitude of imagery that was flooding her optic nerves, impossibly vast machines whose designs only existed—could only have existed—in dreams. The mechanism hearkened back to an age when the boundary between the waking and sleeping worlds had been less defined, when the incredible sat beside the mundane in a man's mind.

Brigid would be lost here, she knew, if it wasn't for one thing—the *anam-chara* bond that tied her to Kane. She had looked into his eyes, allowing herself to go on this perilous journey into the impossible, trusting all along that Kane would be there, that his soul would find hers. Their bond was eternal, and despite the rift that had sprung up between them in the wake of her Brigid Haight brainwashing, they remained tied through the ages, linked at some spiritual level that was difficult to define.

Where Kane had fallen into the world machine powered by the Omniforge, Brigid was tugged by their entwined souls. Kane had appeared amid the machinery, the vast cogs and spindles that brought the fusion of the multiverse, overlaying the new world upon the lines of the old. But Brigid bypassed all of that, rushing ever onward to where Kane's soul called to hers, magnets drawn together.

"I'm coming, Kane," she whispered. "Just hold on."

Hold on to what, she didn't know, but looking around her at the machinescape of mind-dwarfing proportions, she suspected it was to his sanity. And to hers.

KANE STARED AT PERFECTION, the million-man army marching through the underbelly of the vast world machine atop the Omniforge. Everything glistened with the redness of blood, and the air itself stank of it, the ferrous tang of amalgam in his mouth from simply breathing it.

Though faceless, the army of human forms had a fascinating beauty, and Kane could not help but admire them. They marched with exceptional grace, shimmering into existence before making their way to an arched window below the center of the vast mechanism. Kane hurried toward it, scampering over a slow-turning horizontal cog, clambering up another that had been set vertically, using its gigantic teeth like the rungs of a ladder.

He was on a plane of existence where nothing quite made sense, and so, where another man might give in to madness, Kane simply made sense of it as best as he could. He had fought with gods on planes of perception that would humble a lesser man. He treated this problem as he had any other—one where he needed information, which meant the graceful humanoids, ghost figures from the future, needed to be halted and examined, perpetrators of a crime against reality.

Ahead of him, Kane saw the first of them begin to step through the arched window, until it flickered and disappeared.

"Now, where the heck is he going?" Kane muttered as he sprinted across a mile-wide connecting chain between spindles.

DEATH CAME IN MANY GUISES to the world of the adventurer.

Grant hurried around the inner room, tipping the box of leechlike stones to spread them across the floor like a farmer sowing mystery seeds, hoping that just one might take root. Grant kicked at the debris, scooting the stones farther across the floor where the glowing dream writing throbbed, batting them into the walls. The rocks scattered across the floor, running over the bloody glyphs that swelled on the stone tiles, and Grant saw them shudder in place. As he watched, each rock began to break apart, tendrils of stone spreading from its skin like the shoots of a plant. And all around them, the bloodred glyphs dimmed, each one losing potency, the color draining away before it could refill, drawn into the wicked stones.

For a moment, Grant stood there congratulating himself as, for the first time since he had arrived at the mysterious temple, the red glow stuttered and threatened to fail.

But before he could celebrate his victory further, something moved behind him, at the center of the circle that dominated the room. Some sixth sense alerted Grant, and he turned to face it, watching in awe as a willowy figure emerged from the bloodred mist that still billowed from the dead pirate's corpse. Human-like, the figure was seven feet tall and appeared almost emaciated, its slender limbs and wisp of a body so thin that they were painful simply to look at. To describe the figure as naked then was inaccurate, although it wore no clothes. Instead, it seemed not fully formed, a phantom of blood and light, sparkling in the air like a cloud of fireflies.

Before Grant could react, the figure charged across the room on its spindly legs, bird-thin limbs swishing to and fro as it powered across the distance toward him. Grant dropped the box without thinking, the remaining contents spilling across the floor as he commanded the Sin Eater back into the palm of his hand.

The blaster kicked in Grant's hand as soon as it met his fingers, the trigger depressed and the muzzle spitting a stream of 9 mm bullets at the eerie figure that rushed toward him. Instinctively, Grant knew it was an enemy, some ghost of a thing come to life. Yet—and Grant would never have believed it had he not seen it with his own eyes—the figure ran past those bullets, angling its slim body in such a way that none of them managed to meet with it.

Then the figure was upon Grant, lunging at him headfirst, striking his forehead with its own. There was so much to take in, and Grant barely had time to register any of it as the figure struck the first blow. His vision swam as he stumbled back, his nose feeling suddenly heavy as if with the onset of a cold. Before him, the willowy figure was still forming, color painting across its slender body, features becoming whole on its once-blank face.

Grant recognized it despite the swanlike neck, the rangy limbs, the wasp-slender waist and pleasing curve of the hips. The face was his own, made beautiful and perfect, an idealized vision of Grant himself. Death came in many guises to the world of the adventurer, but the last one Grant had expected was a better version of himself.

"KANE!" BRIGID CRIED OUT as she appeared beside him on that great racetracklike chain.

Sprinting, Kane slowed his pace, turning at the sound. "Baptiste? How the—? How did you get here?"

Brigid pointed at her eyes. "I looked in your eyes," she told him as she jogged to meet him. "Worked like a charm."

Beside her now, Kane was angry. "What did I tell you? I said categorically not to look in the eyes."

Atop the swaying, chain-link bridge, Brigid held her hands up in a back-off gesture. "No, you said not to look in the pirate's eyes, which I didn't. But I figured yours were fair game. Besides, we're *anam-charas,* remember? I knew I wouldn't get hurt if I made sure to follow you."

Kane was less than convinced. "You 'knew,' huh? That means you guessed."

Brigid smiled her brilliant smile. "Same difference. Now, where are we and what is all this stuff?"

"Your guess is as good as mine," Kane groused. "Got us a million-strong army over that way and the universe's biggest clock all around us. You want to take a stab at what it all means?"

"It's a mechanism," Brigid said reasonably, "and I think it's been designed to change the world."

MONITORING FROM THE Cerberus redoubt, Lakesh and his team watched in trepidation as the world cloud grew larger, casting east and west into shadow, assaulting Earth with its mighty storm. Monitoring the live feed from just outside the redoubt itself, Farrell leaned closer to his screen, narrowing his eyes in disbelief.

"There's something in there," he said loudly, though he was not addressing anyone in particular.

Lakesh, Domi, Donald Bry and others turned at Farrell's words, several people clustering around his screen.

"There," he explained, pointing to the thick cloud that had painted over the sky, "in the rain. Looks like—*people?*"

Lakesh leaned closer as a rumble of discussion blew up spontaneously all around him. On screen, he could see the dark blanket of cloud with its bloody highlights, the thick shafts of rain driving at the bare ground and the plants beyond, hammering at the mountains all around them. But there, just as Farrell had said, it looked like people, shimmering silhouettes descending in the downpour, floating down to earth with such a breathtaking elegance of movement it was like watching a ballet of autumnal leaves descending in the fall.

"What does it mean?" Farrell asked.

"Everything's changing," Lakesh said, his voice a whisper, "and we're watching it all on a monitor screen."

And if there was proof that the modern world had failed in its progress, Lakesh's astonished statement had somehow summed it all up.

THE WORLD MACHINE TICKED ON, taking the world another step closer to the apocalypse and whatever lay on the far side of the apocalypse. Inside its subtle mechanism, Kane and Brigid had caught up to the marching army of human allotropes, each one walking with a slender, supple grace. They stood on a vast shelf close to the arched window that Kane had spotted, the one that the figures were moving into and disappearing through.

"What are they?" Kane asked, his eyes sweeping over the crowd.

Brigid eyed their swanlike necks and curving backs. "People," she said.

Kane looked at her, his face an expression of shock. "People?"

"Perfect people," Brigid said. "The human race a trillion years from now."

"Then what are they doing here?" Kane asked.

"Something's brought about a leap in evolution," Brigid told him, "or is trying to. This is First Day, Kane—this is Genesis."

As they spoke, two of the impossibly graceful figures stepped from the marching ranks and approached them, moving faster and faster as they neared Kane and Brigid at the edge of the platform. Kane spotted the figures as they began their final sprint toward him and Brigid, saw their featureless faces begin to alter, to take on an idealized vision of himself and of Brigid.

"Evolution's coming. I think we're about to be replaced," Kane said, tensing his body.

"Hold them back," Brigid warned. "I'm going to try to get deeper into the machine."

UNGELA, THE MOTHER SUPERIOR, found Rosalia alone in the dorm room, sitting on Tia's bed, gazing at the window where the vicious rain washed against it, shaking the glass in its frame.

"I heard a noise," Ungela explained. "An explosion, I thought."

"Brigid's gone," Rosalia replied.

The air in the room still smelled of quantum energy, the scent reminding Ungela of the smell of burning hair.

"Is everything—?" she began, and Rosalia nodded.

"Our friends are in trouble," Rosalia said.

"'Our'?" the mother superior queried.

"*Her* friends, Mother," Rosalia corrected.

Ungela nodded. "Your place is here, sweet Rose," she said. "Remember all that we've taught you."

Chastised, Rosalia nodded again. Outside, the winds seemed to be getting even stronger, and they could hear the creaking of trees being uprooted, saw blurs pass the window as leaves and branches were caught up in the storm.

"Amazing," Ungela exclaimed. "I've never known a storm like it."

Rosalia was about to agree, but before she could speak something burst through the window, not exactly breaking the glass so much as passing right through it. In fact, there were two figures, each achingly beautiful. They were tall and rangy with slender limbs, long necks and a graceful arch to their towering backs. Pale and humanoid, each one's skin could be said to truly glow, shimmering on their flesh like the eyes of a cat.

Rosalia leaped up, automatically placing herself before the older woman to protect her as the beautiful figures glided toward them both. From the nearby rooms, she could hear screaming as other creatures materialized in the nunnery, each doubtless as impossibly graceful as the two that had appeared in this room.

"What in the name of all the saints—?" Ungela cried.

The two figures had come from that other world, the one from the fusion, the world that was coming to replace our own. As they stalked across the room, their features seemed to firm up, and Rosalia gasped as she recognized herself and Ungela in those still-forming faces. They were different, each with the air of perfection about it, idealized versions of the women in the room.

These were their successors from the new reality, the allotropes of man. Each had been attracted to its progenitor, like calling to like.

Rosalia ducked as her allotrope reached for her, its long fingers grasping for her hair.

"What are they?" Ungela cried, staggering back on her unsteady leg.

Rosalia flashed her a look, her dark eyes glinting. "Trouble," she said, smiling wickedly.

Dancing across the room, just out of reach of the allotrope forms, Rosalia reached for the one weapon she had stored in the room. It was a *katana* sword, its length charcoal-black. She pulled the blade from beside her bed, whipping it free from the tooled sheath that had been given to her by Grant's girlfriend just a few days before. The blade pulled free with a resounding note of perfectly tuned metal.

And then Rosalia was back among them, bringing all her phenomenal fighting prowess to bear on the two graceful, brilliant figures who had materialized from the world that was coming.

"Did you think attacking a nunnery would be easy?" she taunted as she drove her blade through the chest of the Ungela allotrope. "Joke's on you, you freaks."

From all around, the sounds of battle could be heard as more of the nuns and their students engaged with their own allotropic doubles. They would ask no quarter, and no quarter would be given. It was a battle for survival, and the losers would not simply lose their lives but their whole existence, the history of the planet itself dismissed in an instant. If Rosalia had any inkling of the import of the battle, then she gave no indication. All she knew was survival, that one trick she had been taught so well in these very walls.

ALL ACROSS MEXICO, similar scenes were taking place as the heralds of the new reality invaded Earth. They were more graceful, more beautiful, more perfect than any person had ever been, each one a work of art, as far beyond humans as a human was from the aquatic lifeforms he or she had begun as, millions of years before.

Some people fought and some were too scared to react at all, but most just stopped and stared and marveled at the beautiful forms that emerged through their walls or dropped through their ceilings, appearing from the red-tinged clouds that rolled across the planet. To see true beauty would stop most people in their tracks; it was a far more powerful weapon than any other. The strongest may win the battles, but the beautiful reaped the spoils.

IN THE SHADOW OF THE Omniforge, Kane stood before Brigid Baptiste, his arms wide, blocking the two elegant, naked forms from reaching her. He was running interference until she could work out a plan—and he knew it.

The closest of them had Kane's face, but the hard lines had been smoothed, the natural handsomeness made more ethereal, almost androgynous in its beauty. The bald head turned on the stemlike neck and those familiar features came face-to-face with Kane's own, like looking into a mirror. Kane felt his stomach flip as he stared at it, his gray-blue eyes fixing with those of the duplicate even as hair began to spout atop the allotrope's smooth, pale head.

"Nice look," Kane growled, "but it's already taken."

The Kane-creature opened its mouth to respond, a strange ululation warbling from deep in its throat. Kane responded by swinging his right fist at the humanoid's head. His punch connected with a crack, knocking the long-limbed beauty to the floor, much to its surprise. The thing sprawled there a moment, brown hair taking shape on its head, turning darker until it was black.

Kane glanced back over his shoulder for just a second, seeing Brigid gazing at the vast mechanism that towered over them, her eyes darting back and forth as she took everything in.

"What's the verdict, Baptiste? You got anything?"

Brigid nodded. "The pirate's corrupt soul must be feeding it," she said, "informing the machine. If I can find a way to override that instruction, then maybe— just maybe—I can shut it down."

"Big maybe," Kane said.

Ahead of Kane, the other lanky form came stalking toward him on its spindly legs, the face atop that swanlike neck taking on the familiar features of Brigid Baptiste, mimicking them and improving upon them, making the emerald eyes larger and greener, the lips paler. The other one—the one with Kane's face—was dragging itself up from the floor, brushing at its struck jaw with an expression of surprise and outrage.

Brigid continued to eye the structures looming over her, searching for some pivotal point on the unfathomable network stretching out before her eyes. Just a few dozen yards away, the army of beautiful human allotropes moved onward to the window to Earth, swarming out to take over the redundant prototypes who were now nothing more than placeholders for their new lives.

"Looks like a clock," Brigid muttered as she scanned the shuddering cogs and axles. "An old clock."

Just a few feet away, Kane was tussling with the second of the naked, swan-necked humans, his hand shoved into the idealized face of Brigid's twin. He drew his leg behind her pipelike leg and hooked, throwing her off balance and tossing her to the floor as her long hair switched to another, even more perfect, shade of red. The original Brigid paid it no mind, her prodigious intellect too busy trying to work out the impossibly complex mechanism that ran the world builder.

The process was called "the world fusion," and it would bolt the new world onto the old, using the existing world as foundation stones for a whole new existence, a new age of Earth, just as the Mayans had predicted. For Kane and Brigid—and everyone else on Earth—it meant just one thing: upgrading, death by replacement.

"Come on, Baptiste," Kane urged. "Let's hurry it up."

Before Kane, the two graceful human figures rose from the deck once more. They were eyeing him with suspicion now. Newborns, he had taught them their first lesson in pain and survival. Emissaries for the new age, they were quick learners. Kane swallowed as the two nude figures swept toward him again, their slender limbs blurring in movement, their heads tilted at inquisitive angles as they tried to make sense of his actions.

Brigid finally spotted what she was searching for amid the plethora of moving parts. There, in the center, almost hidden by the whirring structures all around it, lay a glowing red sphere. It looked like a miniature sun, pulsing brighter and darker with every turn of the miles-wide cogs.

"A clock needs a key," Brigid reminded herself, already tracing a path to the glowing heart of the world machine. Then she began to run, sprinting away from Kane and off toward a wall of springs and coils, each one the length of a house.

"Baptiste, what are you—?" Kane asked.

Brigid turned at the call, and her heart leaped as the long-limbed mirror-Kane grabbed her Kane by the head, palms pressed to either side of his face.

"Kane!" she cried.

But it was already too late. The creature of exceptional beauty whose template had been Kane, seemed to wrench Kane himself apart, his DNA unraveling like a pulled thread, corpuscles bursting forth in a froth of blood. Then he was gone.

IN THE UNDERGROUND CHAMBER of the temple, as Grant fenced with the eerily beautiful representation of himself that had stepped from the ether, Kane's collapsed body began to flicker out of existence, disappearing as though it had never been.

Delete.

Replace.

Chapter 27

Brigid ran.

All about her, the mechanism of the world machine was turning, counting down the final seconds to the end of the world. Just thirty minutes ago she had still been sitting on the floor of the nunnery at the Mexican border, and now—as incredible as it seemed—she was caught up in some impossible machine whose purpose was to enact Judgment Day itself. She had battled deranged gods before now, but here was something bigger—a fight with reality itself.

Behind her, the two artful forms that were the Kane and Brigid of the next epoch were just finishing with Kane. To the world that was coming he had been nothing but old data whose deletion was now complete.

All across the world, these same new humans were arriving, seeking out their prototypes, deleting them from existence. The new world had no need of people like Kane and Grant and Brigid. They were old data from another system, one wholly incompatible with the world that was coming through the bleeding wound of the sky.

The two who had eliminated Kane turned, their plant-stem bodies rotating with a subtle grace like swirls of ink in water, watching as Brigid continued to run from them, her primitive body working hard to reach for the clocklike mechanism of the Judgment machine. As one, they began to follow her, while their million companions continued to filter through the window that broke open over the world.

Glancing behind her, Brigid saw them move, chasing her in great sweeps of movement more liquid than flesh.

"Keep going," Brigid urged herself. Kane was dead, and she would deal with that later. Right now, there was the machine, and she had to shut it down. If Grant had done his job, used the living stones to staunch the blood flow from the temple, then she had a chance. All she needed to do was turn the mechanism back on itself—in essence, to turn the clock's key.

She had made it to the wall by then, the towering wall of cogs and spinning bobbins, wheels on rotating axles, colossal pistons that moved with the majesty of clouds. The whole thing was washed in red as if seen through a bloody haze, and up above her, there in what she thought of as the heart of the machine, the red sun glowed.

The machine was so big. Only a mindscape could hold something this size; even the universe itself was too small to hold all of its factions. She was in a fully immersive dream, Brigid realized, a dream that blurred into the waking world with no respect for the boundary that man had carefully erected between the two in the intervening years since this thing had first been brought into being.

But a dream could be changed, she reminded herself. A dream could be tooled and shaped by a canny dreamer, so that it need not overwhelm the person.

ACROSS THE GLOBE, ORDINARY people were coming face-to-face with their future echoes as the rains poured down.

In Russia, a nine-year-old girl called Raisa was awakened by the sound of thunder in the skies above her house, and when she turned over she found her future self staring back from the edge of the bed.

In Iceland, a fisherman called Adalsteinn Adalsteinnson was thrown from his boat in the stormy seas close to his home. Plunged beneath the icy waters, Adalsteinn found himself staring into the eyes of a wave with his own features as his allotrope came into being within the whirring maelstrom.

In the North American territory of Luikkerville, a young street boy named Benqhil ran for his life as something with his face came stalking from the darkness of the alleyways, its beatific smile a thing of sinister wonder.

Across the world, people were menaced by their future iterations as a trillion years of evolution careered into them like a train jumping its tracks.

AT THE WALL OF RED COGS, Brigid Baptiste reached for a jutting screw head, its diameter as large as a writing desk. Behind her, the two idealized humans had caught up, and they grasped for her even as she clambered up the walls. Brigid kicked out, booting the Kane-thing in its face, stamping on the woman's elongated fingers as she tried to snag her ankle. She watched as they both fell, dropping the dozen feet to the floor below, the floor just another shelf of the impossible clockwork structure.

Of course it had to be clockwork, she realized now. The whole system followed the long calendar; the Mayans had foreseen the very same thing that she was a part of now, era superseding era, the world ending to begin afresh. Unless she stopped it.

Brigid moved onward, climbing up through the teeth of a cog, arching her body between the brief gap that appeared as the meeting teeth unclamped.

ON EARTH, THINGS WERE changing. The world fusion hurried faster now, and whole new structures were bubbling into existence from the ether, oozing out of the bleed that rent the clouds that blanketed the globe.

The next world flickered from existence, flickered back, was gone again. The next time it flickered back it would stay, and the old world would be forgotten forever, consigned to a history that no one remembered, that would never have even been recorded. It had happened before.

GRANT DUCKED LOW as the long-limbed figure reached for him again, its slender arm cutting the air above his head. All around him, the walls of the temple were dimming where the stones drew blood, sucking it into themselves. Rocky protrusions burst from their shells, reaching across the floor and up the walls like creeping vines, seeking more sustenance, more life.

Grant's Sin Eater spit another burst of fire, the bullets sounding cacophonous in the enclosed space. His idealized double stepped aside, arching his body in such a way that seemed to disconnect his spine, letting the bullets skim past him by a hairbreadth.

"Lucky," Grant growled, bringing his blaster around for another attempt. To kill himself. To kill the future. Death to the future.

Around the two impossibly matched combatants, the temple seemed to flicker for a moment, a videotape recording ending too soon, turning to static, its narrative broken.

Grant shook his head, willing the effect away, concentrating on blowing the head off the naked human-like creature that stood before him. Old bullets cut toward the new flesh, and to the idealized twin they were like long-forgotten words spoken in a dead language.

THE ANCIENT MAYANS had designed their calendar to accommodate the cyclical nature of the universe. Their long-count calendar had recorded not merely what had occurred, but it also set the placeholders for all that would occur. They speculated that the world followed a cycle like everything else in nature, and that that cycle would come to a natural end, night to dawn, death and rebirth. Kane, Grant and Brigid now found themselves in the heart of that prophesied rebirth, as the old world passed, making way for the new. The transition was violent and traumatic, for it was the birth of a new age.

Brigid had reached the glowing starlike heart of the Omniforge, and she looked at it as the new iteration crossed into the world she had lived in. The red star pulsed with fearsome illumination, getting brighter and then dimming as it went through its incomprehensible sequence, bringing the old history to its traumatic end. Everything would be forgotten. Everything that humankind had ever done dismissed in an instant.

Which meant it was time to remember. Brigid reached forward, her hands outstretched before her as if delivering a baby, perhaps eight and a half inches between each palm, that red fire burning in its circle of light. She was holding something in the redness, but it was something that was not there. Around her, the imago universe, the fiery distillation of all the power of the cosmos, was coalescing, blurring into actuality, pushing through the infinity breach, crossing into her world to replace it forever. The old replaced by the new; the faulty replaced by the ideal.

Brigid saw the redness beyond, the blood of birth, life reduced to liquid. And behind that, she saw another universe, where the stars were tiny specks of light that twinkled all around, watching her with their starbright eyes, an audience following her every move.

In that moment, the history of everything fitted there between the palms of Brigid's hands. The whole world, just eight and a half inches across, held with astonishing ease in the space between her fingers. It was hard to comprehend, to imagine holding all of a reality in a gap of mere inches.

Brigid could feel the roiling currents of time, a river threatening to burst its banks and flood her world. She held it back, the pressure impossible to gauge. She had spent so long trying to forget, but now she saw that what she really needed was to remember. The only way to save her world was to instruct the Omniforge to make it just as it was, to remember *everything*.

The only weapon against a forge on which realities were fashioned was the past. Brigid sensed this instinctively, and she gritted her teeth, summoning every iota of willpower to fight back the new world that was trying to be born, kicking and crying as it burst from the cosmic womb.

Drawing on her incredible eidetic memory, Brigid Baptiste recalled the formulas of life, the construction of DNA, the Periodic Table and all its elements and the way that each interacted with the others. Numbers, prime numbers, odds and evens, how music was the purest expression of mathematical structure, how that structure described our heartbeats, our bodies, our selves. She remembered the alphabet and other alphabets, words and sentences and poems, and she remembered things that could not be expressed in any known alphabet, things that could manifest only in emotions and in feelings, things that existed only in people's hearts. She recalled the life she had once led in Cobaltville, where her role was to hide the past, smoothing over its edges in the name of the baronial rulers who controlled and manipulated humanity for their own ends. She remembered all the things she had done and all the things she had seen, every event she had witnessed and every location she had visited. She recalled them in the most minute detail, every piece of information that had been stored in her eidetic memory over her twenty-something years. The moon, the stars, the constellations, they all flooded through her mind as she rushed to remember every single piece of data that made up the world she inhabited.

If the Omniforge needed more, then she gave it more. But it never asked. Slowly, painfully, that other universe, that other world with its idealized allotropes of man, its imago perfection, receded across the multiversal stream, retreating from the space that Earth occupied, the space where man had made his home.

Brigid remembered trees and grass and plants, sunlight and wind and rain and—oh, how could she forget?—snow, wonderful snow. She remembered the way evening turned to dusk, and how nightfall turned the sky a rich indigo, only to be replaced at dawn by the joyful rays of the sun as if reborn. Every day a new world, a new universe, born afresh. All this she fed the Omniforge, forcing her will, her memories onto the pattern of hatred that Black John Jefferson had instilled, his awful, vengeful catalyst for the eschaton.

She was alive while he was dead, and her will was infinitely stronger than a dead man's. Even a man's dying wish was only as powerful as the people who acted upon it, and Brigid Baptiste's living wish was far more vocal, far more vociferous, far more *alive*.

To remember other days, other summers, that was the key.

IN THE OPERATIONS CENTER of the Cerberus redoubt, Lakesh and his team watched pensively as the ghostly figures stepped out of the falling rain and approached the facility's sliding door. But even as they watched, the rain outside stuttered as if someone had blocked it with an umbrella, before pouring once again.

"Did it just—?" Farrell asked, incredulous.

"I saw it, too, Mr. Farrell," Lakesh confirmed.

Behind them, others of the Cerberus team were watching avidly, while out in the corridors beyond, the security teams were moving into place to defend the redoubt should the doors be breached.

As Lakesh watched the monitor, the rain stuttered a second time, a third, and then it ceased entirely.

Lakesh searched Farrell's monitor screen, feelings of hope welling within him. The ghostly figures had stopped at the doors to the redoubt and were even now beginning to fade, flickering from view as if they had never been.

Across the globe, the same thing was happening, those beautiful allotropes of man failing to hold their form, disappearing from Earth as swiftly as they had arrived.

In Mexico, Rosalia drew her *katana* down to behead one of the ethereally beautiful creatures, only to have it disappear before her eyes, its body elongating to the width of a molecule until it had stretched to nothingness.

In Montana, Lakesh watched the monitor screen, hardly daring to take a breath. There on the screen, the world cloud was parting and shafts of sunlight touched the Bitterroot Mountains once more. Around him, the Cerberus team gave a cheer as they, too, saw what was happening. Lakesh knew that the disaster had been averted, no matter how difficult it was to comprehend its nature.

Already, the memory of the storm and the ghost figures was beginning to recede, backing away from this reality as swiftly as it had arrived. All over the world, the sense that something had happened, that something had changed, was beginning to fade from people's minds, as easily forgotten as the pain of a stubbed toe, important for a critical moment, only to evaporate from one's mind to never be thought of again.

BRIGID STOOD BEFORE the burning red heart of the Omniforge, staring into its smoldering depths, enforcing her will upon it. She had remembered everything in the world, but it had not simply been memory that had won through. Knowledge was meaningless without the understanding of how to apply it. In Brigid's case, she had been inside the Ontic Library, that incredible storehouse of reality that lurked beneath the ocean. She had walked within its sacred halls, seen the rules of reality laid bare. In that moment, she had learned how to put it all together, to remake these, the structures of reality. Like a surgeon reattaching a person's hand, she trusted nature to remake the most important connections over again; all she had needed to do was slot the large pieces back in place.

But there was something else Brigid needed to remember to make this world whole, to put things right.

"Kane," she said, the word expelled between her lips like a bullet.

That word-bullet struck the would-be birth, blasting into its burning redness and changing it, coloring it with white. And above, the stars flickered for a moment, as if bowing in appreciation of Brigid's mastery of the world and its values.

"I did it for you," she whispered.

But if the stars heard they gave no sign. They just watched, as they always had in Brigid's world, as they always would.

In the temple that had formed the link between the Omniforge and reality, the corpse of Black John Jefferson finally burned away to nothingness, consumed by the brilliant red fire that had eventually turned white before dimming forever.

On the temple floor, Grant's fearsome opponent, the one who wore his face, winked out of existence. The walls were dark, that bloody dream writing finally removed, sucked into the stone buds left by Ullikummis. They fidgeted on the floor like insects, their rocky feelers swaying like leaves in a breeze, searching for more life that they would never find, never touch, searching for the last drop of sustenance before they, too, withered and died.

Grant was breathing hard, and his muscles ached. He had been fighting that thing with such intensity he had lost track of time. It felt as if he'd lived a whole lifetime over, but maybe that was just the kind of day it had been, with the pirates and the stones and who knew how many flight hours he and Kane had notched up in between.

"Kane!" Grant cried, even as the thought struck him.

He spun, searching the place where he had last seen his partner, there on the central flagstone of the circular room. Kane had disappeared; he was sure of it. Yet, to his astonishment, Kane's body lay there now, shuddering. He had seemed so close to death before, when Grant had last seen him, but suddenly he rocked as if jolted by electric current. Even as Grant hurried over to check on him, he saw Kane's eyes flicker open. They were red. Bloodshot, but not the scarlet, bloody-red that had consumed Black John Jefferson. That was gone forever.

"You okay?" Grant asked breathlessly.

Kane turned his head, scanning the walls of the underground chamber. The scarlet traces had receded, their power draining away as the living stones sucked it all into them. The stones thrived on blood; they would gorge now until they burst.

"Yeah, I'm okay," Kane muttered, rubbing a hand over his tousled hair. "Where's Baptiste? She make it?"

Before Grant could answer, Kane spotted her, lying flat out just a few feet away.

"Baptiste?" Kane said, scooting over to her side. "Baptiste, come on. Snap out of there now."

Brigid's head lolled atop her shoulders for a moment, and then a bright smile crossed her lips as she opened her eyes. "Kane," she said. "I remembered you after all."

Kane bent and kissed her on the forehead. "Would have been hell to pay if you'd forgotten."

All around them, the world was restarting just the

way it had always been, the storm abating, the parallax points returning to their locations, the pieces resetting for another day.

Chapter 28

They had sealed the temple before leaving the tiny island, and Edwards had led a bombing raid on it eight hours later, blasting the whole sorry structure to dust. Grant and Kane had accompanied him, determined to see the wicked place turned to rubble. Grant could not quite recall all that had happened in those last few moments in the temple's walls. Sometimes he remembered it one way, sometimes another. It was as if there were two stories, and either could have been correct. Ultimately they were all alive—that's all that mattered.

Back at the Cerberus redoubt, Kane, Grant and Brigid had returned not to a hero's welcome but to a physical check-up from Reba DeFore.

"Shot at by pirates," she chided as she checked Kane over, having already sent Grant on his way. "Will you never do things the easy way, Kane?"

"I thought that was the easy way," he replied, and he watched with satisfaction as DeFore's shoulders shook. She was trying to stifle laughter, he knew.

"It's easy to be sure of yourself when you don't get killed," she reminded him.

"How would I know?" Kane asked. "It's not like I'll come back here if the alternative does happen."

While Grant had taken a few scrapes, Kane—much to DeFore's surprise—was the picture of health. If anything, he seemed healthier than when he had left the redoubt more than twenty-four hours before, not even so much as tired after what should have been a very trying day.

Kane shrugged. "What can I tell you? I feel rejuvenated."

"That's adrenaline," DeFore warned him. "You'll come down." Satisfied that there was nothing physically wrong with Kane, DeFore let it go at that.

When Brigid Baptiste arrived for her physical, DeFore reengaged her transponder. It was a simple operation to bring the unit back online, and Brigid felt that she had been out of touch with Cerberus for too long. Whatever the transponder meant in terms of her health monitoring while in the field, it meant more to everyone that she was seen as a team player once more. And somehow, that felt right. No one was asking questions anymore, or if they were they just did not seem so hard to answer now.

Things had changed, Brigid reflected as she lay on the operating table, the numb of the local anesthetic pressing against her back where DeFore was sewing up the tiny incision she had made. Mother Superior Ungela had told Brigid that no matter what way a tree grew, the trunk remained in place. She had been lost when she had left here, unsure of who she was and whether she could ever live with herself. But now she felt whole again. The trunk remained in place, as sturdy as ever, but the rogue branches had been pruned. Now she could grow afresh.

"You'll be a little sore for a day or two," DeFore told Brigid gently once the operation was complete. "Let me know if there are any other complications."

Then, as Brigid watched, DeFore brought up her details on her computer terminal, the live signal from the transponder showing her heart rate, her breathing and her location. All were normal.

"Looking at this, I see the life signs of someone who's tired," the redoubt medic said with a sincere smile.

"Sure am," Brigid agreed. "But you didn't really need all that technology to tell you that, right?"

"Go," DeFore urged. "Sleep. You've earned it."

Brigid thanked her and she made her way to the exit. "Good night, Reba."

"Welcome back, Brigid," DeFore declared as the transponder signal's sine waves ran smoothly across her screen, reengaged at last.

Once she was alone in the medical bay, DeFore peered through the safety glass at the patients who still remained. The rock traceries had been removed from the room now, the Cerberus staff working all day to clear the last of it from the walls and doors using high-intensity ultrasonic beams. Without the rocky trails, the redoubt was finally looking like its former state.

Through the glass, DeFore saw Melanie, the so-called Stone Widow, sitting in bed. She was illuminated by her nightlight, the little beam creating a warm circle of light in the darkened room. Beside her, the acolyte called Danny had taken up position in a chair by her bed, his hand in hers, fingers entwined. His head was lolled back and he was snoring, mouth open, the sound no more than a muffled buzz through the thick glass.

DeFore watched as Melanie stroked the man's patchy hair, watching him with care as he slept.

They were human, DeFore reminded herself. Just human. Caught up in a war they could not possibly have understood, drawn to their deaths by a vengeful alien prince whom it had taken all the might of Cerberus to defeat and whose legacy had almost taken countless more lives.

She would speak to Lakesh in the morning and request that he let them go. They served no purpose as prisoners now. Let them live the last of their days out there in peace.

IN THE MEXICAN NUNNERY close to the border, lessons had already begun and the sounds of girls' laughter rattled through the halls. To Rosalia, the students seemed that little bit more excitable, that little bit happier than they usually did, as if it was the first day of summer.

Dressed in an ankle-length skirt the color of wine with a jet-black top, Rosalia hurried past the excited children on her way to the mother superior's office. After knocking, she let herself in and took up a position in one of the high-backed chairs before the desk.

Behind the desk, two trainee nuns worked a large plate of glass into the frame where the window had broken, easing it carefully into place after having tapped out the last shards of its ruined predecessor. Rosalia watched them for a moment as Ungela, the mother superior, shuffled into the room and took up her place behind the desk, limping along as her sciatica played havoc with the nerves in her leg.

Rosalia stood politely as she took her seat, and when she saw Rosalia eyeing the ruined window, Ungela shrugged with resignation.

"A branch blew in during the night," she explained. "Must have snapped off from one of the trees somewhere. Rain soaked the drapes and left me with a big puddle when I opened the office this morning. Not a good start to the day."

"Must have been quite a storm," Rosalia said. "Guess I slept through it."

"No real harm done," Ungela said. "I'm sorry I didn't get to say goodbye to your friend."

"Brigid's always running about," Rosalia said. "Who can keep up?"

Ungela took a sheaf of papers from her desk, licking her fingers before flicking rapidly through them for the correct document.

"I've had a request for a bodyguard," she started. "A local magnate is shipping some materials via the Panama Canal. He's concerned that there may be some trouble from the authorities, wondered if we might be able to offer him some spiritual guidance."

"He have a big boat?" Rosalia asked.

"Ninety-foot yacht," Ungela replied, checking the details from the sheet of paper she held. "He feels that someone decorous would allay suspicions."

Rosalia smiled. "I love yachts. Fresh air and sun. Who can resist?"

Mother Superior Ungela passed the paperwork over to Rosalia, and together they thrashed out the details of the assignment.

At 7:00 a.m. Kane bounded through the doors of the Cerberus canteen like an excited puppy, and when he spotted Brigid he brought his coffee over to join her. It seemed early, but he had awakened after just four hours' sleep, ready to take on the world.

"Whatever happened yesterday," he said as he took his seat opposite Brigid on the plastic-topped table, "left me feeling on top of the world."

Brigid looked up from her toasted muffin, smiling as she licked raspberry preserve from her lip. "Lucky you. I feel like hell. I'm only here because the anesthetic wore off and I couldn't get back to sleep."

"Anesthetic?" Kane asked.

"Reba reengaged my transponder last night, as soon as we got back."

Kane looked outraged. "What? She couldn't leave it until today?"

"I guess she didn't want to lose me again," Brigid conceded. "She did it while I was in her office for the debrief."

From his seat, Kane stared around at the bustling canteen. As ever, it was busy with Cerberus personnel, familiar faces congregating here to eat before they started their shifts or having just finished an all-nighter. A few days before, the walls had been covered in a webbing of rock, the vestigial fingers of Ullikummis still clear to anyone who entered the facility. Now, at last, they were gone, replaced by plastered walls and the first licks of new paint. Lakesh—did that man ever sleep?—was standing before one wall, discussing the possibility of adding a mural like the one that waited at the entrance to the redoubt. That mural showed a gaudy rendition of Cerberus, the mythical multiheaded dog guarding the gates of Hades. The mural was considered by many to be a lucky charm, and it had served as the source for the redoubt's name. Perhaps another mural would bring further luck, or maybe just remind everyone of who they were after so long in the wilderness.

Kane closed his eyes, thinking back to what had happened in the ten-thousand-year-old temple that had served as a gateway to the dream mechanism. The last thing that he had seen were the ghost figures of the new age reaching for him, those eerily beautiful allotropes of man, each one drawn in color and light. Each form had been more graceful than the most beautiful thing he had ever seen on planet Earth. As he thought about it now, he felt a pang of regret. Had they turned back something wonderful? Had they turned away something that was meant to be, that was supposed to supersede the world of misery and danger and chaos that humankind had inhabited since the dawn of time?

Across from Kane, Brigid was thinking of her time as Brigid Haight, of how much she had wanted to disappear, to have those moments erased. But she had saved Kane now, effectively reconstructed him after he was deleted from the end of time. She peered at him across the table, admiring the line of his square jaw, every inch the hero she remembered. He was gazing off into the distance, thinking faraway thoughts. Brigid recognized that wistful look in his eye and she called to him, bringing him back to reality. "Hey. Forgive me?" she asked.

Kane looked at her and smiled, bewildered. "Whatever it was, it's forgotten," he promised.

As he spoke, he drained his cup and got up. "I should go give Lakesh a hand," he decided.

Brigid watched him go, giving him a little wave as he strode away from the table.

It was good to forget sometimes, Brigid thought as she blew on her cooling mug of hot chocolate, but it was infinitely better to remember.

* * * * *

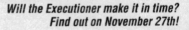